MW00940135

THE
GIRLFRIEND
STAGE

THE GIRLFRIEND STAGE

Cover Design by Melissa Williams Design

Shoes copyright 2019 lukpedclub, Adobestock. Branches copyright 2019 dollitude, Adobestock. Moon copyright 2019 alec_maneewan, Adobestock. Controllers copyright 2019 EVZ, Adobestock

Janci's author photo by Michelle D. Argyle

Megan's author photo by Heather Cavill

Published by Garden Ninja Books

ExtraSeriesBooks.com

First Edition: May 2019

0 9 8 7 6 5 4 3 2 1

THE EXTRA SERIES *Book 2*

MEGAN WALKER & JANCI PATTERSON

For Hannah Ekren
who couldn't stop reading

ONE

Anna-Marie

I can always tell how good a guy is going to be in bed by the type and quality of his sheets.

My roommate Gabby rolled her eyes when I first proclaimed this to her. "Come on, Anna-Marie," she said. "Just because a guy doesn't have a ton of money to buy nice sheets doesn't mean he's bad at sex."

But really, how materialistic does she think I am? (She wisely didn't answer that.) The truth is, this has nothing to do with how much money a man makes. I've been with guys who lived in crappy apartments in WeHo who manage to keep a modest but respectable four-hundred-thread-count cotton blend over the mattress that sits directly on the floor. And I've been with guys who drive Ferraris and wear Armani suits and live in impeccable lofts who cheap out on scratchy nylon/polyester nightmares that would be better used as campfire kindling.

I can tell you right away which of those guys are going to get a second night with me and which ones are going to have to find some other girl to brag to over foie gras about their diversified stock portfolios. And don't get me started on the sleaze-ball guys who think satin sheets are a classy idea.

But then there's Josh Rios.

The moment my bare ass first hit this pristine white Egyptian cotton with a single-ply thread count higher than the SAT score of your typical Harvard attendee, I knew I was going to be spending a lot of quality time rolling around in this bed.

What I didn't quite count on was how much I'd enjoy waking up here, too.

I sigh contentedly and stretch out against those perfect sheets, taking in the sight of the guy sleeping next to me. A lock of dark hair has flopped over his face, but I can still make out the stubble along his jaw, the curve of those lips that can become the most amazing, heart-stopping smile—and can do a fair number of other heart-stopping things, as well.

I roll over and turn off the alarm on my phone before it has a chance to go off and wake him, but my movement must have done that anyway, because he scoots closer and slings an arm around my waist.

"Mmmm, it can't be morning yet," he mumbles sleepily and mostly into his pillow.

"And yet it happens every day. Damn rotation of the planet." Despite how very warm and nice his arm is against my bare skin, I have a ridiculously early call time at work, and so I peel away from him and out of the bed.

He groans. "You're sexy when you talk science. Maybe I'll join you in the shower." But he's barely finished that last word before his breathing goes deep again and he's back asleep, his arm stretched across the bed where I was seconds before.

Josh Rios is many things, but a natural morning person is not one of them. Before his first cup of coffee, he's basically a beautiful Puerto Rican coma patient.

I smile and grab my purse, digging through it for my sleepover essentials. My extra-large blue Kate Spade bucket bag works well for this. It can hold my *Southern Heat* script (which I pull out and set on the bed so I remember to look it over on the way to work), my toiletries and makeup bags, and a rolled up spare shirt and panties. I'm going straight to work, where I'm going to be changed into something else anyway, but I'd rather avoid the complete "walk of shame" feel.

Then I pad quietly out of the room and into the kitchen, where Josh's state-of-the-art coffee machine has just finished automatically brewing the perfect cup of hazelnut roast. I pour us each a cup and breathe in the heavenly scent.

Last week, I suggested to Gabby that I could buy a coffee machine like this for our place.

"We can't replace Bertrude. She has personality," she'd said, looking over at the appliance like she was concerned it might have overheard my blasphemous suggestion.

Yes, our coffee machine is named Bertrude, a name I vaguely remember coining on one of our weekly Wine and Doritos nights, probably after far too much of both those things. And Bertrude does indeed have personality—the personality of someone who makes coffee that tastes like tar and does so with great reluctance and loud grinding noises.

It's a good thing I don't actually drink that much coffee.

I lean against the granite counter top, taking a sip as I look over Josh's condo. It's still dark—despite my comments about planetary rotation, the sun seems to agree with Josh that it's way too early to make an appearance—but the track lighting under the cabinets reflects against the stainless steel of the chef-quality appliances I doubt actually see much use.

The kitchen opens directly into Josh's spacious high-ceilinged living room, which is decorated with lots of heavy, old-world-style furniture. The first time I'd been here, two months ago, I'd been duly impressed with his style. I'd figured he'd have a nice place—or at least I did once I'd realized the gorgeous man I was flirting shamelessly with at the bar was super-agent Josh Rios, number three on *Entertainment Weekly*'s "Top 10 Hottest Behind-the-Scenes Industry Professionals." I knew he was a guy who did well for himself.

Most of the younger rich guys I've dated tend to go for a more sleek, modern look—which can be cool, but is only one weird vagina-shaped vase away from officially trying too hard. Josh's place is decorated in a way that's more classic, and it's a nice change of pace. Even if the constant bubbling of the fountain beside the couch always makes me need to pee.

Now, though, as I look out over the place, something about it makes me feel unsettled. Like it's missing something, though I can't put my finger on what.

Oh well. That's a problem for his interior decorator to solve, not a girl who occasionally spends the night—no matter how much she rocks his world when she does. I grin and bring the coffee back into the bedroom, setting his on the nightstand, so he doesn't have to zombie-shamble out into the kitchen in his boxers in order to become a functional human.

Even though it's downright adorable to watch.

I take a shower that's not nearly as long as I'd actually like, given that Josh's shower, unlike mine, has enough room to turn in without knocking over every single bottle of shampoo and conditioner and Moroccan oil we have. (Contrary to Gabby's complaints, I do not have too many hair care products. I just have very demanding hair.) Then I towel off—another sign of a quality guy are these first-rate fluffy towels that are so comfy I want to wear one as an avant-guard summer dress—and throw on my new shirt with the skirt I wore to dinner last night. I don't bother blow-drying my hair, since my stylist will mess with that plenty anyway, but I do put on makeup. I'm a confident girl, but I'm still not about to face a guy as hot as Josh Rios (who will likely be caffeinated and fully awake by now) without at least some mascara and lip gloss.

When I leave the bathroom, a cloud of steam trailing out behind me, I see that Josh is sitting up in bed, drinking his coffee and flipping through my script.

"You're really getting back together with Vincenzo?" he asks, raising a dark eyebrow at me. "Didn't he steal your baby or something?"

"My *character* Maeve is getting back together with Vincenzo.

Which, yeah, seems like an oversight, given the baby thing. But Maeve has a weakness for cute Latino men."

"Clearly something Anna-Marie and Maeve have in common."

I grin, and let my gaze linger on his bare, toned chest. "Clearly." Then I walk over to him and grab the script from his hands. "Besides, you aren't supposed to be reading that. I have clauses against this kind of thing. You're an agent. You should know better." My scolding tone is all for show. I'm supposed to keep spoilers from getting out in the world, but it's not like I'm carrying around the script for the latest *Star Wars* or something. And I'm pretty sure Josh doesn't even watch *Southern Heat*.

"Hey, you left it out on my bed. I didn't sign anything about not reading it." He gives me that smile, just the teeniest bit crooked and all kinds of mischievous, and then pulls me back down to the bed on top of him.

I don't resist at all. The script falls to the floor as we kiss. He tastes like hazelnut roast and heat, and I suddenly wish I didn't have to go into work today.

But I do, because Maeve needs to reconnect with Vincenzo, and I need to not lose another soap opera gig. I've been at *Southern Heat* now for just over a year, which is definitely better than my short tenure on *Passion Medical*, but after that incident, I am well aware I'm only one framed awards statue theft away from my character dying a tragic poisoning death—or worse, being recast with some actress who has bigger boobs than me.

Josh seems happy enough with my boob size; his hands are already making their way up my shirt when I pull back, and he gives me a sad little sigh. "Fine, I get it. You've got another hot guy to go make out with. Meanwhile, I have a meeting with a client who wants a rider in his contract that will allow his cats to have their own trailer on set. One of us is clearly going to enjoy the day more."

I laugh. I know Josh well enough to know the put-upon agent thing is an act—he loves his job, even when it annoys the hell out of him. "Well, if you really want to make out with

Vincenzo instead, I could probably arrange that."

He tickles my waist and his grin widens when I can't help but giggle. I roll off him so that I'm stretched out along his side. "Thanks, but I'll pass," he says. "Besides, if I'm going to go after one of Maeve's boyfriends, Ben tells me the better catch is Bruce."

"Ben watches *Southern Heat*?" I've never met Josh's best friend, a guy he's known since childhood, but I've heard about him plenty. And nothing Josh has ever said about Ben—other than the fact that he's gay—indicated he's a soap-opera kind of guy. More like a guy who yells at the screen while watching hockey games and eating cereal in his sweatpants.

"No, but Wyatt does. And Ben tells me he's a super-fan of Maeve and Bruce. Posts on the message boards and everything."

"Really." The thought that Josh's best friend's husband is a fan makes me surprisingly happy. Then again, I'm still new enough to the industry that I have to hold in a little squee noise every time someone recognizes me from TV. "Well, Braeve is the more popular ship of the two, that's for sure. The solid choice."

"Brave?" Josh raises an eyebrow.

"Yeah, you know, like a combination of Bruce and Maeve. Braeve." I swat at him when he continues to eye me skeptically. "Hey, I didn't make it up. Blame the fans."

"Yes, blaming the fans. Always good PR advice. But why Braeve? Why not . . ." He pauses for a few seconds, squinting his eyes as he thinks. "Muce?"

The sudden, unexpected hilarity of that—which he pronounces like "Moose"—makes me let out one of my infamous (and thankfully rare) snort-laughs, which sounds like a small weed-whacker has briefly taken up residence in my nose. I feel my soul actually leave my body as I die inside.

Josh Rios has never heard my snort-laugh before, and I would have happily gone on with my life content to keep it that way. But instead of giving me a half-pitying/half-horrified look (trust me, I've gotten that before), Josh's grin gets bigger than

I've ever seen it. And he doesn't say anything to call attention to my embarrassment, which I appreciate.

He does roll over on his side to face me, propping his head up with his hand. It gives his bicep a nice shape, and I know I should encourage him to get clothes on so I'm not late for work, but damn if I don't think he should just stay shirtless and in bed with me all day.

"So which guy do you think Maeve should be with?" he asks. "Solid Bruce or Bad Boy Vincenzo?"

I purse my lips thoughtfully. "Neither. I don't think Maeve has found the right person yet." I pause. "Neither of them really get her, you know? It's like each of them is perfect for a part of her, but Maeve needs more than that. She needs someone more whole, more real."

The moment the words have left my mouth, a kind of warning alarm sounds in my head:

Danger. Danger. Serious relationship talk indicators ahead. Prepare escape vessel.

As if on cue, Josh's amused expression slips, and his dark brown eyes study me carefully. "So is any of Maeve drawn from real life?"

Shit.

Josh and I have been seeing each other for two months now, and this is the closest we've ever come to these dangerous waters—probably because he feels the same way I do, that nothing good ever comes from these talks. He asked the original question jokingly, and then I turned it all . . . serious. And now that I've done that, he feels the need to suss out the threat level himself, make sure I'm not some commitment-hungry agent poacher. Which I am most definitely not.

I've unintentionally led us here; it's up to me to guide us back to safer shores.

I give him my best disarming smile. "Only the part about my newborn child being stolen in the hospital by my jealous lover."

"Only that part?" His lips quirk up in a smile again, and my chest stops feeling quite so tight.

"Real life doesn't come into play very often for Maeve, I'm afraid. Since she's a *soap opera character*," I say with more derision toward the genre than I actually feel. I sit up. "A soap opera I'm going to be late for if we don't eventually get out of bed." I lean in and give him a long, lingering kiss to soften the words.

He makes a little groaning noise when I pull away. "Okay, okay, I'm moving." He slides out of bed and digs around in his dresser drawer until he finds a pair of basketball shorts and one of those sweat-wicking shirts to throw on, then disappears into his closet to gather his work clothes. Josh doesn't need to be at work for a couple hours yet, so after dropping me off on set, he hits the gym and gets ready for work from there.

Despite his hatred of the pre-dawn hours, Josh has never hesitated about taking me to work when I spend the night here, even though it would be far easier if I just drove to his condo in the first place rather than having him pick me up for our dates. I assume he thinks I just like riding around in his Porsche—which, to be fair, is really nice. What he doesn't actually know, because I'm not about volunteer this information, is that I'm irrationally terrified of driving in Los Angeles and don't even own a car. I survive on rides from Gabby or whatever guy I'm currently dating, or, failing that, Uber.

I spend a lot of money on Uber.

I'm in the middle of doing a quick calculation of how many pairs of Gucci heels I could afford if I sweet-talk one of my co-stars into driving me home from set a couple times a week, when I hear Josh's voice, muffled from the closet.

"So do you enjoy working on a soap opera? Like, is that where you ultimately want to be?"

He walks out, carrying a slim-fitted navy blue suit and a pair of brown oxfords. I know this suit; it looks incredibly sexy on him, and it takes me a second to get my mind back on his question.

I shrug. "I mean, not forever. But my agent says I'm in a

good place for now."

Josh looks up sharply from the garment bag he's putting his suit into. "Are you serious? He says that to you? He doesn't have you auditioning anywhere else?"

"No. He thinks I should work for a while here, build up some more experience—"

"That's ridiculous. You're an actress. Unless you actually want a lifelong career in soaps, you need to be auditioning." He zips the garment bag up with a sense of finality. "What you need is a better agent."

"Brent's a good agent," I say, feeling slightly defensive of the man who took a chance on me when my acting experience had been limited to high school theater. In *Wyoming*. "He got me this job, which is pretty damn great for how long I've been in Hollywood."

Josh's expression softens, and he sits on the bed next to me. "Brent got you an audition. You were the one that got the part, which *is* pretty damn great. But just because you're grateful for what you have doesn't mean you can't be ambitious." He pauses. "You should let me represent you."

My heart stops beating for long enough I should probably be worried.

But all I can think is, Josh Rios wants to be my agent.

It's not like this possibility has never entered my mind before. I'm a newbie actress, after all, and Josh is an agent with a capital A. He's not quite at the very top echelon yet, but for being only twenty-eight, he's really close. He represents Chad Montgomery and Asia Phillips and a heaping handful of others who are breaking out, big-time.

The things he could do for my career . . .

And yet.

I *like* Josh. And though I clearly have no problem using guys for car rides, the thought of leveraging the fun I have with him into some stepping stone—like so many in Hollywood do as naturally as popping pills—makes me faintly nauseated.

This thing we have has an expiration date, and the last thing I want is some super awkward agent/client relationship with Josh once it sours.

"That sounds a lot like mixing business with pleasure," I finally manage. "Which I hear isn't a great idea."

Josh leans in close enough that his hair brushes against my forehead. "Lots of agents sleep with their clients. It's really not a big deal."

Suddenly I can't help but wonder if—and how often—Asia Phillips rolls around on these same Egyptian cotton sheets. The image of that gives me a pit in my gut like after Gabby talks me into eating at Fong's.

Which is stupid. Who he sleeps with isn't any of my business. We're super casual, Josh and I, and that works for us.

"Thanks," I say, even though part of me is wailing in disbelief at what I'm about to say. "But I'm going to stay with Brent."

Josh winces in mock pain. "You're breaking my heart, Halsey."

I run my foot up his leg, under the basketball shorts. "I know one way to ease the pain of my rejection."

He raises an eyebrow. "I thought you didn't want to be late for work."

"I don't." I hold up my phone, showing him the time. "Turns out we have a few extra minutes. Seems like we always do, don't we?"

A sly smile spreads across his face. "Wait a minute. Are you telling me that even as you're rushing me out of bed, you build in time for this? Every morning?"

I grin back at him. "Took you long enough to catch on, Rios."

He chuckles, and then his hands are in my hair and his lips are on mine, and I lose myself happily in all things Josh.

That expiration date could happen any day now, and I'm determined to enjoy this while it lasts.

TWO

Anna-Marie

I'm sitting in the cramped backseat of a Ford Focus on the way home from work, listening to the middle-aged Uber driver up front as she hums tunelessly to radio music turned so low only she can hear it, when my dad calls.

I grimace at the phone. I love my dad, but we only ever call each other if there's a Reason.

And I have a pretty good idea what that is.

I answer the phone. "Hi, Daddy," I say, my voice far more cheerful than I myself feel.

The Uber driver gives me a look in the rearview mirror and I glare back at her. Yes, I call my dad "Daddy." No, I do not call any of the guys I sleep with that.

I'm not sure if she can read all that from my expression, but she goes back to her humming.

"Hi, Pumpkin," my dad says. "We missed you today."

I sigh. "I'm sorry I couldn't make it to the funeral, my work schedule is so—"

"It's fine! I get it. You're a successful actress, and you have work commitments." He says this with no small amount of pride. "And besides, I know you weren't ever all that close to Aunt Ida."

That's kind of an understatement. Aunt Ida is—was—actually my dad's aunt, a crotchety old woman with the fragile bone structure of a baby bird and a habit of saying whatever crossed her mind. And the things that crossed her mind grew increasingly meaner—and shockingly anti-Semitic—as the years went on.

"Well, the last time I talked with her, she called my soap opera 'an ad for legalized prostitution' and ranted about relations with Israel. So there's that."

My dad laughs. "Yeah, I kept expecting her to sit up in the coffin and chew us all out one last time."

"If that had happened, then I really would have been sorry to miss it."

There's a pause of heavy silence, and I know the Reason is coming now, and it wasn't the funeral of my great-aunt. "You're still coming to the reunion, though, right?" Dad asks. "I know how busy you are, but I'd love for you to meet Tanya."

And there it is, the thing I've been avoiding thinking about ever since I asked for the time off of work a few months ago: the Halsey Family Reunion, in my hometown of Everett, Wyoming. A yearly event, and one I've managed to avoid since I left for LA, four years ago.

But my dad's getting married again, and I know if I don't show up, it'll look like I'm making some kind of stand against this woman I've never met and my dad's happiness. Which would make me a total bitch, if it were true.

The truth is, I don't have any problem with Tanya. What I do have a problem with is the thought of being back in Wyoming. With all of the rest of them.

Which puts me at only semi-bitch level, I'd like to think.

"I'll be there. I promise," I say, curling and uncurling my toes in my new red Fendi slingbacks, which were already growing uncomfortable at the restaurant last night with Josh and are now slowly turning my feet into two giant throbbing blisters. But they are adorable.

"Good. Good." My dad tends to repeat himself when he's

nervous, and it hits me then how worried he was that I'd bail. Which makes me feel like the worst daughter ever.

"I'm leaving tomorrow," I say. "Driving. So I'll be there in a few days."

Dad doesn't question the driving part; he also doesn't know about my aversion to doing so in Los Angeles. "I'm so glad, Pumpkin. I can't wait to have both my favorite girls with me."

I'm not sure he realizes how many times he's lumped me in as one of his "favorite girls" over the years with women who have very quickly lost that title. But I know he means it, every time.

"I'll see you soon," I say, and with the Reason taken care of, we quickly end the call.

We get to my apartment not long after, and the moment I'm inside and close the door behind me, I kick off my beautiful designer feet tenderizers with a low moan of relief.

"Oh, damn," Gabby says, poking her head out from the kitchen and startling me enough that I jump. "For a second there I thought maybe you'd finally brought Josh here."

"And while I'm making *that* noise, that's really when you want to meet a guy I'm seeing?"

"Wouldn't be the first time."

She's not wrong. She's walked in on no small number of my make-out sessions with guys over the years, until I finally just started taking them straight to my bedroom rather than bothering with the living room couch pre-show.

But Josh . . . I look around our cramped apartment, with its thrift store furniture and only semi-functional appliances and the threadbare carpet with that wine stain that looks like a Rorschach test, and I think: no way. Not that I don't love our apartment. It's been my home ever since I came to Los Angeles. It's like a part of me. And it's not that I think Josh would be a jerk about how much nicer his place is than mine—he's too good a guy for that. But Josh is a rich boy from Bel-Air who became a rich agent in Hollywood. He's a man of fancy restaurants and Porsches and coffee machines that don't have to have a "personality" to make up for the fact they can't actually make coffee.

I can't imagine him sleeping over in my bed that's raised up on cinder blocks so it can fit my ever-growing shoe collection underneath. Or taking a shower in the stall so small and dimly lit you feel like you're getting washed in an MRI machine.

Which is fine. Some guys I date, I bring here, but would never take to a swanky industry party. It's best to keep parts of my life separate. It's easier that way.

"Do you want some chicken-fried teriyaki steak?" Gabby holds up a styrofoam container, and the smell of teriyaki and grease wafts out, making me queasy. "Fong's gave me way too much."

"Um, no thanks. I had a big lunch."

Gabby looks dubious, and she probably wouldn't consider the cobb salad I ate to be an actual lunch at all, let alone a big one. But she's also not on camera every day, playing a character with a great fondness for crop tops.

"Your loss." She scoops some onto a plate. She bounces on the balls of her feet a bit as she does so, which is odd. There's something off about Gabby's energy today.

"You okay?" I ask, pulling a bottled water from the fridge.

She tugs at her hair, which is pulled back into a ponytail that's draped over her shoulder. She's wearing her scrubs pants from work and a black t-shirt that says "I heart Nursing," with the heart as an actual anatomical heart. There's a yellowish stain just above her left boob that I convince myself is mustard. Which is likely, because Gabby. But since she's working as a nursing assistant while she's getting her degree, you can never be totally certain.

"Yeah, I'm great." Her eyes widen. "But I got you something!" Still with that strange manic energy, she darts to the counter and rifles through her purse, then pulls out a bottle of shampoo. Mango Sunrise.

I sigh, though I can't help but smile. "You didn't have to—"

"No, I did! Or Will did, anyway. I'm sorry he used up the

last of your shampoo the other day."

"Yeah, well. I could have handled it better." Which is true, given that I stomped out of the shower in an ill-fitting towel and dropped the empty bottle into the cereal bowl from which he was eating. Though I was already running late and had to use the crappy dollar store brand he brings over that makes me smell like raisins and old pennies, so he's lucky I didn't do far worse.

"He feels terrible," she says.

"Seriously, Gabs, it's fine."

"Well, he's never going to do that again. Which is good, because having him and you both smell the same coming out of the shower gave me some very confusing sexual feelings."

I laugh, and Gabby grins back at me. For all that Will can be an obnoxious occasional roommate—Gabby clearly didn't start dating him for his ability to throw pizza boxes away—I love how happy he makes her. Between being with Will and her new nursing career, this past year she's in the best place, emotionally, that I've ever seen her.

Besides which, now I can actually talk about sex with her and she can comment on things that don't come from those *Sultry Sins* novels she loves so much.

"Soooo," she says, and I know she's going to bring up Josh again. She gets this fascination with the guys I date somewhere around the two to three month mark, because she keeps hoping it'll turn into something serious. Unfortunately, she tends to get this fascination right around the same time I'm ready to end things. I don't think Gabby has that kind of power over the winds of fate, but I cringe inwardly anyway.

I'm not ready to end things with Josh.

"Are you going to be seeing Josh again before you leave for the reunion?" She takes a huge bite of chicken-fried steak, and teriyaki sauce drips down onto her other boob.

Now I cringe outwardly. "I was supposed to go to this movie premiere with him tonight, which I had totally forgotten about until he reminded me this morning on the way to work. But I told him I couldn't make it. I said I had decided to leave for the reunion tonight."

"What? Why'd you do that?"

I scrunch my face up. "Ummm . . ."

"Spill it," she orders, pointing at me with a fried breading covered fork for emphasis.

"Because tonight's the midnight release of *Death Arsenal 6*!" I say, like it's been bottled up in me all day. Which it has been. I've been waiting for this game forever and there is no one I can geek out with about it other than weirdos online on the forums.

Among which I am known as ZomBGrrrl and have an avatar of Captain Jane Jennings in fishnet tights, so yeah. I'm one of the weirdos.

Her eyebrows knit together. "Anna-Marie! You canceled a movie premiere date with your hot agent boyfriend so you can wait in line to buy a video game? Who are you?"

"Okay, first off, he's not my boyfriend. And second, it's not just any video game, it's a long-awaited installment in a well-beloved series that—"

"And you *lied* to him about it?" She shakes her head. "Why didn't you just tell him?"

One thing I'm not as keen about new, madly-in-love Gabby: she's gotten a hell of a lot more judgmental about my dating life.

"Because he wouldn't understand. He's . . . he's Josh Rios! I can't tell him I'm obsessed with a zombie shooter marketed to fifteen-year-old boys." Or that I've been so since high school, well before they started making the crap-fest movies that do unreasonably well overseas. Or that I got a bit drunk after senior prom and got a tramp stamp of *Death Arsenal*'s evil Millipede Corporation logo—a costly and painful mistake I've since had removed.

Gabby rolls her eyes. "Yeah. Because most guys hate it when girls are into video games."

"Josh isn't most guys." Which is clearly the wrong thing to say, because Gabby gets a sly little smile on her face, which she tries to hide behind a chunk of dripping steak.

"So how'd he take it when you canceled on him?"

I shrug. "He was fine. He said he was sad he wouldn't get to see me again before I left for Wyoming. But really, I'm not going to be gone for that long, and it's not like he won't have plenty to keep him busy in the meantime."

I wish the thought of Asia Phillips didn't jump to mind.

"But it's so last minute. Is he going to take someone else?" She bites her lower lip in clear concern.

"Probably. It's a movie premiere. He's not going to go *alone*. And it's not like he'll have trouble finding a date. Which," I add, because she looks like she's ready to go from concern to pity, "is fine. We're not together like that. Really."

"That's not what that gossip column last week seems to think."

She's referring to a picture taken of Josh and me at a club. We're dancing close, and I'm saying something in his ear that's making him laugh, but from the angle of the shot, it looks like I'm sucking his earlobe. You can't see much more than my profile—and the fact that my ass was looking downright spectacular in that red dress—but they ID'd me anyway. The pic got posted on a lesser TMZ-type site with the caption "Hot Nights with Soap Star for Josh Rios."

Well, they got *that* right.

Ever since then, I've had friends and co-stars sending me links of places that pic has popped up, with other captions: "New Love For Hot Agent Rios," "Talk Dirty to Me, Josh!" and "Maeve's Real-Life Hottie!" (that last one from *Soap Opera Digest* online, the only place on earth where I'm a bigger deal than Josh).

It doesn't bother me that even though I'm the actress, it's Josh who's the more famous of the two of us. He was a model in college, and was already getting attention in Hollywood even before he switched career tracks to agenting. Being seen with Josh has only been helpful for my own name-recognition. But it does bother me when these articles imply that's why I'm seeing him. I get why they'd think that, but really—that part's just a perk, like his nice car.

"It's click bait, Gabs. These people get paid to make everything seem like a big deal. But we're just having fun. I don't do the girlfriend thing."

"You did in high school. What was his name?"

Now it's my turn to roll my eyes. "Shane. So I had a boyfriend in high school. I also had a truly terrible bobbed haircut around that same time. Years ago. Now I have great hair and I don't get serious. Both of which I'm pretty sure Josh appreciates about me."

She smiles, but there's a troubled aspect to it that goes beyond her investment in my dating life. Something else is going on here.

"Gabby. What's going on? Are you and Will okay?"

She cringes, and suddenly I'm imagining that she found racy texts in his phone to another woman, or maybe even pics. And god help me, if he's cheating on her something more sinister than my Mango Sunrise is going to end up in his breakfast cereal.

"Will asked me to move in with him and I said yes!" she blurts out.

I gape. "Is it because of the shampoo? Because I didn't mean to—"

"No, no," she says quickly. "It's just, you know, he's been staying over here so much anyway, and this place is a little too small for the three of us, and his place is closer to the hospital . . ." She trails off, and then nods, as if reassuring herself of something. "And I just want to. I think we're ready for this."

"That's . . . that's great!" I say, because I know I'm supposed to. But inwardly, I feel like my insides are squeezing. Will makes Gabby happy and is a guy I genuinely like, as long as he's not cheating on her *and* he keeps his hands off my shampoo. But right now, I kind of hate him a little for stealing my best friend.

Jealousy does not look good on anyone, and I am no exception.

"It's okay if it's not," Gabby says. "Great, I mean." She looks down at her plate forlornly. I remember how the two of us bought those plates at a yard sale, because I thought the random purple-splattered pattern looked like they had been wept on by Prince himself, and she thought it looked like they'd been found at the murder scene of the purple Teletubby, and we figured either way that made them awesome plates, especially at five for fifty cents.

Is she really not going to be my roommate anymore?

She's been my roommate since the second month I lived here. I can't imagine how empty this place will feel with her gone. Even the thought of all the extra shoe storage I'll have doesn't thrill me the way it should.

"It is," I assure her, and maybe myself. "I mean, it's going to suck not being roommates. But you'll be happy with Will. And it's not like we won't see each other all the time, right?"

"Right," she says, emphatically. Maybe too emphatically. "All the time."

But it won't be the same, and we both know it.

"When were you planning on moving out?" I ask.

She squirms a little before answering. "I was going to start bringing over some stuff this week. But I'll still be here when you get back! Like, for a few days, at least. Maybe we can have a *Buffy the Vampire Slayer* marathon."

I smile at her, though my chest feels empty. I wonder how much of her stuff will still be here when I get back from Wyoming. "We totally should."

There's a beat where neither of us know what to say, and I'm about to fill it with some stupid joke about how I'll fight her for Bertrude, when she looks at the clock on the kitchen wall and swears. Well, mildly swears. It is Gabby, after all. "I've gotta go," she says, dropping the plate into the sink. "I'm working night shift tonight. But if I don't see you before you leave, you'll call me from the road, yeah?"

"Of course, yes."

She grabs her purse, her hand on the doorknob and then wheels around. "Oh, and I know you, and I know that if you get this game tonight, you'll be up all night playing it. Promise me you'll get at least five hours of sleep before you get behind the wheel. Promise."

"I promise, *Mom*."

Gabby smiles, and gives me a hug, and I wish it didn't feel so much like the end of something important. Then she's gone, and I sit alone in the apartment, staring at the wine stain on the floor for long enough it becomes blurry. I consider calling Josh, but he's probably getting ready for the premiere. Maybe even on the way to pick up his date.

I decide to stop feeling sorry for myself and go buy my game. It's time to shoot the hell out of a bunch of zombies.

THREE

Anna-Marie

I leave the Los Angeles area around noon in a rented Nissan that smells like dashboard wax with a faint whiff of cigarette smoke. I'm feeling awake enough on the promised five hours of sleep, and emotionally satisfied after a full night of zombie slaughter. Steeling myself for the road trip ahead—and mainly the dreaded destination—I crank up the first song that comes on the satellite radio's pop station. It's a sweet duet by one my fave new bands, Alec and Jenna. They're a real-life couple, and to watch them perform, you'd think there never were two attractive people so attractively in love.

Unfortunately for them, they're bound to come up against the law of Hollywood sooner or later. It's only a matter of time before he's out banging groupies and she develops a prescription drug addiction and they release some plagiarized statement about an amicable breakup full of the utmost respect that everyone knows is a bald-faced lie. The more adorable they are now, the bigger the backlash is going to be.

Why risk all that pain when you can just have fun instead?

I sing along to the song anyway, and enjoy the swoony feeling the words about "forever love" make in my heart. I may not believe that exists in real life, but I don't believe in vampires either and I still love watching *Buffy*.

I drive for hours, singing to the radio, checking in with Gabby, rolling my eyes through a phone call with my dad's sister, Patrice, who ostensibly has called to get my ETA, but proceeds to fill me in at length about the weather there, as if I'm not going to actually be experiencing it soon.

I stop in St. George to stay the night, and as I curl up, I can't help but check a website I know will be posting pics from the movie premiere I ditched.

I'm curious who he ended up taking, is all.

I scroll furiously down, through pics of celebrities whose choice of dress and date will be dissected at length on fashion and gossip sites, until—there he is. Josh Rios, looking every kind of gorgeous with his black hair slicked back and wearing a deep gray Tom Ford suit, grinning for the camera.

And next to him, a tall blond woman in a sleek navy blue gown cut practically down to her belly button. Not Asia Phillips, but an up-and-coming actress named Macy Mayfield he signed last month. She's around my age, early twenties, and is the kind of beautiful often described as statuesque—like she stepped straight from the set of some Jane Austen period film, but somehow lost the top half of her gown along the way. His hand is on her lower back, and it's like I'm suddenly aware of the absence of it against mine.

"Josh Rios and Macy Mayfield: agent and client, or much more?" reads the caption on this one. I think of him just yesterday morning, so close to me I could feel the warmth of his skin, telling me how agents sleep with their clients all the time. It's not a big deal.

And it's not. We're not exclusive. We're having fun, and he's free to do that with whoever he wants.

I pull the covers up and as I try to go to sleep, I wish they hadn't given me a king-sized bed. All that extra space just feels vast and cold and empty. Just how I remember Wyoming.

The next day, I'm up fairly early, and after picking through the few relatively healthy choices I could scrounge from the hotel's shoddy excuse for a continental breakfast, I'm on the road. I blast the radio and cruise down the long stretches of scrubby desert that comprises most of this drive, and I definitely don't look for more pics of the movie premiere when I stop for gas.

Eight hours later, I pass the faded wooden sign that announces "Everett, Wyoming: Home of Friendly People and Cattle." Some teenager has turned the 'y' in Friendly into a penis with permanent marker. It's not as artistically rendered—or generous—as the one Shane and I drew there one bored night our junior year, but I'm glad traditions are being kept up.

The sight makes me smile, despite the fact that I'm driving into town and not fleeing quickly from it. It's nice to remember that I did actually have some good times here.

I head down main street, which has gotten a new stoplight in the years I've been gone, bringing the total number of stoplights in the town to a whopping two. I pass Bleeker's auto-parts shop, the bank, Sheila's Bakery, and the lone grocery store, half of which is actually another auto-parts shop (why two would be needed in a town with fewer cars than cattle is a mystery I've never solved). I get waves from the same old ladies who have been sitting outside the post office ever since I can remember, knitting what appears to be the same scarf over and over.

Two streets down and a left, and there it is: the Halsey family home. It's a two-story that is actually not terrible looking, thanks to it being older than the cheap vinyl siding most of the houses in Everett seem made of. It has a nice wrap-around porch, and it looks like Dad has put a fresh coat of lemon yellow paint on it at some point in the last few years.

It would, however, look better were it not for the handful of pickup trucks parked haphazardly on the front lawn like giant redneck lawn ornaments. I crunch my Nissan up onto the gravel of the actual driveway and take a deep breath.

Showtime, Anna-Marie.

I ready myself with a TV-worthy smile and step out of the car.

Right into a large pile of shit.

I make an undignified squeal, and then swear, loudly and emphatically. These ankle boots are suede!

A little girl's giggle sounds from behind me and I whirl around to see two kids I don't know watching me. One, the source of the giggle, is a small girl tugging at her long honey-blond braid and wearing overalls with sparkly ballet flats. She's grinning at me. The other is a gangly teenage boy with the same round face and blond hair, only he's watching me with wide brown eyes, looking more startled than anything else. He tugs at one of his earlobes nervously.

"Sorry," I say, looking around, confused. Did I forget some important information, like that my dad moved since I was here last? "I probably shouldn't have said that word in front of . . ." I pause. "Who are you?"

The girl bounces up to me. "I'm Ginnie. And this is my brother Byron. We've seen you on your show. Mom says you're famous."

Ginnie and Byron. Right. Tanya's kids. Honestly, I had kind of forgotten about them, which seems horrible, given that they'll eventually be my stepsiblings. But I've learned over the years that stepsiblings, like stepmoms, have a tendency of coming and going pretty quickly.

Still, the girl clearly knows how to get on my good side. I smile at her, even as I'm scraping the poop off onto the grass. "I don't know about *famous*, but thanks," I say. "It's nice to meet you. So did my dad start letting the neighbors park their cows on our driveway?" I gesture to the giant shit patty.

Ginnie giggles again. "No, that's from our dog, Buckley. He's staying here with us, too."

Of course he is. And from the green, grassy quality of this shit, there must be something seriously wrong with that dog.

"I play football," Byron blurts out, mostly to my chest.

I don't know what to say to that, but suddenly I'm wishing

I were wearing a less tight t-shirt.

"Ginnie! Byron!" a woman's voice calls, sparing me from further conversation about dog poop and being ogled by my teenage future stepbrother. "Your mom says you should come inside and eat, before the food gets—Anna-Marie! You've made it!"

My aunt Patrice jogs down the porch steps in her usual outdated pant-suit, her dyed-brown hair in the stiff bouffant she's had ever since I've been alive. She thinks it makes her look like Liz Taylor, but really it just looks like she needs a new stylist who isn't a hundred years old. Patrice's arms are stretched wide for a hug, even though she's still several yards away. I meet her halfway and am enveloped in the scent of grilled burgers and some epically strong perfume that I can only imagine is named "Lilacs and Even More Lilacs: In Case You Missed It the First Time."

Slightly dizzying, but I imagine it's better than what I smell like after two days in the car and with dog crap on my shoes.

Patrice squeezes me hard enough I grunt, and then pulls back. "So good to see our little star! Such a *shame* you were trapped in the limelight for Aunt Ida's funeral."

She gives me a look that tells me she suspects that this was entirely my choice, which, to be fair, it was. As she continues, I find that's not a decision I regret.

"We talk about you all the time, you know. Your hair has some red in it now! That's for your show, I assume? Lily says it looks like they feed you well on set, but you're still slim as a reed! Guess the camera really does add ten pounds."

I'm sure my smile is more of a grimace, but Patrice doesn't seem to notice. She's right about the red tint to my normally medium-brown hair, at least—my on-set stylist keeps it dyed for my character. But I really could have done without the signature Aunt Patrice backhanded compliment.

The world in general could do without those, but it's never going to stop Patrice.

She's got her arm linked tightly in mine, guiding me up the

stairs like I'm a blind flight risk. "Speaking of weight," she says, "did you hear that Sheila over at the bakery had the gastric bypass? I told her she looks like a new woman, you know, and she does. A much smaller woman. I think she's got a real chance of landing a husband now, especially since she's started taping down all those skin flaps . . ."

There's more, but my brain remembers its atrophying defense mechanism of Tuning Out Patrice, or simply TOP, as my dad and I call it.

I enter the house, and there's Patrice's daughter, my cousin Lily, sitting at the kitchen table filing her nails while her father, my uncle Joe, can be seen outside through the screen door swearing at the grill. They live a whopping twenty minutes out of town where Joe manages a cattle ranch, but as per reunion tradition, we all pile into Dad's house anyway, him being the one with a residence "in town."

Lily looks me up and down when I enter and narrows her eyes, but doesn't bother getting up. "Anna-Marie," she says, as if my arrival is the most tedious part of her glamour-filled life.

"Lily," I respond in kind.

We've never been friends, and that's clearly not about to start now. She's been jealous of me since we were in fourth grade and the boy she liked, Jimmy Sears, asked me if I would kiss him at recess. Which I did, and was put off enough by the whole experience that I didn't kiss a boy again until freshman year of high school. (And soon thereafter learned that Jimmy Sears wasn't representative of the kissing experience as a whole.)

But with that gross kiss that involved a surprising amount of tongue and tasted like onion rings, the gauntlet had apparently been thrown down. Lily made it her goal to kiss every boy in school that liked me, or that I had a crush on. It started going further than kissing at some point in high school, and though I'm hardly one to judge anyone for an active sex life, it's not a reach to say that Lily's vagina became one of Everett's most-visited attractions.

None of which would have actually bothered me all that much if she hadn't tried so blatantly to sleep with Shane. She never succeeded—as far as I know—but I could only endure my cousin having wardrobe malfunctions in front of my first (and only) serious boyfriend so many times before I broke into her house one night and shaved her eyebrows off while she was sleeping.

I'd like to say I wasn't proud of my actions, that I regretted it the next morning when she came to school with brown marker lines drawn above her eyes. But that would be a lie.

Lily's eyebrows have long since grown back, and hopefully both of us are past that sort of thing. But judging by the glare she gives me, I'm definitely locking the door to my room while I sleep.

"Pumpkin!" my dad's booming voice rings out from down the hall, and soon he's there, hugging me. Dad's got the same blue eyes I have and hair the same chestnut brown as my natural color—though his is graying at the edges and thinning at the top. He's a handsome man for his age, though he's gotten a bit thicker around the middle since I last saw him. Or maybe it's just that the v-neck shirt he's wearing is a size too small, and dear god, are those—?

"Skinny jeans," my dad says, seeing my horrified gaze at his legs. He doesn't appear nearly as abashed as a man his age should be for wearing those things, no matter how good looking he is. Especially tucked as they are into cowboy boots. "Tanya likes the way they make my ass look. And what Tanya likes . . ." He trails off with a suggestive waggle of his eyebrows.

I heroically hold in a gag.

"Bill, I was just telling Anna-Marie about Sheila's gastric bypass," Patrice says, sweeping by us with a thick cloud of lilac scent. "You should tell her how good Sheila looks now. Oh! And tell her about the nice Muslim family that moved down the street! They are the sweetest people, and . . . wait. Maybe they're Indian. Well, sweet all the same, and—Dad!" she calls down to the basement, to where my Grandpa is likely sleeping in his favorite chair in front of the TV. "Dad! Anna-Marie is here and dinner is ready and . . . is that dog sleeping on the couch?" Her voice trails off as she heads downstairs, and Dad grins at me.

"Activating TOP systems?" he asks.

"TOP systems are go," I say, smiling back.

"So have you met Ginnie and Byron yet?" He looks over my shoulder. I turn to see the two of them in the front doorway, Ginnie beaming at me and Byron with his hands shoved in his jeans pockets and staring at the floor.

"Yes, just outside." I try to think of anything I can say to make it seem like I actually invested energy in getting to know them. "Ginnie has really fabulous taste in shoes"—the girl's smile stretches even wider, and she shifts in her sparkly ballet flats so that the sunlight catches the sequins—"and Byron plays football."

My dad raises an eyebrow. "Oh?"

Byron's face flushes crimson. "I mean, I *have* played football," he mumbles. "With friends."

Dad nods. "Well, Byron, why don't you get Anna-Marie's suitcase from the car and bring it in for her."

Byron runs back outside like he's fleeing a crime scene. I realize that I never shut the door to my car, let alone locked it, but I suppose that doesn't matter. This is Everett, not Los Angeles. I could leave the car totally open and running all week and the worst I'd have to fear would be a dead battery and some raccoons nesting in the front seat.

"And while he's doing that," Dad continues, "I'll go find Tanya so you ladies can finally meet."

"Don't bother, I'm here," a voice calls from upstairs, and a woman quickly bounds down the steps. "Anna-Marie," she says, when she's nearing the bottom, "I'm so excited to finally meet you."

I try to say the same, but I'm having trouble forming words that aren't "Oh my god, are you younger than me?" So I just smile like an idiot in return.

Tanya is really pretty, with the same honey-blond hair as her kids, cut in a face-framing bob. She's wearing frayed jean shorts and a t-shirt that says "A woman's place is in the House and the Senate," and feather earrings that dangle down to brush her shoulders.

I know Dad said she's a bookkeeper from Evanston but she looks like she could be a co-ed at the University of Wyoming. I know she can't actually be as young as she looks, given that she has a teenage son. But it's super disconcerting.

"Tanya loves your show," my dad says. "She didn't watch many soaps before, but you should hear her go on about who Maeve should end up with."

"That's great," I manage. Tanya's lips twist to the side in a knowing smile.

"They have awards for soap operas, don't they?" Dad asks. "I imagine you'll be getting one of those soon."

The thought of me getting a Daytime Emmy—something Bridget Messler herself has yet to achieve—is crazy laughable. Which isn't to say I haven't, on occasion, practiced my acceptance speech in the bathroom, holding a bottle of conditioner like it's the golden statue.

But I can't exactly tell my dad how unlikely the possibility is. He'd never believe me, anyway.

"Maybe," I say.

There is an awkward pause, which I know I should fill, but I'm still trying to do the math on Tanya's age and my brain seems to be stuck on my mom's bitter voice on repeat: *He keeps finding them younger and younger, doesn't he?*

"I'll just go help Byron with the luggage," Dad says, as if he thinks I've brought my entire apartment's worth of clothes with me, and flees the scene almost as quickly as Byron. My dad is not great with awkward pauses.

"I'm sorry, I just—" I start, but Tanya shakes her head.

"Really, it's okay," she says. "I know I look young. And I

figured you'd be kind of shocked by that. I'm thirty-two. I had Byron when I was sixteen."

"Wow," I say, though I'm not sure if I'm saying that to the fact that my soon-to-be stepmom was eight years old when I was born or that she had a son herself only eight years after that.

"I know, right? And don't worry, I'm not going to try to be like some kind of mom to you. That would be weird." She wrinkles her nose, and I smile.

"Yeah, maybe a bit." I'm surprised by how much I like her already.

Surprised, and a little concerned.

After all, she'll be my dad's fourth wife. And just like each of his wives has been younger than the one that came before, each of his marriages has been shorter. I love my dad, but he doesn't have a great track record when it comes to his romantic attention span.

Never trust a man, Anna-Marie, I can hear my mom say, her words slurred by too much wine. *You'll give them your best years and they still go screw the one auto mechanic in town with big tits.*

I need to get out of here.

Dad and Byron shuffle back in with my suitcase and purse, and I see a temporary escape.

"Thanks, you guys, you're the best. I'll take that," I say, grabbing both items from their hands before they can protest. "Am I still up in my old room?"

"Yeah," Dad says, looking a bit surprised by my haste to escape. "Of course. Just the way you left it."

I dearly hope my room hasn't been sitting there gathering four years of dust and rats. Though since the one thing Wyoming doesn't lack for is space, this house, like most others, is enormous enough it's possible Dad hasn't needed it for anything, even with Tanya and the kids living here, and Patrice and Joe and Grandpa staying for the reunion. "It's great meeting you, Tanya," I say. "I'll go get settled in, and we'll chat more later, yeah? Fabulous." This is the same idiotically breezy tone industry people use as brush-offs at parties, usually followed by some quick air kisses and a "darling" or two.

I have a feeling she's smart enough to pick up on this, but all I care about right now is hauling ass upstairs and closing myself off in my old bedroom. Which I do. The moment the door is shut behind me, I can breathe again.

I leave my suitcase and purse by the door and sit down on my bed, just taking in the room I haven't seen in years. It looks exactly the same as before—same sky-blue bedding on the brass-framed bed, same long-expired bottles of perfume and pots of makeup on the dresser, same tiny holes in the walls from where I took down my *Death Arsenal* and *Firefly* posters the day before I moved. Same row of shiny trophies and dangling medals on a special shelf Dad built for them.

Clearly someone has cleaned in here since then because it doesn't smell like four years of trapped air and I'm not choking on dust, but other than that it looks like the room is being kept in some weird stasis. A memorial for someone who is never really coming back.

I walk to the large mirror over the dresser and run my fingers over the photographs shoved into the edges. Younger versions of me, smiling back. Me and girlfriends I wasn't actually that close to. Me holding trophies that now sit on that shelf. Me graduating as salutatorian (damn you, Kelsey Sprack, for edging me out by one one-hundredth of a point). Lots of me and Shane.

My phone buzzes in my purse, shaking me out of my thoughts. Gabby, most likely, checking to make sure I haven't already turned tail and headed back to LA. I grab my phone, and my heart pounds harder when I see that it's not Gabby calling me.

It's Josh.

FOUR

Anna-Marie

I stare dumbly at my phone. Why is Josh calling me? Not that we never talk on the phone, but it's mainly to arrange our next date. In lieu of having Gabby around to debate with, my brain chooses to argue with itself.

Me: Maybe he's calling to break up with me.

Also Me: How can he do that? You aren't his girlfriend, remember? There's nothing to break up.

Me: True. But maybe he decided he wants someone else to be, and so he's just giving me the heads up. Maybe he really wants to be serious with Macy.

Also Me: *Macy*? Really? She didn't look *that* good at the premiere.

Me: Maybe I should just answer the damn phone and stop being an insane person who talks to myself.

Also Me: Yeah, okay.

And with that matter settled, I answer the phone.

"Hey," I say, as if I haven't just had a brief mental breakdown, likely from being back in Wyoming.

"Hey," he says back, and I can hear the smile in it. Just that one word, and something tight in my chest eases. Talking to Josh is kind of like that. "So I take it you made it to Wyoming okay?"

"I did." I settle onto my bed cross-legged, leaning against the brass frame. A familiar position from years of phone calls with cute boys. "Already regretting it, though," I say with a small laugh. "Please tell me something about Los Angeles that will make me not want to drive back tonight."

"That doesn't sound in my best interest," he says. "But sure, okay. How about this—I spent my whole day in meetings about volumizer. *Volumizer*, Anna-Marie."

I laugh. "What? Have you started taking on stylist clients now?"

"God, maybe I should," he says with a groan. "So one of my clients has a clause in her contract about how nothing irreversible can be done to her hair. And she calls me at *five in the morning*, all hysterical about how the volumizer they've started using is damaging it."

"Five? Were you even able to have a coherent conversation at that ungodly time?" I try not to think about some other girl having brought him his mug of coffee, taking a shower while he talks his client down off the hair-emergency ledge.

"Probably not. Though she wasn't exactly coherent herself, so I doubt she noticed."

"Well, that helps."

"So I schedule meetings with the heads of wardrobe and cosmetology on set, in which they're bringing me long lists and charts of the chemical breakdowns of their products. And I have to actually pay attention to this shit, and all the while make sure they know how hard I will fight to protect the 'integrity of my client's hair' "—I can practically see the air quotes from his tone— "even though both they and I know she'll be totally over this tomorrow."

I groan in empathy. And decide never to tell him how mad I got when Will used up the last of my shampoo. "So what happened?"

"Well, I'm a little worried I'm going to be blackballed in the hair-care community from now on. But they agreed to switch product lines."

"You really are a good agent. Brent would tell me to bring my own damn volumizer to work if I cared about it that much."

"Having second thoughts about my offer?" he says, a note of teasing in his voice.

I am, but the reasons I declined him originally are all still unfortunately valid. "Your concern for the integrity of my hair is tempting. But maybe you'd be the one having second thoughts. After all, you don't know what kind of demands I'd make on you."

He laughs, clearly picking up on my suggestive tone. "I think I have a pretty good idea. And you haven't heard me complaining."

I picture myself pressing up next to him in bed as he says this, his hand trailing lazily along my back.

I stretch out in my own bed. "Well, you've clearly failed at one of my demands. Because all of that still sounds way better than being here."

There's a pause. "Has it really been that bad? You've only been there a day." He doesn't sound judgmental, just curious. Which makes sense. He knows the basics about my family, like I do about his—two brothers, parents still married, a few nephews and a newborn niece—but we haven't really talked about family stuff in depth. I don't talk about family stuff much with anyone, if I can help it.

Also, I remember that because I lied to him about the movie premiere, he thinks that I've been here nearly a full day, not twenty minutes.

"No, I mean . . ." I shrug, even though he can't see it. "I don't know. My family isn't terrible, it's just . . ." I trail off, thinking of how best to phrase what I'm feeling.

"You don't have to talk about them if you don't want to," he says cautiously. Which is the perfect excuse not to.

But surprisingly, I kind of do. "It's not that. I just don't know how to describe it. Being back here and seeing them again." I pause. "I told you my dad's getting re-married, right?"

"Yeah. Part of why you needed to go was to meet her. Is she awful?"

"Actually, no. Like, I think she's the kind of person I could be friends with. Hell, she's not much older than I am. But I can't, because . . ." I let out a breath. "She'll be his fourth wife, you know? And other than to my mom, he's never been married longer than a couple years. He's not great at it."

"At being married?"

"At *not* being a cheating asshole would be how my mom and his other ex-wives would put it, but yeah."

"Yikes. Yeah, that sounds difficult." His voice is gentle and sincere, and I find myself continuing, possibly against my better judgment.

"I love my dad, and I think he goes in each time with the best intentions. But it's frustrating. Like getting to know these women and their kids, and . . . I tried before, you know? Like I tried to be the good stepdaughter and stepsister and be family, and . . . why bother when I'll never see them again?" I sigh. "Sorry, I don't mean to be all heavy about it."

"God, no, it's—I'm happy to listen. Really. Is your mom there, too? Is she remarried?"

"No way. To both. She stayed here in Everett in a house at the edge of town until I graduated high school, and then she got about as far away from my dad as she could. She lives in Connecticut now, in some community that as far as I can tell is at least half lesbian. She's not gay herself, but she's pretty much sworn off men and dating entirely, and she's insistent that life is much better that way." I smile despite myself. "Clearly, I don't share her views."

"Well, I'm glad for that." But he still sounds troubled, and I wonder what it is I'm doing, telling him all this. Really, if I need to unload all this stuff, I should do so with Gabby, not the guy I'm casually dating. Though Gabby's moving, and I don't know how much I'm going to get to see her anymore, since most of our interactions revolve around her giving me rides or being my roommate. And Josh is—has always been—really easy to talk to. I suppose this doesn't hurt anything, really.

"What about the rest of your family?" he asks.

"They're fine. I mean, my dad's sister Patrice is well-meaning but super offensive to pretty much every race, religion, and heavy-set person in existence. And my cousin Lily hates me. And my teenage soon-to-be stepbrother won't stop staring at my chest. But other than that . . ."

He laughs, though it's in clear sympathy. "I'm sorry to hear all that. The only thing about my family that really compares is their constant harping on me being a college dropout."

I hesitate. I'm pretty sure Josh graduated from UC Irvine. "You dropped out?"

"Yeah, right after getting my bachelors degree. You haven't finished school in my family until you have a PhD. My little brother Adrian at least got his MBA, so I'm the family deadbeat."

I can't tell if this bothers him or not, so I try not to laugh. "You're way up on me. I never went to college."

"And in a normal family, that's not a problem."

"I wouldn't exactly call my family *normal*."

Josh makes a sympathetic noise. "I wish you were having a better time. There's got to be something good there. Otherwise, I'm really going to have a hard time making LA seem like a worse place to be."

He's already lost that battle. If I was home now, I'd be out to dinner with him and we'd be laughing about his client's hair crisis over Thai curry, or getting ready to go to some club, where we'd dance close for hours and go back to his place to dance even closer. Or I'd be at my apartment watching some romantic comedy with Gabby and we'd be criticizing Reese Witherspoon's inability to choose between hot men (though Gabby and I would vehemently disagree on which hot man she should pick).

All of these options sound like bliss. But I do love my family, and I can't just leave a half hour after I got here. He's right.

There's got to be something good.

And then I think of it.

"Hot dogs," I say. "My uncle Joe makes the world's best hot dogs."

"Wait, what? Are you serious? That's a pretty big claim."

"I stand by it. Every year at the reunion, we have the Halsey Grillmaster Championship, and Uncle Joe always wins. He makes these amazing hot dogs, that he's marinated in like, I don't know, unicorn tears and crack or something. He won't tell us."

"I feel like unicorn tears and crack sounds like a reasonable assumption," Josh says, and I can practically hear the wide grin. "These sound incredible. I'm not sure you know this, but I'm a bit of a hot dog snob."

Now I'm incredulous. "You. A hot dog snob."

"It's true. Not to disparage the Halsey Championship, but the best hot dogs in the world are actually at the ballpark. I have clients who give me box seats sometimes, and I think they'd be horrified to know that what I'm excited about is going there for the food."

"I've never seen you eat a hot dog. Not once."

"Yeah, well," he says slowly. "Maybe you should come with me sometime."

"To watch a baseball game. And eat stadium hot dogs."

"To eat the best hot dogs in the world. The game is beside the point. I don't even know what the hell's going on most of the time."

I grin. It should be hard to imagine, him and me at a baseball game we don't actually care about, eating hot dogs and waving those big foam hands at all the wrong times. But right now, it's not. And out of all the options of what I could be doing back home, somehow this sounds like the very best one.

"I'm in. Absolutely," I say. "If only to know for sure that you're wrong and Uncle Joe's dogs are better."

He groans and laughs, all at once, and it's an adorable sound. "No way, Halsey. Unicorn tears or no, I refuse to believe."

"Well, Josh Rios, hot dog connoisseur, you're welcome to drive out here and try them for yourself."

There's a pause, and then, "Maybe I will. Uncle Joe's award-winning hot dogs don't sound like an opportunity I can pass up."

I laugh. "Yes, I'm sure you're ready to drive all the way out to Everett, Wyoming, on my hot dog recommendation."

"You don't understand how much I love hot dogs. I just might."

A knock sounds at my door. "Anna-Marie?" Aunt Patrice calls. "Are you going to join us? We're setting up Scrabble!"

I sigh. "I'll be right there!" I call back. Then to Josh: "Sorry. It's Scrabble time. I missed Aunt Ida's funeral, and if I also skip reunion game night, there'll be serious hell to pay."

"I wouldn't want that," he says. There's a moment where neither of us says anything, and I realize I don't want to say goodbye. Like it will physically hurt to say the words.

I miss him.

The silence stretches on, and my heart pounds.

"Save some of those dogs for me," he eventually says.

"Will do," I reply, though my mind is racing through the ramifications of that single stark thought, and suddenly I do want to say goodbye. I *need* to say goodbye. "I'll talk to you later," is what I actually say, and barely hear his response before I hang up.

Then I toss the phone on my bed and stare at it like it's some kind of giant hairy spider that just crawled out of the shower drain.

How can I *miss* him? I haven't been gone that long. It's not like we haven't gone days without seeing each other before, and I've been fine. More than fine.

It's just being back here, back with my crazy family and stiflingly small home town. I've barely been here thirty minutes and it's messing with me already. Missing someone like that after only a couple days, wishing you could talk and talk and never have to say goodbye—that's not how I am. That's for serious relationships with labels and commitment and joint rewards accounts at restaurants. And that's not what I do.

Josh is a great guy and we have fun and we have incredible sex, but that's it. We both know this. And that's all either of us wants. It's a good thing, what we have. No pain, no jealousy, no expectations.

And I'm not going to muck it up by letting my crazy Wyoming brain interfere. I probably shouldn't call him while I'm here. Or pick up the phone if he calls me. We can talk when I get back.

And go to that baseball game. Or not. Either way.

I let out a breath, and leave my phone on my bed while I go and rejoin my family. I smile, and I hug my grandpa and I pet Buckley, the giant dog that looks like a cross between a Shetland pony and a huge mop. I Tune Out Patrice and I ignore jibes from Lily and I make small talk with Tanya that I keep very deliberately small, even though I can tell she's onto me. I win the first round of Scrabble and pretend to be devastated when I lose the next one to my dad, and the one after that to Lily (okay, that one does sting).

In short, I am being the Anna-Marie they want me to be, the same girl who left Wyoming years ago. And I am definitely not thinking about missing Josh.

Hours later, I fall back into bed, and I turn the lights out and I lie there in the dark with some kind of ache in my chest I can't even begin to identify and don't want to try.

Something splats against my window. And again. And a third time.

I turn on my light, but I already know what it was.

One bright red gummy bear sticks to the warm glass of the window pane. There's a smear of yellow from one sliding down the pane, and a green splotch from one that hit and bounced off.

The ache in my chest doesn't seem so strong anymore, and I smile as I climb out of bed and open the window to see a familiar sight from years ago.

Shane Beckstrom, standing on the grass below my window,

leaning against the trunk of the poplar tree my dad threatened to cut down many times and never did, even when he knew how often my boyfriend used it as a ladder into my room.

Shane's blond hair hangs in his face, and he brushes it back with his hand, the way he always used to. "Hey, Beautiful," he says. "Mind if I come up and say hi?"

"Not at all," I say, and watch him start to climb, as I've watched him do a hundred times before.

FIVE

Josh

Ten minutes after I hang up with Anna-Marie, I'm still sitting in my basement, holding my phone, looking down at her name on my screen.

Anna-Marie Halsey.

I stretch out in my La-Z-Boy, and my worn copy of *Harry Potter and the Goblet of Fire* falls off the arm and lands on top of a half-open bag of Doritos. I look down at it and see that the spine has split about an inch right around the part of the book where Harry is announced as one of the contestants in the Tri-Wizard Tournament. That's been coming for a while, and it's about time I replaced it.

Save some of those dogs for me.

Will do.

I rub my forehead. I'm not sure what possessed me to tell Anna-Marie Halsey, of all people, of my unreasonable affection for ballpark hot dogs. This mundane obsession, like my love of books, isn't something I've ever shared with a woman I'm dating—not since my girlfriend in college, before I entered the flashiest industry on earth. Anna-Marie's new in Hollywood, but she's climbing rapidly. She's a damn good actress, though she blows me off every time I say anything like that. I'm pretty sure she still thinks I never watch her soap, as if I would pass up on the opportunity to watch her do just about anything. But the point is, she's the kind of girl you take out for lobster, not hot dogs.

Still, something about talking to her today felt different, in a nice kind of way.

I search on my phone to see where exactly Everett is in the state of Wyoming, and frankly how exactly one gets to Wyoming, because at least for this California native, there's basically the east coast, the west coast, and that big cluster in the middle. Wyoming is above Colorado, and Everett is a bit west of the middle of the state. Google tells me it's a fifteen hour drive, which means it would have to be broken up into two pieces. Not that I'm planning on driving it.

But the way she suggested I wasn't going to sounded like a challenge.

I shift in my chair, picking what's probably petrified Cheeto dust out of one of the arms. There was some of that on *The Goblet of Fire* as well—my mom always complained that for loving books so much, I sure didn't take very good care of them.

She's right, but the great thing about books is you can always buy another copy, as evidenced by the varying states of repair of the books sprawling across my shelves, spanning everything from *A Song of Ice and Fire* to my extensive Tolkien collection to everything that's ever been written in the Star Wars universe. Ben keeps telling me I need to get a video game system down here, but I like it this way, just me and my books. I love movies, but they're work, and if I try to unwind with them, I inevitably end up falling down the Google rabbit hole of who is represented by whom and how happy they appear to be with their current representation.

I love the rest of my life, but it's nice to have a sanctuary that doesn't ask anything of me.

I lean forward and gather up the pieces of the white model Ford Anglia I've been assembling. My mother would also have a fit if she saw me shaving plastic flash off the bumper of the Weasley family car and assembling it, all while reclining in my chair. She'd have even more of a fit when she noticed the large super-glue stain that has now joined the other hardened bits of glue all over the chair arm.

Why don't you take care of your things, Josh? she'd say.

The truth is, I do. The upstairs of my condo is always immaculate—partly, of course, because my cleaning service keeps it that way. Down here in my basement, on the other hand, I'm allowed to spill super-glue on my chair, and grind chip crumbs into the carpet.

My mother might not see the importance of a space where one is allowed to relax, but I do. There's a reason I keep the door to my condo basement locked at all times, and never mention to the women I'm dating—or anyone else, for that matter—that it's anything other than a utility closet.

But my inability to keep the place clean is only part of that reason.

I Google Halseys in Everett and find a William Halsey of about the right age on a White Horse Lane.

I lift the partially-assembled Ford Anglia, checking to make sure I haven't ended up with any fuzz from the worn chair upholstery stuck in any of the crevices, and carry it through the door into the basement storage room, which I affectionately named the Chamber of Secrets. I can't walk in more than about three feet, because the room is owned by an enormous table—two tables, actually, fastened together with a Formica tabletop bolted down on top. I walk past my model of Platform Nine and Three-Quarters, along the train track that circles the table, to the miniature Whomping Willow I spent six nights over the last two weeks flocking, gluing, and assembling out of wire, floral tape, and bits of plastic vines I ordered from a hobby shop online.

I test the size of the car against the branches. It looks reasonably in-scale, so once I've finished my assembly it should be ready to affix and position in the branches. I look out over the table, which is covered in an O-scale mish-mash of locations from the *Harry Potter* novels, all crowded much closer together than they are in the actual books. Between the train station and the Whomping Willow are unconnected twisting renditions of Diagon Alley and Knockturn Alley, which in such a small space are backed unfortunately up against the town of Hogsmeade. Beyond that, dominating the table and dwarfing the other pieces, is the four-foot open-backed Hogwarts Castle. There's enough rooms in the castle to feature the majority of the places mentioned in the books, most of which are finished, though my Room of Requirement is unfortunately empty, as I haven't yet decided what I need to put in there. It's gotten large and elaborate over the years—my own way of bringing the stories to life without all the politics and trappings of Hollywood.

I'd intended to take advantage of Anna-Marie's absence and spend every night this week finishing the tree, and then possibly working on some centaurs for the Forbidden Forest. Since my last meeting today got cancelled, I'm home earlier than usual, so I could get a solid start on it tonight. But now all I can think about is hanging out with Anna-Marie in Wyoming, in a setting where we can eat hot dogs and talk about family.

There's this voice in the back of my head—not just any voice, but my best friend Ben's. And right now he's rolling his eyes at me and reminding me that we could do those things *here*. My dating life doesn't have to be all industry parties and movie premieres and five-star restaurants.

Except it does. I'm an agent in LA. My clients—not to mention the girls I date—expect me to live a certain lifestyle. I suppose if I want to date a girl who could hang out with me in my basement I could start hitting on women in Luna Lovegood cosplay at Comic Con, but Hollywood is my life, and while I can resign myself to settling down with a girl who doesn't understand my obsession with fictional wizards, being in a longterm relationship with a girl who's not comfortable with the industry scene would be next to impossible.

Besides, I've grown used to dating hot actresses and my standards are embarrassingly high. Anna-Marie blows all those standards out of the water, and while I'm confident from the amount of time she's willing to spend with me privately that she's after more than just someone to be seen with, I can't imagine what she'd say if she knew what was behind the locked door I pretend is a utility closet, if she knew what I did with the nights I'm not with her.

I lean back, dusting flock from my hands onto my paint-stained basement jeans. I adjust my tiny miniature Ron Weasley, who at this moment is standing on the steps of Hogwarts, looking down at Hermione, who is paying him no attention.

And I put my finger on what was different about that conversation with Anna-Marie. I love talking to her. I wouldn't have been out with her so often over the last two months if I didn't. But that conversation wasn't all joking and banter. Those elements were there, but underneath it . . . she seemed less guarded, real in a way she didn't when we went out in LA.

I rest my hands on the edge of the table and take a deep breath.

Against my better judgment, I want to get in my car and drive to Everett, Wyoming, and have one of Uncle Joe's hot dogs with Anna-Marie.

There's no shortage of hot actresses to take out in Hollywood, but I never seem to get past the casual stuff—dating, sex, industry parties and clubs, introducing each other around to our mutual contacts. Not that I don't love all that stuff. It's necessary, and even if it wasn't, I like loud music and bright lights and dancing in big crowds with beautiful women.

My parents think my lifestyle is too "fast," and maybe they're right. I can't ever seem to make the transition from casually dating to a stable, serious relationship. It's not that I don't want that—I want to fall in love and get married someday to someone I adore, and serious relationships are pretty much a requirement for that. Maybe it's just the expectations of the industry, or maybe it's my inability to be direct about what I want; I don't know. I can fight all day for my clients, but when it comes to myself, I prefer to let things happen naturally, and I think what naturally happens with me and women is that they naturally overlook the signals I send them until one or the other of us moves on to someone else.

If I drive to Wyoming, she won't be able to miss *that.*

I know if I think about this too hard, I'm going to talk myself out of it, and I don't want to. I miss her, and whatever that was on the phone with the hot dogs and the personal stuff—I liked it, and I'd like it to someday be more.

So I climb the stairs, lock the door to my basement, and go into my bedroom to pack.

I don't call Ben until I get to the Travelodge in Parowan, because I don't want him to talk me out of it. I'm too far away, now. I'm committed, and also far enough away that Ben can't have me committed, which is a plus. It's past eleven, so he and his husband Wyatt may be in bed already, but it's Ben, so I don't care.

"Hey," Ben says. "What's up?"

He sounds like it's totally normal for me to call him at eleven o'clock at night, which to be fair, it is.

"I'm in Utah," I say.

There's a pause on the other end, during which I collapse back on the double bed.

"Did you get on a bus while drunk again?" Ben asks.

"First, that was nine years ago. And second, it was definitely your idea."

"Hmm," Ben says. "That's not how I remember it."

I sigh. "Aren't you going to ask me what I'm doing here?"

"No," Ben says, "because you're going to tell me anyway." There's a murmuring on the other end. "No, I don't think he needs a ride. Josh, do you need a ride?"

"No," I say. "I'm going to Wyoming to visit Anna-Marie."

"*Really*. I thought you were going to spend all week on that walloping tree."

"The Whomping Willow," I say. "And you know perfectly well what it's called." Wyatt and Ben are the only other people who are allowed in my basement. A few others know it exists—my family, and my friend Trevor who used to work for Weta and now does miniatures photography for *Game of Thrones*—but none of them have seen anything but pictures. My older brother keeps threatening to come see it someday, but he spent most of our childhood teasing me for reading books about dragons and spaceships and dragons on spaceships, and it's only gotten worse since I failed to grow out of it, so I keep putting him off.

"So what you're saying is, your condo is available."

"I suppose I am." Ben has a key, and he and Wyatt have a habit of staying at my place while I'm traveling. They claimed it was because of my sheets, but I bought them a set of really nice Egyptian cotton last Christmas, and still somehow this happens. "But if you put Harry in bed with Hermione again, so help me, I will change the locks."

"Right," Ben says. Then, to Wyatt, "No, he's not drunk. He's going to Wyoming to visit Anna-Marie. No, a *different* Anna-Marie. Of course it's *that* Anna-Marie." His voice grows louder again. "Wyatt is squealing."

I laugh. Wyatt is a huge *Southern Heat* fan, and he has an equally-huge crush on Anna-Marie's co-star—the one who plays Bruce, though I can never remember his real name. "As usual," I say, "not a word of this on the forums."

"He says not to put it on the forums," Ben says. "No, Wyatt, he trusts you. Wyatt crosses his heart."

"I bet he does," I say. "Because he knows if he doesn't, he's not going to hear about my love life anymore."

"Please," Ben says. "It doesn't matter what Wyatt does. You're still going to tell me everything and I'm still going to tell him."

"This is true, but I don't appreciate you saying that to Wyatt."

"No, Wyatt, he knows you can keep your mouth shut." Then, to me: "Now you've offended him."

"Tell Wyatt I'm sorry," I say. "But could we focus on me please?"

"Fine. Diva Josh has my attention."

I hear another squeal from Wyatt, which I assume means he forgives me. "I'm driving across the country for a woman," I say. "Tell me I'm crazy."

"You're crazy," Ben says. "Though I'm not sure Wyoming counts as across the country. You're not even fully crossing the Rockies."

Ben grew up down the street from me in Bel Air, so he has no more reason to know exactly where Wyoming is than I do, but of course he does. "Oh my god, can we just talk about me driving fifteen hours to see a girl?"

"She invited you?" Ben asks.

I hesitate. "Technically."

"Technically?"

"Yeah. I mean, it was a joke. She told me her uncle Joe makes the world's best hot dogs."

"Oh, no," Ben says. "I bet she got an earful about that."

"She did. I don't know why I told her, but I may have invited her to come to a game with me sometime."

"Speaking of, Wyatt wants to know when he can get tickets from you again."

Wyatt, unlike me, can actually follow baseball. He played as a kid, while the combined sports experience of Ben and me consists of trying to get picked for the same team so we could stand in the outfield and talk about Pokémon.

"He has dibs on the next set after I take Anna-Marie," I say. "If I had some for this week, they'd be yours. But could we please—"

"Yeah, yeah," Ben says. "Back to your girlfriend."

"She's not my girlfriend." I've been pretty careful not to monopolize Anna-Marie's time, even though I easily could have, the needs of my Whomping Willow notwithstanding. Three nights a week is my absolute date-cap, which means we have to spend at least two nights in a row apart. I'd love to have her around even more than that, but I don't want to crowd her.

For example, by crashing her family reunion.

I grab a pillow and hug it with my free arm.

"Are you sure about that?" Ben asks. "Because you called her your girlfriend at least twice in the last week."

"Seriously?" I say. "I hope I didn't say that to her."

"I'm pretty sure if you had, you'd have gotten a reaction."

"I would, right?" I'm not sure. It's all well and good for me to want things to be more serious, but I know better than to just assume they are. For all I know, on the nights she's not with me, she's sleeping with her co-stars, guys she picks up at parties, even her director.

The thought of *him* pressuring her makes me wish she'd let me represent her. It really pisses me off when industry people treat my clients like prostitutes, and I feel even more protective of Anna-Marie.

"You're driving to Wyoming, mostly uninvited. Which story you haven't finished telling me, by the way. But you don't want this girl to be your girlfriend."

"No," I say, "I do."

"Whoa," Ben says. "Really? You're admitting that?"

That's warranted. Ben calls me a serial dater for never getting serious with the girls I date. I pretend I like it that way, but I know Ben sees through me. "Yeah," I say. "I really do."

I'm becoming alarmingly aware of all the implications of this on the drive here. It's hard for me to imagine giving up my basement, or living with someone who resents it, or frankly even telling a girl about it. In college I didn't hide it as much, but in the six years since I joined the Hollywood scene I haven't known many people I can geek out with about things that aren't cars or clothes or net worths.

"Anna-Marie isn't a basement girl. But I enjoy her company, and we laugh a lot." It's more than that; it's a genuine pleasure every time I get to see her.

"And yet you can't tell her your lobster joke."

I groan. I do this impression of a lobster that Ben mocks me unceasingly for. All lobsters are French, and my French accent is terrible, but I've been laughing at my own joke since we were in high school and I'll probably never stop. I may have totally choked last week when Anna-Marie and I were waiting to be seated at Le Papillon and we were watching the lobsters jockey for position in the tank. She turned to me with that dazzling smile and those gorgeous blue eyes of hers and asked me what I thought they would say if they could talk.

I brushed her off, and Ben is never going to let me live it down.

It's embarrassing how hard it is for me to even directly admit to my best friend that I want more with this girl. "I've been thinking a lot lately that maybe this is what it would feel like to find somebody I could actually be serious with, even if she's not into all the same things I am, you know?"

"That's awesome," Ben says. "But she really doesn't know you're coming?"

"She said I'm welcome to come try the hot dogs, but she clearly didn't think I would. I told her to save some for me. Honestly, I didn't think I would either."

"But now you're in Utah."

"Yeah," I say. "Tell me I'm crazy."

"You're crazy," Ben says. "Hey! Cut that out. No, I'm not talking him out of it."

"You can't," I say. "I'm already gone." And this is exactly why: if I was still back in LA, Ben would be talking me out of this without giving it a second thought. With the distance, he still could, but only if he thinks I'm making a truly terrible mistake.

Given his reaction, I'm gathering he expects this particular mistake to be only mildly humiliating—something he'll mock me about for years, but only after the sting wears off.

"For what it's worth," Ben says, "Wyatt thinks this is impossibly romantic."

From the sound of it, Ben does, too, though he'd never admit it. "Too bad I'm not trying to impress you or Wyatt."

"Yeah, sorry, man. But you're not my type."

That's been a running joke since Ben came out when we were fourteen—after I'd been watching him be twitchy and terrified to tell me for months, even though I already knew.

"I'm scared," I say.

"Yeah," Ben says. "That and you being in Utah are pretty good signs you're in this deep."

That only makes the whole thing scarier. "I have no idea if she feels the same way."

"Yeah. I remember something about that. I also remember the advice you gave me."

"Just talk to him already before I punch you in the face?"

Ben laughs. He told me to shut up every day for four months when he dragged me to the pool hall where Wyatt worked and proceeded not to talk to the guy.

"How the tables have turned," Ben says.

"All right," I say. "If we've reached the gloating part of this conversation, I'm going to crash before I drive to Wyoming tomorrow and probably scare off Anna-Marie for good. Have fun with my sheets. Leave Harry and Hermione *alone*."

"Just for that, I'm going to make Ron watch."

I hang up on him, which is how many of our conversations end. Just one of the many reasons he calls me a diva.

I stare at the blank ceiling and stretch out on the empty bed. I wish Anna-Marie was here, something I've been thinking increasingly, even at night in the basement. Last night after I dropped off my client Macy after the movie premiere—where she flirted and made in-roads with everyone in the room, just like I knew she would—I'd gone back to my basement and let myself imagine what it would be like to curl up with Anna-Marie in the La-Z-Boy and read a book together.

I know if that's what I want, I shouldn't be dating actresses. But the truth is, I want it all. I'm a romantic, and watching Ben and Wyatt fawn over each other doesn't help. I want what I have with Anna-Marie—a woman I can take to premieres and clubs and dance and drink with and laugh about the absurdity of all things Hollywood. But I also want someone who'll watch *Star Wars* and read *Harry Potter* with me without mocking or acting put out about it.

If I'm honest, I'd like someone who'd enjoy quiet nights at home as much as going out and being seen.

I know I can't have all that, but being with Anna-Marie makes me want to let some parts of it go—not like settling, but like giving up old dreams in favor of new ones. But as with everyone else I've dated, our conversations never seem to veer toward the serious—with the exception of that last one—and I'm colossally bad at guiding them that way.

I wish I had the first clue what she was going to think about me showing up out of the blue, or a much shorter drive between here and there during which to sweat about it. I wish I'd gotten a plane ticket, but the closest major airports were still hours away.

It doesn't matter now.

Whatever's going to happen, by tomorrow night, I'll know.

SIX

Anna-Marie

Gummy bears?" I say. "Still?" Shane pulls himself through the window, his shirt catching on the latch like it always did, pulling up to expose his abs.

Which are more defined than I remember. Apparently Shane has taken to working out.

He frees himself, and bounds to his feet with the careless grin that has always been his trademark, along with those bright blue eyes. "It felt fitting. I can't believe the grocery store still carries those things. They're clearly toxic. Gummy bears aren't supposed to do this."

He holds up his fingers, which are stained with unnaturally bright candy colors.

"Please." I fold my arms across my chest. "Don't pretend that's not why you started using those off-brand radioactive hazards in the first place. You wanted me to have to get up earlier than my dad to wash the gummy rainbow off my window before he saw."

His smile becomes all feigned innocence. "I thought it was a cute, fun quirk in a relationship filled with cute, fun quirks. If you want to read malicious intent into my actions . . ."

I laugh, then sit back on my bed against the frame again,

drawing my knees up to my chest. He sprawls out across the foot of my bed, propping his head up on his elbow. He's wearing faded jeans and some t-shirt for a band I've never heard of. His straw-blond hair flops over his hand and he grins up at me.

The déjà vu is so strong, I may have actually traveled back in time.

Except now, I can't help but think of Josh in bed, his head propped up like that. Smiling over at me.

"Shane Beckstrom," I say, firmly pushing away thoughts of deep brown eyes and baseball games and whether he's eaten hot dogs with Asia or Macy. "It's been a long time."

"Five years, just about," he says. "Crazy, right?"

It is. Shane and I were such a constant in each other's lives, even as we broke up and got back together over and over again through the years, that even when I abruptly packed up and left for Los Angeles—and hadn't seen him nearly for a year before *then*—I don't think I could have imagined five years would go by without us running into each other somehow.

"How did you know I'd be back?" I can't help but ask. I didn't tell anyone but Dad. And Patrice.

Before he even speaks, I know the answer.

"Seriously?" he says. "You don't think Aunt Patrice was telling everyone in town about how 'our little Anna-Marie' was finally coming to the reunion this year?"

I groan, but laugh a little too. Because obviously she did.

"I mean, it's not like she told me directly," he says with a smile that says he couldn't give a shit if Patrice talks to him or not. "But word gets around. It's Everett. What the hell else is there to talk about?"

"Sounds like about how I left it." I smile back, because however he found out, and despite all the mess of our past, it *is* good to see him again. "So how are things? How's the band? Is Mikey still an ass?"

"Ha. Well, yeah, probably. But he left us a couple years ago. I think he's in rehab now? Anyway, not my shit to deal with anymore. We have a guy named Dylan on drums now. He whines about his girlfriend constantly, but otherwise he's pretty cool." Shane shrugs. "But no, the band is doing great, actually. We just got back from playing in Denver. This massive show with some really big-name groups. It was kind of mind-blowing."

"Nice!" I'm impressed, but not overly surprised. Shane and I had started dating soon after he first formed his band, Accidental Erotica, and so I was there from the humble garage beginnings. Which mainly involved a lot of noise masquerading as music and Mikey drinking too much and throwing his drumsticks around when he got pissed. But by the last time Shane and I broke up, they had gotten legitimately good, and were starting to play in places that weren't predominantly cattle-populated.

"Well, it's nothing compared to Everett's real shining star," he says, raising an eyebrow. "*Maeve LaBlanche*."

"Okay fine, make fun of the soap opera actress. She's an easy target." I poke him in the chest with my toes.

"I'm not making fun of you! God, you've become paranoid." He smiles, and grabs my foot, holding it in his hand. He rubs the arch with his thumb, and a shiver runs up my leg. "No, I'm really proud of you, Anna. You're making it. I never doubted you would, you know."

"Oh, come on." I shift my foot to poke him again. "You can't say that. I didn't even decide to try for the whole acting thing until well after we'd broken up."

"Okay, fine, I didn't exactly know you'd be some big Hollywood actress. But you were never going to stay here forever, no matter what you thought. You're Anna-Marie Halsey. You were going to take over the world, one way or another." He gestures back at the shelf of trophies and dangling medals lining my wall. "The rest of us just needed to stay out of your way."

I should feel good about his confidence in me, but I think of Josh saying that I should be auditioning more and for some reason the thought scares me.

I think of that phone call, and it's not only the thought of auditioning that scares me.

"Staying out of my way? Is that why we broke up? Because I seem to remember it having more to do with a waitress in Lander you couldn't stop flirting with."

Shane groans. "Yeah, I suppose that may have had something to do with it. I didn't sleep with her, you know."

"Really."

"Well . . ." He scrunches up his face. "Not until after you and I broke up, anyway."

"*There* it is." I laugh, and am happy to find I don't have to force it. This was a common thread back in the day, Shane's wandering eyes—and occasional hands, I assumed, though he's always claimed he never actually cheated on me. He did manage to make the most out of the short gaps in which we were broken up, though. Not that I didn't do the same myself, mostly to get back at him.

God, it's good to not be emotionally invested in that kind of thing anymore.

He tugs on my pinkie toe gently. "I heard about that Reid guy you started seeing after. Sounds like a dick. Is he why you left Wyoming?"

Reid. Ugh. I haven't thought about that bastard in a long time.

"I don't know. He was part of it, I suppose. Like why I left *then*, at least. But I just needed to get out."

Shane nods. If there's one thing he and I will always have in common, it's that neither of us ever felt like we fit in Everett. We'd talk about that sometimes, in our more introspective moments, when we were done groping each other behind the bleachers. How we felt too big for this town, how we sometimes felt like we couldn't breathe here, no matter how much open sky Wyoming held.

I left, and only regret I didn't do it sooner. Shane is still here, and even though things are going well for his band, I feel bad he hasn't fully made his escape yet.

"So tell me about what life is like for a TV star," Shane says, the grin creeping back onto his face. If he resents me for getting out before him, there's no way in hell he's going to tell me.

"Hmmm. Well, I wake up way too early to get to hair and makeup on time, and then spend most of my day in uncomfortably tight clothes waiting around on set for my scene to be up. I work with lots of hot people who are all primarily concerned about how hot they are relative to everyone else. I live in a shitty apartment in a shitty part of town with my awesome roommate, and I probably drink too much because god knows I can't *eat* too much or I won't fit into those tight clothes again the next day. I think that about sums it up."

"And you *love* it."

"I do," I agree, grinning back at him. "Though I just found out that my awesome roommate is going to be moving in with her boyfriend soon. So that's going to suck."

"Really?" His lips twist, as if considering something. "So you're going to be needing a new roommate."

"I don't know, I pay most of the rent myself anyway, since she drives me—wait. Are you trying to get at something here?"

He shrugs. "Maybe. The guys and I have been talking about moving to LA, getting more exposure. Kevin and JT want us all to get a place together, but I see enough of these guys as is, you know? I love them, but I don't need to stare across the breakfast table every morning at their ugly faces." His eyes glint. "Especially if I could be staring at a face that's *way* better looking."

I shake my head incredulously, and shove his chest with my foot. "You're insane. You and me? Roommates?"

"Why not? No matter what, we've always been friends, haven't we?"

"Friends who haven't spoken to each other in like five years." But I get what he means. Like how even after five years, we can still hang out like this and it feels . . . I don't know, familiar.

"Yeah, so?" He dismisses that half a decade with a wave of his hand. "It'd be fun. And I'd pay my fair share of rent, and you wouldn't have to live alone in some shitty apartment in a shitty part of town. We could help each other out, you know?"

When he says it like that, like it's the easiest decision in the world, I can't help but be the tiniest bit tempted. The thought of going back to my Gabby-less apartment, watching *Buffy the Vampire Slayer* alone on our weekly Wine and Doritos night—which will no longer be a thing, I'm guessing?—even not having to smell the god-awful scents of whatever Fong's daily special she's brought home . . .

My gut twists, not just because of how lonely that sounds. But because I suddenly can't help imagining Josh there on my crappy wine-stained couch with me, cuddled up while watching *Dollhouse* and talking about how much better the last movie premiere we've been to would have been if Joss Whedon had written it. Coming back from a fun night at the latest trendy club and then playing *Death Arsenal*, him listening to me rant about the latest DA forum debate.

Josh Rios.

Yeah, like *that* could happen.

Although he does like *hot dogs*, apparently. Which doesn't really have anything to do with my geeky interests, but—

"Unless," Shane continues, breaking into my Josh-related speculation, "you're worried I'll intimidate your boyfriend."

"I don't have a boyfriend," I sputter, and feel my face flush. Sputtering is not the most convincing way to say something. Even if it is true.

"Yeah? Not even that agent guy?" When he sees my surprise, he grins. "I might have Googled you when I heard you were coming back to town. You looked great in that red dress, by the way."

"We're . . . it's super casual. He's not the kind of guy that does serious. And neither am I."

Shane raises an eyebrow. "Really? I don't remember you having problems being serious with me." His fingers tickle the side of my foot and up my ankle.

I pull my foot away then, too fast, and his smile slips. "Hey, I'm just playing. It's cool. If you want me to go—"

"No," I say. "No, it's just . . ."

What? What is wrong with me?

It's just that I miss Josh. It's just that I wish he was the one joking with me and touching me and I wish he wasn't probably doing that with some other girl right now and—

And I can't think that, because I know where it all leads. I've seen it, over and over and over again.

I can't and I *won't*.

"It's nothing," I say, forcing a smile, as I scoot closer to Shane. "Want to get out of here?"

I pull a hoodie on over my cotton tank top and pajama shorts when Shane and I leave through the window. Shane puts a finger to his lips and points upward as he climbs out the window. I lean out to see who exactly he thinks is going to hear us from up on the roof, and spot a family of bats just spreading their wings for the evening.

Lovely. I'm so happy to be back in Wyoming, where the rodents have wings. I duck my head and I lower myself onto a thick branch—and as my top gets tugged up a couple inches by a smaller branch, I note Shane's unabashed appraisal of my bare stomach. Yes, I have been kicking ass on the Roman Chair, thanks.

Even with the hoodie, I immediately regret not putting on more clothes. I had forgotten how freaking cold Wyoming can be, even in the summer. But I'm not going to mention that to him. Without really discussing where we're going, we walk back to his house the next street over and get in his van—the same old beater van he had in high school and used to move band equipment around in.

He starts the engine, and it makes some alarming creaking noises before roaring to life.

"I can't believe you still have this thing." I run my fingers over the ripped fabric of the seat. I'd caused one of those rips when my bracelet caught on it during a particularly good make-out session.

He gives me a side-look. "This van and I have had some pretty great times together. Why would I want to get rid of something like that?"

I don't remember him feeling so charitable towards this van when it wouldn't start in the winter—or moderately cold spring, for that matter—but he clearly isn't talking about cars.

And maybe he's right. I mean, I'm not the girlfriend, serious commitment type. But if I *was*, well—every rom-com I've ever seen, especially those starring my girl Reese, would indicate that Shane is the one I should actually be with. The small town boy, the one I grew up with. Hell, he's one street away from literally being the boy next door (that proximity being a large part of why I spent most of my time at my dad's house rather than my mom's).

We have history. We have chemistry. We have all the freaking school subjects.

I don't answer him, but I do smile over at him, which is enough to make him grin knowingly back as he shifts the van into gear and we head down the street and out the east end of town.

It doesn't take me long to realize we're headed to the hot springs at the edge of the Randalls' property. It's always been one of our favorite spots to hang out and hook up and occasionally get back together after one of our break-ups. Locals know about it, but given that there aren't a ton of locals, it's usually empty.

We chat a bit as we drive, him asking how my mom's been, me asking more about the guys in the band. As we talk, his eyes keep drifting over to my bare legs, and he runs his hand along the back of my arm almost absently, like he used to.

The small talk is all just mindless prelude, but that's okay by me. I don't want to talk or think much, either.

We crunch down the winding trail, the occasional long branch scraping against Shane's van, and he pulls off to the side at one of the patches of dirt and gravel that used to be grassy before people took to parking there. It's not as far in as he could drive—technically the wide dirt path goes pretty much right into the springs—but this, too, is tradition. He squeezes my arm once before opening his car door.

I flash back to how Josh squeezed my knee before dropping me off at work Monday morning. How he does that every time he drops me off for work now—he has for the last few weeks, like our own little tradition.

My chest tightens, and I force the thought away. Because I can't think about it like that.

I can't and I won't.

We get out, my knock-off Uggs (because there was no way in hell I was bringing my real Uggs to Wyoming) tamping down a lone swath of long grass. I've barely had time to slam the door shut behind me before Shane comes around the front of the van and slings an arm around my waist. And then I'm pressed up against the cold metal of the van door and Shane's mouth is on mine and he tastes like cheap gummy bears. His hands tug up my sweatshirt and tank top, and even after five years this all feels so familiar.

"God, I've missed you," he says after a few minutes of us making out against the van.

"Me too," I say, and it feels true, though it occurs to me I haven't actually thought about him all that much the last several years.

There's a lot about Wyoming I haven't let myself think much about the last several years.

He grabs my hand and pulls me forward along the path, which is cleared enough that we don't trip over anything, even in the dark. My eyes adjust and I can see the evergreens and jagged rocks. The air smells like Wyoming. It's earthy and somehow sparse, like after being in LA for so long among the constant deluge of scents there—people and car exhaust and skinny foam lattes—my senses are confused by breathing in just nature.

We reach the first pool of the hot springs. The moonlight reflects on its surface and casts a portion of the pool in a kind of hazy glow. The heat from it wafts against my skin, which should feel comforting, but instead I'm nervous. Unsettled.

Which is crazy. This is what I want. Something uncomplicated and unburdened by anything other than what feels good.

I let out a breath and smile over at Shane. "I don't think either of us brought swimsuits."

"I don't think we've ever brought swimsuits," he says with a chuckle, and pulls his shirt off.

I follow suit, and soon my clothes and his are piles at the edge of the pool. I ease myself into the water, and now, finally, the heat of it is soothing and my nerves start to unwind. Shane splashes in next to me and lets out a low moan as we settle onto our usual shelf of smooth rock and he pulls my body against his.

He *has* been working out. His abs are harder, his arms stronger. We begin kissing again and I feel my body respond to his, my heart pounding, and as our hands explore each other, I am totally not thinking about Josh—who, really, is totally not thinking about me right now, and is probably at some party with Macy dancing up close against him. Which, you know, good for him, because I bet Macy is a great dancer and can also rock a tight red dress.

"You have a condom, right?" I ask, too suddenly and partially into Shane's mouth.

He pulls back and grins. "Of course." Then he reaches back around him towards his crumpled jeans.

There's a splash in the darkness towards the opposite end of the pool, and my nerves ratchet up again. "What was that?" I whisper.

"Probably nothing. Like the wind or something. Don't worry about—"

"Shane Beckstrom, is that you?" a man's voice calls out, and I jump back enough in surprise that I bang my shoulder painfully against some rock.

Shane squints towards the voice. "Who's asking?"

"It's me, Jim Dart!" More splashing and suddenly we can see an old, balding man wading toward us—not just any old, balding man. Our high school guidance counselor, the one who had a tendency of calling girls in for counseling on the days they were wearing their cheerleading uniforms. "How's your dad doing? I haven't seen him in—Why, is that little Anna-Marie Halsey with you?"

I want to sink under the water and die, but I don't think having my obituary read "died while naked in a hot springs with both her ex-boyfriend and Mr. Dart, the creepy guidance counselor," will help my overall mortification.

"Hi, Mr. Dart," Shane says, and judging by his tone, he's only barely holding in his laughter. "My dad's good. And yeah, Anna-Marie's back in town for their reunion."

"Hi, Mr. Dart," I mumble, far less amused. I want to get out of the pool, but I definitely don't want to be seen buck-naked by *him*.

"That's wonderful!" Mr. Dart swims closer, though I really, really wish he wouldn't. He's not wearing those thick square-framed glasses of his, which I'm grateful for. But I also don't want him blindly—or maybe not so blindly—swimming so close he grabs a fistful of my boob. "Nice night for a swim, don't you think?"

"We sure thought so," Shane says, and grins over at me. I respond with a clear, "do something about this" glare. Or maybe just a glare. Either way, Shane ignores the message.

"Congratulations on your success, Anna-Marie," Mr. Dart says, his arms swishing back and forth in the water and causing little waves. I slump down under the water further to keep my chest from being exposed as the water dips. "I always knew you had so many talents to share with the world. I enjoy watching you on your show."

I bet he does. This is coming from a man who once kept me in his office for an hour, trying to talk me into applying to law school, because "those judges won't be able to say no to a pretty girl like you. Especially if you wear things like that."

I wrinkle my nose in disgust at the memory, and am about to say something nasty back, but Shane just laughs.

"She *does* have incredible talents," he says. "Isn't that nice, Anna? Mr. Dart remembers your talents."

Shane has always found guys like Mr. Dart to be pervy in a harmless sort of way, and this is far from the first time he's been overly amused at my expense. But I am growing increasingly pissed and I swear Mr. Dart is floating closer. I can almost count his sparse patches of chest hair.

I pinch Shane hard on his inner thigh, close enough to some more delicate parts of him that he yelps. Then he turns that into a cough and clears his throat. "Hey, Mr. Dart, if you don't mind, Anna-Marie and I were hoping for some, you know, alone time—"

His words are cut off by the sound of an engine approaching from the path. A large outcropping of rock keeps us from being able to see the vehicle—or them from seeing us until they make the last turn—but the glow of oncoming headlights brightens the distant trees in bobbing patches. And that's it for me hanging out here. I have this horrible image of us being joined in the hot springs by more members of Everett's unofficial Creepy Old Men Brigade, summoned by my nakedness like I've sent out a boob-shaped Bat Signal.

I have time to get my clothes on and get the hell out of here before more people arrive. Not much, but some.

"Turn the hell around, Mr. Dart," I growl.

And without looking to see whether he listens to me or whether I'm giving him the peep-show he's always wanted, I scramble out of the springs and grab at my pile of clothes.

"Anna-Marie," Shane groans, disappointed. But I ignore him.

My shorts are caught on a patch of sagebrush, and I swear as I attempt to disentangle them. "Hey, dude, stay turned around, she's changing," I hear him say. "In fact, why don't you back away a few feet."

His chivalry is a little late, but at least it's something.

Mr. Dart chuckles. "She better hurry up, with those Boy Scouts coming back from their day hike."

"Boy Scouts?" My voice is a thin squeak, and I finally manage to get my damn shorts free.

"Their camp is set up back in the clearing there," Mr. Dart says, and thankfully he's at least still facing the other direction, and is further away in the pool. "One of those high adventure week-long campouts that—"

But before I can do more than get one of my feet into my shorts, the van—dear god, it's a whole vanful of them—swings around past the outcropping and I am caught naked and bent over, right in the blinding headlights.

SEVEN

Anna-Marie

The whole "deer in the headlights" thing is real. I've driven in Wyoming enough and nearly hit my share of idiot deer that freeze in the middle of the road.

Right now, though, I share their stupidity and freeze.

No, worse, I instinctively throw my arm up to shield my eyes from the headlights, which I only realize long frozen seconds later has just shown my chest at a more advantageous angle.

Van doors slide open, and I hear a male voice, sounding almost as panicked as I feel, saying, "Boys, wait, don't get out, don't—"

This voice jostles me into movement, and I try to cover my chest, while still trying to tug on my shorts with one hand.

This is not effective at accomplishing either task.

The bright headlights make it so I can't see much from the direction of the van, but I can make out the outlines of kids—Boy Scouts—of all sizes bobbing out of the van. And I can certainly hear the babble of voices, and the growing hush as they see me.

"Awesome," one kid says, in the reverent tones he might reserve for seeing a real-life superhero.

Or a real-life naked woman, I suppose.

Shane bursts out laughing, and I am torn between desperately wrangling on my shorts and deciding whether murdering my ex in front of a troop of Boy Scouts would really make my life any worse at this moment.

I settle for the shorts.

"Boys! Don't look! Get back in the van!" Their equally desperate leader is calling out to them, but apparently hasn't considered turning off the freaking headlights, and I want to yell at him to do so, but talking seems like it would take away much needed brain space from trying to locate my hoodie—where the hell is it? I settle for pulling on my tank top, a task which is normally easy but right now feels like trying to put on really elaborate lingerie in the dark. There are too many straps and holes and I can't seem to get the right end up, and oh my god why couldn't the van have kept driving and hit me instead?

Finally, the leader gets a clue and turns off the headlights—which I suppose I should have run *away* from instead of fumbling with my clothes, but I'm barefoot and would probably have tripped over my own shorts. A second later, I see another, smaller beam of light.

Is that a phone flashlight?

Shit, are they taking *pictures*?

There's a splash and Shane pulls himself out of the water, still laughing, totally unconcerned about his own nakedness, just as I manage to pull my tank top down. Now that I am at least reasonably covered, I should feel better, but I don't. My nerves are still screaming at me as I fumble for my Uggs, and finally find my hoodie under Shane's pants. My re-adjusting eyes make out the taller form of the leader standing in front of the group of boys, trying to herd them back into the van.

The flashlight—hopefully it was just a flashlight—is turned off.

With my boots on, I storm past Shane, who is struggling to pull his jeans up over his wet legs. "Anna-Marie, wait—" he starts, and then swears. Hopefully he caught something painfully in his zipper.

I can feel my whole body burning with embarrassment as I jog past the van of Boy Scouts, most of whom are back inside and at least one of whom is giggling hysterically. I am almost back to Shane's van when he catches up with me, his jeans and shoes on, his shirt balled up in one hand. "Hey, Anna, hey. Stop, okay?"

I don't. I open the door to his van and climb in, and then I sit, wet and cold and shivering in damp clothes, my arms folded across my chest.

Shane sighs as he climbs in the driver seat and shuts the door. "You're mad," he says.

I give him an incredulous look. Which I think is warranted, and much more merciful than the middle finger I should be giving him. "Do you have any idea how humiliating that was?"

Shane's expression softens, though his lips still tilt upward in amusement. "Come on. What do you have to be embarrassed about? Your amazing body? Giving those boys an image they'll cherish well into old age?"

"I was naked. And they were kids!"

"They were teenage boys. They may be Boy Scouts, but I can assure you they've seen a lot more than that on the internet."

I glare at him, but he's probably got a point there.

Shane leans in closer, his smile broadening. Damn the charm of that smile. "And hey, you can bet that recruitment will be at an all-time high after this. Every kid in central Wyoming is going to be signing up for the next campout."

I purse my lips and look steadfastly away. "This is not helping."

But it sort of is. Shane has always been too good at disarming my righteous anger. And he knows it.

"Come on, you have to admit it was funny," he says. "Just a little bit?"

I'm not as cold now, sitting in the van, and I'm no longer being ogled by Mr. Dart or a bunch of teenage boys who thought a knot-tying workshop was going to be the most exciting thing they'd see this weekend.

His fingers lightly tickle my side, and I squirm away, but he does manage to tease a small smile out of me. "Okay, fine," I say, relaxing a bit. "Maybe a little bit."

"See? I knew my Anna-Marie was still in there. None of this LA-girl prissiness, 'I'm too good to flash a few Boy Scouts.' " He winks and starts the car, and by the time we're halfway back to his house, he's got me actually laughing as he does an impression of the panicked troop leader.

But even as I laugh, there's some part of me that can't help but wonder what Josh would have done in that situation. Josh, who is willing to fight battles for his clients about volumizer and who doesn't like Brent trying to pigeonhole me into just working soaps—even though I am pretty new to the industry. Josh, whose mom is a professor of women's studies, and who apparently lectured him all of his growing-up years about how not to be a dick to women. I can't imagine he would have encouraged Mr. Dart like that. Or just sat there and laughed at my humiliation.

Not that I need anyone to fight my battles, I tell myself firmly. And maybe I was just taking myself too seriously. Shane didn't seem care who saw him.

But there's a sharp twinge in my chest that doesn't go away, even as we get to Shane's house and drop off the van. Even as we walk back to my house and creep quietly through the back door (which is always unlocked, because Everett) and up the stairs to my room. The window is still open part-way from when we climbed out earlier, and I leave it despite the cold, hoping Shane will soon decide to use it as an exit, but instead he sprawls out on my bed. He never bothered putting his shirt back on. I'm pretty sure he left it in the van.

"So, is the whole Halsey clan here this year?"

"Well, everyone but Aunt Ida."

Shane grimaces and makes a one-fingered salute to the heavens. "Rest in peace, you crazy old bitch."

I laugh. Which maybe I shouldn't do, considering it's about

the death of a family member, but really, Aunt Ida's passing isn't going to tear anyone up. "But yeah. Cherstie's getting in tomorrow, I think, but everyone else is here. My dad and his latest fiancée, and her kids. Aunt Patrice and Uncle Joe are staying over, and they brought Grandpa with them. And Lily."

Shane makes a disgusted face at that last mention, which pleases me an inordinate amount. Still, I can't resist. "Come on. Are you telling me she never had her way with you? I sure remember her trying an awful lot."

"Yeah. Because desperation and showing me at every possible opportunity how she can give a blow job to a pickle always get me going." Shane gives a mock shudder. "No. I never got with Lily. I have standards, you know."

"Standards? That diner waitress?"

He shrugs and gives me a lopsided smile. "I didn't say they were particularly high."

I roll my eyes. Probably I should be offended, but really I'm not. This is Shane, after all.

"So how are all these people fitting in your house?" Shane asks. "And how did you end up with this big bed, all to yourself?" There's a teasing note in his voice, and he gestures to the bed as if inviting me to join him.

I take off my fake Uggs while I consider, which have been squishing with every step and are starting to smell like wet dog.

"Dad finally made that extra bedroom in the basement, for one thing," I say. "And I also think he knew that if I had to share my bed with Lily—or anyone else for that matter—I'd be driving back to LA first thing tomorrow morning."

"*Anyone* else?" He sits up and leans forward just enough to tug at my fingers. I let him pull me closer.

The truth is, I'm tired and still a little irritated and really just want to change into something dry and warm and sleep until the week is over. But maybe Shane's right, maybe I have gotten a little prissy over the years. Old Anna-Marie wouldn't have let a little mishap at the hot springs keep her from a good time with Shane.

And she definitely wouldn't have let thoughts of another guy—a guy who is hundreds of miles away and surely having his own good times right now—keep her from doing so.

It's really not a big deal, I can hear Josh say in my memory.

Right.

"Yeah, okay, maybe not *anyone*," I say, stepping into his arms. And that's all it takes. We're kissing again, and his hands are up my damp shirt, and before I know it, that shirt is back to being a pile on the floor, along with my shorts and his jeans.

And then we're on the bed together, his body tangled with mine, and well, this really isn't a bad way to get warm, I suppose. His skin is smooth and his hands confident, and my blood heats up as it rushes through me. We've both learned some new things over the past few years, it turns out. Which is nice. But ultimately, it's me and Shane, and we know our way around each other, our motions syncing up naturally, without thought or much in the way of effort.

We're syncing pretty hard when I hear a rustling sound from my curtains.

I freeze. "What was that?" I squint in the direction of my window, but I can't see anything. The light from my bedside lamp isn't that bright.

Shane pauses just enough to groan. "Nothing. It's nothing."

I grab him by his shoulders and hold him still. "That's what you said last time."

"Well, it's not going to be Mr. Dart here in your bedroom, is it?" He's clearly exasperated, but I don't care. Especially once I hear the sound again.

"There it is again," I say, cringing back.

"Come on, Anna, just a few more seconds, I'm almost—"

And then a furry black shape with an impossibly large wingspan launches itself across the ceiling and I have the barest moment to register the fact that there is a *bat in my bedroom* before I yelp and shove Shane away.

"Get it out, Shane, get it out!" I shriek, because that bat is huge and my room is suddenly very very small and confining and oh my god if I end up getting rabies in Wyoming I am officially done with life.

"It's out," he grumbles. "Trust me."

"The bat, you ass! Get the—" My tirade is cut short when the bat swoops again, perilously close to the bed. I scream and roll off the side of the bed, landing on my knees on the carpet, painfully and with a loud thump.

Somewhere below me in the house, a dog starts howling.

Shit. Shit shit shit.

But the bat swoops again, even though Shane isn't doing much more than sitting up naked in bed and glaring at it.

I'm all for feminism and women being able to save themselves, but when there is a clearly rabid monster-bat in my bedroom, I don't care how sexist it is. This is a man's responsibility.

"Shane, do something!"

"What do you want me to—"

And that's when my bedroom door bursts open, and my dad comes in, wild-eyed and in nothing but a pair of boxers, carrying a baseball bat.

That sight gets Shane moving, at least in as much as he jumps off the bed and backs up a few steps toward the dresser. Which just means he's standing there buck naked, condom still hanging from his penis while I'm on my knees next to him, also naked.

"Hi, Mr. Halsey," Shane says.

My dad's face turns a shade of purply-red normally reserved for cartoon characters before steam shoots out of their ears. But before that can happen, my uncle Joe is in the doorway, Aunt Patrice behind him.

"What's going on?" Patrice demands. "Is Anna-Marie all right?"

"I'd say so," Uncle Joe says with a chuckle, taking in the scene and scratching at his thick mustache.

"Get out!" I yell, scrambling for the nearest blanket on my

bed. But the bat swoops across the room again, and I duck and shriek—as does Patrice, and, rewardingly, Uncle Joe—and at the very least, now everybody has their eyes on the bat and not me.

Everyone, that is, except Byron, my future stepbrother, who has somehow entered the room in all the panic and is staring at me, transfixed. And behind him, Lily, her dark hair a mess, and mascara smudges around her eyes, but still managing to look a thousand times more composed than me right now as she takes in the scene with visible glee.

"That's it," I hear Tanya announce from behind them all in the hallway. "Bill will take care of the bat. The rest of you, out. Now." She pushes her small frame through the growing crowd and grabs Byron's ear. "Especially you," she says, tugging her son from the room.

If I wasn't still huddled on the ground, tugging a blanket around me, I'd have kissed the woman, I am so damn grateful to her.

The others file out, Lily giving Shane one last long look-over that he is clearly trying to pretend he doesn't see, though he does finally notice the condom and slides it off with one hand. Tanya closes the door with a definitive slam.

And then there are just the four of us: me, Shane, my weapon-wielding dad, and the bat, who is a dark blob on the ceiling beside my bookshelf. There's a moment of silence, in which we all four regard each other, and then my dad finally speaks.

"Get your damn pants on, Shane," he says. "And then help me with the bat."

"Yes, sir," Shane replies, and pulls his jeans on.

It takes about ten minutes and several failed attempts, as well as multiple times in which I burrow under my blanket to avoid getting swooped upon. But eventually, my dad traps the bat in my small desk garbage can (which theoretically means that the bat probably isn't the ginormous vampire-legend monstrosity it seemed a few minutes earlier) and flings it back out the open window.

Then he glares at both of us—but mainly Shane—and walks out of the room, not saying a word. I groan and put my head in my hands.

"So . . . any chance you want to—" Shane starts, but I glare at him and the look on my face shuts him up. He nods. "Yeah, okay. See you, Anna-Marie." He climbs out the window and down the tree.

I hurriedly close the window to prevent the return of either bats or ex-boyfriends. Then I crawl into bed and wish I wasn't too exhausted to drive back to LA.

EIGHT

Anna-Marie

Despite the events of last night being reason enough to never emerge from my bedroom ever again, I do manage to gather courage and dignity enough to do so. Sometime around noon, but still.

It doesn't matter that my entire family has seen me naked now, I decide. Well, my entire family and several soon-to-be members of my family. And a whole troop of Boy Scouts. And my high school guidance counselor.

Honestly, at this rate I should probably just ride through town on horseback like Lady Freaking Godiva and get it over with.

When I get downstairs, I am cheered by the fact that my cousin Cherstie has arrived and is sitting at the kitchen table, flipping through a magazine—*People*, it looks like—with Ginnie. The younger girl is tugging on her braid and studying the pictures with a strangely intense concentration. Buckley the dog is a huge mop-like pile on the kitchen floor that barely stirs when I enter.

Cherstie grins when she sees me. "Anna-Marie!" she cries and jumps up to give me a hug, which I happily return. Cherstie may look a lot like her older sister Lily—same dark hair and big brown eyes, same scattering of freckles across her nose—but the two couldn't be more different. For one, Cherstie has a nice habit of not being a total bitch. When she graduated high school she moved to Cheyenne, which is as far from her parents as she could get and still be in Wyoming, and that I had to respect.

"Hey," I say. "How have you been? How's cosmetology school?"

"Good! I've only got about two months left, and then I can finally start making some money."

"Nice."

Ginnie makes a little squeak and bounces in her chair. "This one," she says, pointing at a picture in the magazine. Then she looks up at me and smiles shyly. "I think you'll look beautiful like this."

"Um . . . what?" I raise my eyebrow at Cherstie, who is clearly trying to hold in a laugh.

"So I heard about your . . . adventure last night," Cherstie says, carefully. "And Ginnie and I thought maybe you could use some cheering up. And I remember how when we were younger, you and I always had fun when I would do your hair and makeup and—"

"The fashion shows," I say with a groan, but one that is more amused than miserable. Those were always fun.

"Exactly." Cherstie grins. "So I told Ginnie to flip through the magazine and find the very best hairstyle for you. And she has chosen . . . wow." Her eyes widen and practically gleam with joy. I have a bad feeling about this all of a sudden.

Cherstie holds up the magazine and it takes everything in me not to cringe when I see the huge, hair-sprayed mass of teased hair. "Melanie Griffith in *Working Girl*, huh?" I manage. "How old is this magazine?"

"It's so glamorous," Ginnie says in a dreamy tone. I don't know much about kids her age, but I don't get the feeling she's punking me. And really, if you're going to do a fashion show at a family reunion in Everett, Wyoming, hair from the 1980s is probably fitting.

"Okay, I'm in," I say, which prompts an excited squeal from Ginnie and a laugh from Cherstie. "Just let me get something to eat first."

"There's sandwich meat in the fridge," Aunt Patrice says, sweeping in from the living room as if she'd been waiting all day for the chance to tell this to someone. She gives me a look like she's trying not to judge me but can't figure out how one goes about not judging. "You look . . . well rested."

I have no idea how to respond to that, but before I can even take a stab at it, my dad walks in from the backyard, the screen door banging shut behind him. "Hey, Pumpkin," he says, not quite meeting my eyes as he hurries through the kitchen.

Ugh. I can't spend the whole reunion pretending last night didn't happen.

"Hey, Daddy," I say, striding into the hallway to catch up with him. He turns around, and gives a faint smile in a kind of "we're really doing this, I guess" resignation. "I'm sorry you had to see that last night. It's your house, and I should have warned you about Shane sleeping over—"

He lets out a chuckle. "Not that you ever did that before."

But he seems legitimately amused, so I smile back. "Yeah, well. I probably should start at some point."

"Look, Pumpkin, it's okay." He sighs. "It was awkward as hell, but it's okay. You're a grown woman. You've been one for a long time. I have to accept that you're not my baby girl anymore."

Well, if anything was going to make him finally come to that realization, it was last night—which is certainly not the first time he'd caught me in some compromising situation with Shane, but definitely the most flagrant. But I feel a pang of loss at his words, and I can tell by his expression that he does, too.

"Maybe," I venture. "I can still be both?"

He smiles gently. "Sure thing, Pumpkin." He gives me a hug and I realize how much I've missed my dad. How rare moments like this are, and always have been, even when I saw him every day. "Really, though," he says, as he draws back. "Shane? Still? I'd hoped you'd be on to a higher quality of man by now."

I laugh, though suddenly I wonder what Dad would think of Josh. Which leads to me thinking about that phone call again, and about *missing* him—no. I can't and I won't.

"Old habits are hard to break," I say.

Dad pats me on the shoulder. "Ain't that the truth."

"Bill," Aunt Patrice says, leaning into the hallway from the kitchen, brandishing a pack of lunch meat. "Has the UPS fellow come by yet? The reunion shirts are supposed to be in today."

"Reunion shirts?" I ask as Dad shakes his head.

Patrice's eyes narrow in irritation. "They have that fancy tracking thing on the internet, and it says they're in Farson, which is close enough, if they're actually doing their work and not sitting around eating donuts."

I'm fairly certain she's confusing UPS driver stereotypes with police officer stereotypes, but that hardly seems worth mentioning to her. "Reunion shirts?" I say again. "Like the matching kind? Are we going to Disneyland or something? Ooh, are we finally taking that family tour of Everett's two auto-parts shops?"

Dad laughs, but Patrice doesn't seem amused. "I thought it would be nice. For the Grillmaster Championship." She purses her lips. "I should call UPS. Here, Anna-Marie, make a sandwich for yourself. You looked a little pale last night, you probably need the iron."

I take the package of sliced roast beef from her and only roll my eyes once she's taken off to go track down her missing t-shirts.

Later that afternoon, I'm back in my room, sitting in my desk chair, while Cherstie begins the process of turning me into an eighties style nightmare. I remind her not to do anything damaging to it, and fear I sound like Josh's client with the volumizer, but Cherstie shakes her head at me and tells me that she remembers how picky I am about my hair, and besides, she's now a *professional.* Ginnie bounces on my bed as she watches. Cherstie and I chat, and I flip through that *People* magazine, which as it turns out is a brand-new issue that just happened to be featuring a retrospective of Melanie Griffith's Hollywood career.

Lucky me.

I turn to a page talking about the recent breakup of Blake Pless and Kim Watterson, Hollywood super-couple with a six-year marriage during which they gushed regularly about each other, and their adorable little kids, and about their "perfectly normal" marriage.

Well, I suppose it ended up being pretty normal, after all.

"Isn't that sad?" Cherstie says, peeking over my shoulder. "I really thought they had a chance."

"Really? You saw how gorgeous their nanny is, right?" The article doesn't specify that she factored into their divorce, but I've seen pics online of Blake standing awfully close to their nanny, and from the way she's smiling back at him, it's pretty clear she's been taking care of more than just the kids.

Cherstie tugs at my hair, as she teases a big chunk near my crown. "You're just cynical."

"I'm a realist. Who knows you don't hire a nanny who could be Sweden's Next Top Model and not expect this to happen."

Cherstie chuckles and starts teasing another section.

RIP, Watterpless, who have officially joined the ranks of Brangelina and Bennifer and all the many, many others. Even my beloved Joss Whedon, for all his talk about respecting women, couldn't keep it in his pants. Maybe I am cynical, but I'd rather be that than an idiot who thinks these things don't inevitably end in total heartbreak.

Cherstie finishes teasing my hair and sprays the contents of an entire can of extra-firm hold hair spray over it (we open the window so as to not choke to death during this part, and I pray the fumes will ward away future bat attacks), and then Ginnie begs to do my makeup. Cherstie has a huge case filled with every color of eyeshadow and lipstick imaginable, and Ginnie and I have way too much fun picking through it, though I tell her she can choose what colors I wear. She takes her time, chewing her lower lip and studying each bright little eyeshadow pot and eyeliner, narrowing down the choices seemingly based on quantity of glitter. It's pretty cute, actually—so much so that when she finally chooses two very sparkly eyeshadows named "Indigo Revolution" and "Screaming Pink" that should never be combined outside of a drag queen show, I compliment her on her impeccable taste and happily submit to the rest of the makeover.

Makeup takes a long time, with Ginnie fussing adorably over blush and lipstick just as much as the eyeshadow. It's already past dinnertime by the time Cherstie tells Ginnie she should pick out my runway outfit. She starts rifling through my closet, which unfortunately for me still holds all sorts of outfits I didn't feel the need to bring with me to LA when I left years ago. My cheerleading uniforms, prom dresses, graduation gown, that sort of thing. Practically a little girl's costuming dream. Ginnie eventually emerges with an emerald green spandex number from one of my old dance recitals. The sheer number of sequins are blinding, and the short skirt has honest-to-god fringe.

"This one," she says in a rapturous tone.

Of course that one.

When I'm in my outfit and with my huge helmet of teased hair and my shockingly bright makeup, I look like some combination of an off-Vegas showgirl and one of those Ladies of WWE Wrestling from the eighties.

But I can't help smiling; despite how awful yesterday was, I've actually had fun this afternoon. Maybe this reunion won't *all* be awkward family interactions and animal attacks and accidental nudity.

Cherstie and Ginnie gather everyone in the basement and announce that I'm going to be showing off the "latest in Hollywood superstar fashion." When everyone is settled (and I'm waiting at the top of the stairs for my cue), I hear Ginnie say, “Wait! We need music!”

“Maybe we can sing something,” Cherstie says.

“Fat-Bottomed Girls?” Lily suggests, and I wish a particularly nasty herpes outbreak upon her.

“I’ve got a song,” Grandpa says. “Anna-Marie always liked this one. Does anyone have spoons?”

And thus it is that I walk down the stairs and along the makeshift runway—a long line of towels laid out in a path between the pushed-back ratty couches—to the sound of my eighty-two-year-old grandfather singing “You Are My Sunshine” and playing a set of spoons on his knee.

The Milan Fashion Show, this is not.

But I’m playing it up, striking dramatic modeling poses because each time I do Ginnie cheers, and most everyone is laughing and having a good time. Grandpa is on the second verse of the song when the doorbell rings. Buckley, who is parked firmly across both my dad’s and Tanya’s laps, raises his head and utters one lonesome “wooooof” before deciding he’d rather go back to sleep.

“I bet it’s finally that lazy UPS driver,” Aunt Patrice says. “Keep the show going. I’ll be right back.”

I’m not sure what else I’m supposed to do—this is a fashion show consisting of one model and one outfit, after all. I ask Ginnie to join me in my next trip down the catwalk, and she eagerly does so, even though she’s far more reasonably dressed in jeans, a t-shirt, and my homecoming queen tiara.

Grandpa circles back around to the first verse of “You Are My Sunshine,” the spoons clattering away on his knee, and Ginnie follows behind me as I make another trip on the runway, copying my poses, which I do my best to make increasingly ridiculous. I barely hear Patrice’s footsteps on the stairs as she comes back down, so caught up am I in my dramatic rendition of John Travolta’s *Saturday Night Fever* dance. Ginnie is giggling so hard behind me that I think she’s going to choke, and I whirl around with my finger thrust in the air and my hip thrust to the side, and then I freeze.

Because standing there at the bottom of the steps, just behind Aunt Patrice, is—

"Josh!" I blurt out, so stunned I forget for a long second to drop my pose.

Josh Rios.

Here, in a short-sleeve button down shirt and cargo shorts and flip-flops, dressed way more casually than I usually see him, and yet looking no less hot.

Watching me do *this*.

For what it's worth, he looks almost as surprised as I am, though his wide-eyed, slightly gaping shock is rapidly turning into one of those gorgeous grins of delight that never fail to make my heart beat faster. "Hey," he says, his dark eyes gleaming.

Grandpa trails off on his song when he realizes I'm no longer walking the runway.

"Anna-Marie, you have a visitor," my Aunt Patrice announces, super helpfully. She turns to Josh. "You didn't happen to see a UPS truck on the way in, did you?"

Josh blinks. "Um. No, sorry. Lots of cows, though."

I want to laugh, but I think I've lost the ability to even breathe. Because I have just remembered what I currently look like.

Patrice sighs, and it's unclear whether it's in disappointment about the lack of reunion shirts or at Josh's joke. "Well, why don't you introduce us, Anna-Marie?"

I stand there stupidly, because all I can think is "Why on earth is Josh here?" and I remember us joking about hot dogs and him saying "Maybe I will" and me missing him even though I know how ridiculous that is and now he's actually here in Everett and—

"Right," I say, blinking back into the present. I take the couple steps to go stand by Josh. He smells like his usual deliciously spicy cologne and . . . Doritos? "Hey everyone, this is my . . ."

My brain has a minor stroke. My what?

My boyfriend? Um, *no*.

My friend? Obviously not.

My super hot guy I have amazing sex with and a relationship of a happily undetermined nature?

Josh is watching me expectantly, his eyebrow raised. He's clearly not about to bail me out.

". . . Josh," is all I manage. And then I flush as I realize I've just called him "my Josh," which is a potentially worse answer than any of the ones I mentally discarded. But he just smiles knowingly at me. "Josh Rios," I clarify to my family, lest they think he's some diva who insists on only having one name, like Cher or Adele. "Josh, this is . . . well, everybody." I name them off, one by one, and try not to glare at Lily as I do so, even though she's eyeing Josh like she's a starving wolf and he's a large piece of untended flank steak.

"Nice to meet you all," he says, and he's smiling so broadly I actually believe he does find it nice to meet my motley band of family members at a basement fashion show in Everett, Wyoming.

They all stare at him, and I know that every single one of them—with the exception, perhaps, of Ginnie and Buckley—is thinking about Shane last night in my bedroom and wondering how Josh fits into to all of this. Lily sits forward on the couch, practically squirming with bottled vengeance.

Please please please let none of them say anything about last night.

"So what brings you here, Josh?" my dad says, and I give him a warning look, which he ignores. I'm wondering the same thing, but I don't really want Josh answering that question in front of my entire family, the eldest of which is still jouncing his knee up and down like he's just waiting to return to the spoons.

"Um," Josh says. "Anna-Marie invited me to try the best hot dogs in the world, and I couldn't pass that up."

If Josh really drove fifteen hours to try hot dogs, he must be even more of a fanatic than he let on. But I don't think for one minute this is really why he's here. The warning klaxons are blaring, but under that, there's a steady, sweet note of something else.

Am I *thrilled* to see him? Even here, like this? Oh, god. This is—

"She had a hot dog last night," Lily says, and it is only my mortification that prevents me from vaulting over the coffee table and strangling her. Josh looks at me, concerned, possibly because my face is likely the same color as my dad's was last night when he was faced with full-frontal Shane. I'm pretty sure I can't get anymore embarrassed than I am at that moment, and then—

"*Rios*," Uncle Joe says slowly. "Is that Mexican?"

Oh no.

"Puerto Rican, actually," Josh says.

"Do you know Julio?" Uncle Joe asks. "Nice fellow. He works down at the auto shop. The real one, not the grocery store one."

"Um, no. Is he Puerto Rican?" Josh asks.

"Maybe." Joe shrugs. "Never asked. Somewhere like that, though, I bet, with a name like Julio."

I make a little squeak of embarrassment, because I cannot believe this is actually happening and that I'm trapped in an even worse nightmare than last night's Boy Scout escapade.

But Josh doesn't seem fazed. His eyes cut over to me, and I see the mischievous turn to his smile. "Sorry, don't know Julio. Hey, do you any of you know my friend Ryan? He's from Wyoming, I think. Or maybe Nevada."

I find myself smiling back at him, my mortification fading at seeing that Josh isn't already so offended by my family's casual racism that he's going to leave as soon as he arrived.

I see Tanya grinning, and Dad looks cautiously amused.

"No, I don't think so." Uncle Joe squints as he searches his memory.

"I know a Ryan," Lily says, and runs her tongue over her upper lip.

I bet she does.

"Well, Josh and I should—" I start, but Aunt Patrice cuts me off.

"Puerto Rico!" she exclaims. "How fascinating? Isn't that fascinating, everyone? I'm a bit of a student of cultures," she tells Josh, with a humble little wave of her hand.

I bite my lip to keep from making a comment about the Muslim family she went on about yesterday that might or might not be Indian, or even Muslim. I see Cherstie rolling her eyes.

"Now, Josh," Patrice says, placing a hand on his upper arm, and suddenly I wonder if I'm going to have to protect him from both Lily and her mother. "That doesn't sound like a very Hispanic name."

"Well, my given name is actually Josué. But I've gone by Josh ever since I can remember."

"*In*-teresting," Patrice says. "That sounds like 'Joe's Way.' Isn't that funny, Joe? Well, you don't need to worry about the Halseys not respecting your culture. We are happy to call you by your real name."

"Really, it's not—" he starts, at the same time that I say "Patrice, that's not—"

She steamrolls over both of us. "Why doesn't everyone try saying it together. Joe's Way. Joe's Way."

My family mumbles this with varying degrees of enthusiasm—Ginnie on the upper end, bouncing as she shouts the words. Tanya mouthing something at my dad that is clearly not "Joe's Way" and shaking her head.

"Oh my god," I say under my breath. Or maybe not under my breath, because next to me Josh glances at me and lets out a laugh that he quickly smothers when Patrice turns back to him.

"So how about you tell us something interesting about your people?" she asks.

"Patrice, let's not—" I try again.

"Puerto Ricans, I mean," she says, and I'm not sure if she thought she had been too subtle in her racism before, like she'd been asking about his "people" being hot guys in their late twenties.

Josh just gives me a quick smile and squeezes my hand. Warmth rushes up my arm, entirely different from the hot flush of pure embarrassment I've been feeling since he arrived.

"My people are actually called Bel-Airians," he says with a completely straight face. "It's a regional term."

Tanya snickers, and I find myself liking her even more. My dad is just closing his eyes and rubbing his temple like he has a migraine. The rest of them totally miss the joke, and Patrice nods seriously. "Well, I have never heard that term before. Fascinating."

"I dropped one of my damn spoons," Grandpa says, and starts digging around under the seat cushions.

We need to get out of here. "Josh is a fascinating guy," I say, and squeeze his hand back, not sure if I'm holding in hysterical laughter or hysterical tears, but sure as hell holding back something. "Okay, well, we're going to—"

"So when did your family immigrate, Joe's Way?" Patrice asks.

I'm about to inform her that they didn't immigrate, because Puerto Rico is in fact a part of the United States, but Josh speaks first. "Before I was born," he says. "My dad was a brain surgeon in San Juan for several years, before he started teaching neurosurgery at UCLA."

At this, Grandpa stops digging for his lost spoon. "Your dad's a doctor, you say? I've had this growth on my netherregions. It's like a big grape right there on the end of my—"

"Dad, stop," my dad tries, finally doing something to spare me from this hell.

"He's a doctor! He sees netherregions all the damn time, doesn't he? I just think he could take a look and see what he thinks it is."

Josh blanches at this. He's starting to look dazed. He's probably—and very sanely, I might add—thinking that there is no hot dog in the world worth this. Or girl, for that matter. "Um. I'm an agent, not a doctor. My *dad* is a *brain surgeon*."

"Okay, that's enough!" I step in front of Josh like I've seen managers do in front of A-list clients who are being hassled by the press. "Josh will be able to answer questions later. Maybe. But right now, we're going to talk. Him and me. Alone."

And then I pull Josh along after me as I head up the stairs to my bedroom.

NINE

Anna-Marie

I close the door behind us and find myself leaning against it, my hands up in front of my face, partly from embarrassment, and partly because the fact that Josh Rios is here, in my bedroom—seeing me dressed like I'm the second most famous hooker from the eighties after *Pretty Woman*—makes me want to hyperventilate. "Oh my god, I am so sorry about them. Seriously."

"Hey, it's fine," Josh says, and his touch is gentle as he tugs on my elbow, and suddenly I'm in Josh's arms and it feels so good and right and—

Panic floods my brain and I pull back. I am in very serious trouble, and if I was back in LA I would force myself to delete Josh's number from my phone and never talk to him again.

But I can't. Because he's *here*.

"My Uncle Joe pestering you about immigrating was not fine," I say. "My Aunt Patrice talking about your 'people' was not fine. Grandpa practically whipping out his dick at you—" I shudder, and Josh laughs.

"Yeah, okay, it was a little overwhelming. And I'm kind of worried about your grandpa; I think someone needs to take him to an actual doctor. But none of that is your fault." He ducks his head down to meet my eyes, smiling.

"You must be regretting your decision to come here," I say. "Into the den of crazy people who apparently don't know that Puerto Ricans are American."

"Hey, but you do. You'd be surprised how many people don't, at least not until it was wiped out by that hurricane and suddenly started impacting their tax dollars."

I cringe and step around him to sit, rather ungracefully and forcefully, onto my bed. "Don't be too impressed. I may have Googled Puerto Rico after our first date, when I realized I knew absolutely nothing about it."

"Really?"

"Yeah," I say, wanting to bury my head in my hands again. Instead I just look sheepishly up at him. "Pretty sad, huh? I blame the Wyoming educational system."

He sits next to me and I'm struck by the fact that Josh Rios is sitting on my childhood bed. Not that my teenage self would have had any idea who he was back then—since he was only a college student who did some modeling on the side—but she damn well would have been impressed at just the sight of him there.

I feel a little less like running away.

"I think it's kind of sweet, actually," he says. "That you cared enough to do that."

I smile at him, feeling a flush spreading through me that may still be residual embarrassment, but probably has much more to do with the whole aforementioned Josh being on my bed thing and my body trying to figure out why in the hell we're both still clothed.

God, even back in LA I would have had a hard time deleting his number. "Well, it was a pretty great date."

"It was," he agrees, his brown eyes gleaming. "And if it makes you feel better, I had to Google Wyoming to get here. And I don't just mean your address. I mean *Wyoming*. So there's that."

"Yeah, there's that." In what is a rare moment in all my time with Josh, I'm at a serious loss for what to say. "So you're here," I finally manage.

And with that insightful statement, I have officially lost the right to ever again complain about the terrible dialogue on *Southern Heat*.

Josh rakes a hand through his hair. "Yeah. I'm here." He studies my worn carpet for a bit before looking back up at me, and I'm surprised to see he looks . . . nervous. "Is that okay? I probably should have called you from the road but—"

"You *drove* all the way out here?"

He bites his lower lip. "A little bit, yeah."

I'm still not entirely sure why he's here at all, let alone why he would have driven fifteen hours to do so—certainly not for the hot dogs.

But the fact that he did so, the fact that he's here, makes my heart swell and my palms feel sweaty and I'm afraid to examine too closely why, mostly because some traitorous part of me is *glad* this didn't happen in LA, where I had the option to delete his number.

"Wow," I say. "I mean, that's a long drive. I know, because I just drove it."

Score another revenge victory for soap opera writers everywhere. My god, where have my powers of reasonably intelligent speech gone?

He blinks, and swallows. "I can go, you know. If this is too weird, I can just—"

"No," I say, too quickly. But the thought of him leaving hits me like a punch to the gut. "No, I don't want you to go. Really. I'm just surprised, that's all."

He looks cautiously hopeful. "Yeah? Good surprised?"

And partly because he looks so unaccountably vulnerable, but mostly because I've been wanting to do this ever since I saw him in my family's basement, I lean into him and kiss him. Soft at first, and then deeply, until I've pretty much crawled onto his lap and we're making out like we've been apart for months instead of days and my whole body is on fire, just alight with Josh, and his hands are in my hair and—

"Ow," I say, and I realize after another scalp tug that his hand is stuck in my hair.

Which, I had forgotten, is sprayed up with a lifetime supply of Aquanet.

"Sorry," he says, grimacing as he carefully extricates his hand from the bird's nest that is my hair.

But once I pull back from the kiss, I see my hot pink lipstick is now smeared all over his lips and beyond, and he has splotches of glittery blush in random places on his cheeks.

I should just give up on life right then and there. Well done, Wyoming. After twenty-four years, you've finally embarrassed me to death.

Instead, I let out a giggle that turns into a full-out belly laugh. Josh raises his eyebrows at me, grinning but clearly not getting why I'm laughing so hard. This only makes me laugh harder, especially as the glitter catches the light.

I point at the mirror over my vanity, and he turns and then groans.

"Oh my god, Halsey," he says. "What have you done to me? I look like I'm auditioning for some all-clown version of *Moulin Rouge*."

This summons a fresh peal of laughter from me, and I'm literally curled up on the bed, laughing so hard tears are starting to roll down my cheeks.

The absurdity of the last day and a half has finally caught up to me. And none of it is funnier or more absurd than Josh Rios, here in my childhood bedroom, in his flip-flops—nice ones, granted, but he owns these things?—emerging from a make-out session looking like Ronald McDonald gone drag.

"Totally worth it, though." He grins and flops down on the bed in a way that makes the whole mattress bounce and I laugh some more.

I swipe at my eyes, undoubtedly smearing more makeup

around my face. "Yeah? Because I gotta say, this is a good look for you."

He laughs. "Yeah, you too. Especially the hair. How many woodland creatures can you house in there, exactly?"

"Oh my god." I roll my eyes. "I can't believe you walked in to see me like this." I gesture broadly at myself, making sure to include the sequined green outfit in the tally of awfulness.

"The best part was definitely the dance moves. I've never seen someone shake like that to 'You Are My Sunshine.' "

I groan. "Don't remind me."

"Come on, it was adorable. That little girl, Ginnie? She was copying your every move, and having the best time." He grins at me, and I melt a little inside.

"Well, that's good. Because I think she has better prospects as a dancer than as a makeup artist." I grin back as I roll off the bed and grab some makeup removal wipes from the vanity. I toss a few to him. "Speaking of which, here. You've got to get that makeup off. I can't stand not being the prettiest one in the relationship."

He blinks, and I catch the word I used too late.

Relationship.

I mean, yeah, we have *a* relationship. But there are relationships and there are *relationships*, and what if he thinks I meant the non-casual kind?

What if, for just a second there, I did?

The panic klaxons in my head sound even louder than ever.

I very carefully don't look at him as I wipe my face as clean as I can. He stands next to me and does the same. I'm searching for the words to play off what I've just said, but he beats me to it.

"You know that word you avoided using before," he says. "When you introduced me, I mean." He swipes one last time, adding the wadded up, glitter-covered wipe to the growing stack on my vanity, and then looks at me sideways. His voice is artificially casual. "If you wanted to use it, I wouldn't hate it."

And now I'm blinking at him in surprise. Is Josh saying he wants to be my boyfriend? There's a part of me that lights up, that feels giddy with the idea, giddy and warm and—

And naive. And idiotic. Because I know better. But a large part of me does not want to know better right now, and that terrifies me.

"Yeah, I turned into a stuttering mess in there, didn't I?" is what I say. "Like some combination of the shock of seeing you and the chemical fumes from this much hair spray caused me to have a mini-stroke."

He smiles, but it's forced, and I know he did not miss my total dodge of the boyfriend issue. But I can't tell him it's not what I want, and I don't trust myself to address it until I can.

What I do know is that I can't agree to be his girlfriend, because when we go back to LA and it takes him five seconds to hook up with the next hot actress who throws herself his way, that will make me the biggest idiot on the planet. And that's the best case scenario. Worst case, I'm Kai Cole getting letters from my ex about all the times he couldn't resist the "needy, aggressive" women in Hollywood.

No, thank you.

Josh clears his throat and shrugs. "Yeah, well, you should know my real reason for driving out all this way was in fact the hot dogs. I have to taste these championship-winning dogs you bragged so much about."

I smile, and wonder if mine looks as fake as his does. I hope not. I'm the actress, after all.

"In fact," he continues, looking over my shoulder. "Are any of those trophies over there from the Halsey Grilling Championship?"

"Halsey Grillmaster Championship," I correct him. "And no. I have never won the Golden Weiner. It's pretty much always Uncle Joe."

"The Golden Weiner, huh? Sounds prestigious." He walks over to the trophies on the shelf. "First place, National Debate Team. First place dance. First place science fair. First place . . . blueberry pie eating?" He looks back at me with eyebrow raised.

"Anna-Marie Halsey. I knew you were a woman of many talents, but damn."

I settle myself back on my bed, pulling my legs up under me, grateful that Josh seems to want to get away from the relationship subject as fast as I do. "There's not a lot to do in Wyoming. So I kind of got involved in everything."

"I can see that." The dangling golden track medal from junior year swings as he touches it. "Did you ever not come in first place?"

"Lots of times." I play with the eyelet hem on my comforter. "I only have the first place trophies, though. My parents always threw out the others."

"Really?" His smile drops as he looks back at me. "Why?"

I shrug. "My mom and dad are both really concerned with my success. They always have been. It may be the only thing they ever had in common. And they always wanted me to be the best."

His eyebrows draw together in concern and he sits down on the bed next to me. "That sounds . . . stressful."

"Only when I couldn't be," I say. Then I shake my head. "It's okay, though. It's not like they were mean about it, they just . . . have high expectations. I think because neither of them felt like they really amounted to much."

He nods, but I don't get the feeling he quite understands. "So I bet they're pretty proud of you now, being on TV and all."

"Yeah, I'd say. When I was on the cover of *Soap Opera Digest*, even though it was just one of those inset pictures in the corner, I think my dad bought up every copy in the county to send to everyone he knew." I smile, but it still feels forced, which is strange. I really had been so happy to hear my dad gush about me like that. "I'm a little surprised he hasn't completely papered the walls with them."

Josh kicks off his flip-flops, then repositions himself so his back is against the brass headboard. The same position I was in when we talked on the phone about hot dogs and baseball games.

A pit forms in my gut, as I think about Shane on that bed, just last night. About *Shane and I* on that bed.

Should I tell him about that? Would he even *want* to know?

We've never said we weren't seeing other people. He may want to be my boyfriend now, but that doesn't mean he hasn't been dating other girls the whole time he was seeing me—in fact, though I tried not to think about it much, I fully assumed he was.

But the guilt churns in me anyway.

"Well, I'm a little surprised," he says, and I have a panicked second of thinking he could read my thoughts. "I gotta admit, when I was thinking about seeing the bedroom you grew up in, I imagined it covered in posters of boy bands or, I don't know, Zac Efron."

"Zac? Really?" I can't help but scoot in closer.

"Robert Pattinson? A Hemsworth brother? A *Franco* brother?"

"Mmmm, nope. No posters of any of them. I didn't really do the celebrity crush thing. At least, not until I was out in LA."

"Not until then, huh?" He moves in closer as well. "So who had the honors of being Anna-Marie Halsey's first big celebrity crush?"

"Ummm . . . " I wrinkle my nose.

Josh leans in close. "Please don't tell me it's one of my clients. Chad Montgomery?"

"No, not one of your clients. But it was one of my previous co-workers."

He squints, searching his memory, and then his eyes widen. "Not—"

"Yep. Ryan Lansing. The guy whose sexcapades in Bridget Messler's dressing room ended up getting me fired." I laugh, but don't bother explaining that mess further. Josh already knows all about the 'stolen' fake Emmy that eventually led to my current job. "Honestly, I was pretty much over the crush part as soon as I met him and found him incapable of stringing a single sentence together that wasn't about himself."

"Really. So there was nothing to those rumors about the two

of you." He gives me a look that says he knows well otherwise.

"I didn't say that. I mean, egotistical idiot or not, he was still Ryan Lansing."

He laughs. "Fair enough. I can't blame you. If I'd had the opportunity to hook up with my celebrity crush, I would've taken it." He pauses. "If I'd met her when she was much younger. And not dead."

"What?" I've scooted close enough that I'm back to being practically in his lap again. "Please tell me about this."

He covers his eyes. "No way. I can't. It's too embarrassing."

"Come on, more embarrassing than this?" I strike the pose he caught me in downstairs, my disco-John Travolta. "Or this?" I press down my hair and can feel it bounce back up to its lofty heights.

He laughs again and pulls me down onto him, and I'm not about to resist that. "Yes. Definitely. But okay, I suppose it's only fair." He cringes. "Carrie Fisher. As Princess Leia."

I laugh, trying to picture Josh watching *Star Wars*. As a kid, maybe. "*Star Wars*? Really? Let me guess, the gold bikini?"

He groans. "I know, right? It's such a cliché."

I lean in so my forehead is just inches away from his. "Maybe it's a cliché because it's hot. And maybe I could pick myself up one of those gold bikinis. And put my hair in a nice long braid . . ."

"Mmmm . . ." He closes his eyes and starts to lean in like he's going to kiss me, and then suddenly pulls back. "Wait. You know she's not wearing the buns?"

I shrug. "Yeah, of course. It's iconic." And then, because I can't help myself, I add, "And I actually love *Star Wars*."

His eyes widen. "Seriously?"

I've been keeping this part of me from him, but the guy has met my family, so at this point, this is the least of the embarrassment. And him admitting his Princess Leia crush means he can't judge me too much, right?

"I may be a bit of a geek," I say cautiously. "*Star Wars*,

science fiction movies in general, some anime, pretty much anything Joss Whedon-related . . . what?"

This last bit because he's giving me this strange look, like he's seeing me for the first time. His hands run up the sides of my sparkly leotard, and his body tenses. "I—I just . . . really? You like that stuff?"

I chew on my lip, suddenly self-conscious, and move to roll off him, but his hands move to my hips, holding me still. "No, I mean—" he shakes his head. "Me too. I've read everything in the Star Wars expanded universe. I have book shelves filled with it, and all sorts of fantasy series, like Jordan and Martin and Tolkien, of course, and—"

And now I think I'm looking at him that same way, because his cheeks flush.

"—And yeah," he says. "You may be a bit of a geek, but I'm like the biggest geek. Maybe not the admission I should have followed up with after showing up in Wyoming like an idiot."

Is it possible? Josh Rios, super-hot, famous agent and all-around great guy who makes me laugh like no one else. Could he also be someone I could slaughter hordes of video game zombies with, or debate the highlights of *Firefly* episodes?

"If that's true," I say, "why did you never tell me?" I hesitate, suddenly sure he's setting me up for some humiliating punchline. "I've been in your house and I haven't seen these book shelves."

Josh laughs. "Because I hide them well. And I sweep the house before I come to pick you up. His expression turns sheepish, then accusatory. "And wait. What do you mean why didn't I tell you? I didn't hear you ever mention wanting to watch any anime."

"Right. Because I'm going to suggest to the super hot agent I'm dating that we should stay home and watch *Death Note*."

"Yeah. Because I would have told you you were crazy if you think it's better than *Brotherhood*."

That giddiness is back, and my heart is beating faster. I feel like I pulled him out of some perfect-guy fantasy I didn't even have the imagination to dream up.

"Oh my god," I say. "Those posters you were asking about? I had one for *Full Metal Alchemist* right there." I point above the vanity. "Also posters from *Buffy*. And *Firefly*. And mostly *Death Arsenal*."

He's grinning, and it lights up his whole face. I'm not sure I've ever seen him look this happy. "I took an online course to learn to speak Dothraki. From *Game of Thrones*."

I giggle. "Yeah, well, I've written some well-received *Death Arsenal* fan fiction, in which Captain Jane Jennings hooks up with ship mechanic Curtis Huang. A lot."

He looks confused. "Aren't those two characters in totally different timelines? Are they ever even together?"

Oh my god. He knows who Jane and Curtis are, and Curtis isn't even in any of the crappy DA movies. "In my world they are. Repeatedly."

He laughs and from the sound of it, I know he's feeling shocked and giddy in the same way I am. Our bodies are twining together, and I want him, badly, and I can tell he wants me, but I also desperately want to keep talking.

"I may have canceled a date once," he says, "—not with you— to stay home and watch the *Highlander* marathon on Syfy."

"Umm . . ." I say, and he leans forward eagerly.

"What? Tell me."

Oh, god. Am I really going to tell him this? "So you know how I said I couldn't go to the movie premiere with you because I was driving here that night?" I grimace as he waits expectantly. "I lied. I went to the midnight release of the new *Death Arsenal* game. I wanted to be first in line. I didn't leave until the next day."

His arms wrap tight around me."Whaaaat?" But he doesn't sound upset, just incredulous. "You should have told me! I would totally have come with you! Or at least come back after the premiere and joined you in line."

The thought that he would prefer a night waiting outside

of GameStop with me (and a bunch of fellow geeks in DA cosplay) over a night spent doing, well, whatever, with Macy Mayfield—it floors me.

"Do you play?" I ask, not sure my life can get any better.

He wobbles his hand. "I've played some of them, because Ben's a fan, though when he and I play together it's usually JRPGs. My own fandoms run more along books and comics. But still."

But still.

We grin at each other like idiots. And I don't care that I look like a deranged eighties Melanie Griffith or that my family is still downstairs waiting to barrage Josh with racially insensitive questions. I just want to freeze time here in this bedroom with Josh, just like this.

The talking, the laughing, the just being in his arms . . . All things that were already great with him, but somehow now feel like so much more than before.

Maybe more than I've ever felt before.

He lets me go and pulls back enough to take my hand in his, gently, and shake it. "It's nice to meet you, Anna-Marie."

"You too, Josh Rios." I can't stop smiling, especially as his arms work their way around my waist again and draw me closer to him. I breathe him in, nuzzling my nose against his jaw, which is unshaven and stubbly. "So is there anything else? Any other deeply geeky confessions? Because I know I could keep going."

He lets out a long breath. "There are. I may happen to have the geekiest of all secrets in my basement—"

"You have a basement?" I'm trying to figure out where that would fit in the layout to his condo. "Is this some *Fifty Shades of Grey* sex dungeon?"

He chuckles, and his fingers trace along my arm, raising goosebumps along my skin. "Trust me, I would have showed you that already. But no, this is what proves me to be the geekiest guy ever. But I've already vowed that I'm not telling any woman about that. Not until I've put a ring on her finger, at least."

My breath catches. Because for this one moment, it's like I can picture it. Him down on one knee looking at me like I'm the only woman in the world for him. And more than picture it, I can feel it, feel how amazing it would be to be that person for him, and it makes me dizzy.

I'm glad when he speaks again, so I don't have to.

"There is one thing. It's more of a dumb joke than a geeky thing, but . . ."

I force myself to breath evenly again, hoping he didn't notice how I was struggling mere seconds ago. "Well, you should definitely tell me this dumb, not-geeky joke. Especially if you aren't going to tell me about this basement secret of yours."

He looks like he wants to say something, and then kisses my forehead instead. I close my eyes against the feel of his lips on my skin. Something I've felt before, often and in much better places, but it feels different now. Like maybe every little touch means something important.

Like maybe I want them to.

"Okay," he says. "So you remember when we went on that date to Le Papillon and we were watching those lobsters? And you asked me what I thought they could say if they could talk."

I sit up straighter. "I do remember that! And I also remember you got the weirdest look on your face. And I just thought, 'Okay, so he doesn't like pretending sea creatures can talk. Or maybe just the ones we're about to eat. Either way, noted.' "

Josh groans and smacks his head back against the headboard—not hard enough it would hurt, but the brass makes a ringing sound. "You want to hear what I was thinking?"

"Absolutely." I'm not sure I can get enough of that. Not now when I'm realizing how much of it he held back before.

Not that I was sharing enough of my own thinking either.

"So what I wanted to tell you was that lobsters are all French. You knew that about lobsters, right?" He's saying this seriously, but he's got a twitch to lips hinting at a smile.

"French, huh? I did not."

"And they all climb over each other to get to the top, right?"

"Right."

"All so that the one at the top, so that he can say—" and here Josh gets a snooty look on his face, and removes his hands from my waist to wave his fingers in front of his mouth like alarming little whiskers—"'I am ze king of ze tank!' " he says, in the most tragic French accent I have ever heard. He shifts slightly, as if he's hopping from one lobster's head to another. "No! It is I! I am ze king! All who challenge ze king shall suffer and despaaaaair."

It's like the Muce joke all over again. It's not even that funny, but the random hilarity of Josh Rios impersonating a lobster in my childhood bed induces another of my snort-giggles—one of the loudest, most obnoxious ones I've ever made, and I bury my head in his shoulder, both laughing uncontrollably again and also dying of humiliation.

"Ahhhhh!" I say into his shirt. "Why do I keep *doing* that in front of you? Can you please please please just forget you have ever heard me make that sound?"

But he's laughing too, and rolls over on top of me, propped up on his elbows on either side. "Never. I'm never going to forget that. Because that is my new favorite sound. And I've heard you make a lot of *really* great sounds."

I thought just a few minutes ago that he looked the happiest I'd ever seen him. But no, this is the happiest, and I wonder if I look the same way, because I sure as hell feel it.

And then he's kissing me, and my legs are wrapped tight around his waist and, well, now I sure want more than just talking. His hands are finding their way under my spandex and I'm working at the buttons on his shirt when there's a sharp knocking at my door that makes us both jump.

"Anna-Marie, are you decent?" calls my Aunt Patrice. "I'm coming in."

Josh rolls back off me just as the door opens and Patrice walks in, but his shirt is mostly unbuttoned and his hair sticking up in about a dozen different ways and it couldn't be more obvious what was going on.

Then I remember last night with Shane. *That* was more obvious.

What would Josh say if he knew? Or worse yet, saw those pictures the Boy Scouts may have taken?

Patrice looks at us both, and sighs. Then she puts on a forced smile. "Joe's Way," she says, as sweet as pie, "I assume you're staying with us for the night?"

Josh struggles to keep from laughing, and mostly succeeds. "Um. Yes, I was hoping to. Yes."

"Wonderful! I've made up a bed for you in the storage room."

Oh god. I know exactly what she's done, because this was the set-up my dad used when the basement wasn't finished and his bedroom was being re-painted. A sad little twin-sized mattress lying on top of a large pallet of canned food storage we've had for longer than I've been alive.

I sit up. "No, Aunt Patrice, he can sleep with me, it's—"

"*I think*," Patrice says in a voice which indicates that her thoughts and commandments from deity are one and the same, "that we'd all be much more comfortable if Joe's Way slept in his own bed while he's here. There are children here, after all."

Those same children know very well that their mom and my dad are sleeping in the same bed, so I'm tempted to argue with her. But then I remember that at least one of those children has already seen me naked with a guy in the last twenty-four hours.

And I very much don't want Patrice bringing that up to support her case.

I look over at Josh, and he smiles. "It's okay," he says. "The bed in the storage room sounds great, thank you." He gives Patrice one of his gorgeous grins, and her expression softens noticeably and she actually blushes. Then she nods at us and leaves the room.

She keeps the door open, though.

"The storage room is not great," I warn him as soon as she's out of sight.

"I'll survive. And I'm really good at sneaking around in the middle of the night." His dark eyes gleam mischievously.

"A skill that will come in handy," I say. But that pit in my stomach is starting to feel heavier. Do I tell Josh about Shane? Do I not?

We aren't committed, and we weren't last night. But I care about Josh. A lot. Even more, now. I don't want to lie to him.

"I'm going to go get my stuff from the car," Josh says. "And I've got some work calls to make that might take a little while. But we'll continue this later, yeah?"

"Yes. Very much so, yes."

And I find there's nothing I want more.

TEN

Anna-Marie

While Josh is off making his work calls, I decide to take a shower so the next time he sees me I will be back to looking more like the Anna-Marie that isn't a crazy person. It's a longer process than normal—the sheer amount of hairspray Cherstie put in requires several rounds of "lather, rinse, repeat"—but eventually I emerge victorious.

I have, however, forgotten to bring my pajamas into the bathroom with me. And there's no way in hell I'm putting the sparkly leotard back on. So using one towel as a makeshift turban for my wet hair, I wrap another around myself and poke my head out into the hallway to make sure no one is there. The towels aren't super big, and too many people in this house have seen too much of my body.

Luckily, the path is clear, with the exception of Buckley, who trots down the hallway when he sees me and starts licking my wet feet.

"Hey, stop that." I've never been a pet person, and being slobbered on doesn't help. Buckley looks up at me—or at least I think he does; I have yet to actually see eyes beneath that big mop of shaggy fur—and makes a snuffling noise. As I dash down the hallway to my bedroom, he trots along beside me and makes a sad little whining sound when I block him from entering.

"Prove you can scare away bats and maybe I'll consider letting you in," I say, and then close the door.

I'm just about to drop my towel when I hear a tapping on the window. Too loud to be gummy bears, but I still know exactly who it is.

Shit. Shane is back.

The curtains are mostly closed, but I can see movement through the crack of black night that shows between them. Shane is right out there on the closest branch and can probably see me, too, which means there's no pretending I'm not in my room.

Naked, of course.

Not that it's a good idea to ignore him. He'd just come back later, which with Josh here could be much, much worse. I've got to get rid of Shane now and give myself more time to figure out what to do about telling Josh.

Tap-tap-tap.

I grab a soft cotton t-shirt from my suitcase and another pair of pajama shorts and hurriedly put them on, and then slide the curtains apart and unlock the window before tugging it open.

"I don't think you need the lock to keep bats out," Shane says with a grin.

"Maybe it's not bats I'm trying to keep out," I say pointedly, folding my arms across my chest.

Shane sighs. "I'm sorry, Anna-Marie. Seriously. I was an ass, and—actually, you mind if I come in to apologize? I've been straddling this branch for the last twenty minutes and I'm starting to lose feeling in some sensitive areas here."

"The state of your sensitive areas isn't exactly a concern of mine," I say. He opens his mouth, but I cut him off. "And if you say 'it was last night,' I'm going to push you off that branch."

He shuts his mouth again and tries to hide a grin.

"And anyway," I continue, "now's not a good time."

"I'll just be a minute." He gives me that sheepish look I've received a hundred times before, and yet somehow always fall for. "Come on, babe. Don't leave things like that."

And the truth is, I don't want to leave things like that. Shane's . . . well, I don't know what he is to me, really, but he's at the very least a friend. And an important part of my past. A part that I find that I do still care about, one way or another.

Besides, if Josh is going to be here for the rest of the reunion—something I realize I have no idea of—then I need to make sure Shane knows to stay well away. And it's just now occurring to me that Josh went out to make work calls, but I have no idea *where* exactly he intended to do that and if he's pacing in front of the house, he might see Shane up in the tree.

I stand back, letting Shane climb in. He looks very much the same as yesterday—a different vintage band t-shirt, worn-in jeans. He's got a faded multi-colored friendship bracelet on his left wrist that I recognize immediately. I worked as a camp counselor the summer after my junior year, and had to make a million of the stupid things with my group of ten-year-old girls. So I made one for him, ironically, and he wore it for years, also ironically. Except he still has it, so I'm not sure how ironic it was, after all.

My throat goes dry.

"Shane, I—" I start, but he steps right up to me, and puts his hands on my waist.

"I shouldn't have joked around with Mr. Dart when you were clearly uncomfortable," he says, leaning down so his forehead is right up against mine. "I shouldn't have laughed about the Boy Scouts. And I should have been more helpful with getting the bat out. Does that about cover it? Or is there more assery to apologize for? Because I'll apologize for it all. I'm sorry."

He sounds sincere enough, and really, nothing he did was *that* bad.

"Whatever, it's fine," I say. "I'm not actually all that mad anymore."

He brings his hands up to the towel turban on my head and

massages it like he's trying to dry my hair, then takes the turban off. My wet hair tumbles down around my shoulders, a strand of it sticking to my cheek.

"Good." He peels the strand off, and raises an eyebrow. "So you want to get out of here again? We can just stay at my house this time. I already checked the house for bats. And Boy Scouts."

"I can't." But I know it's more than that. I don't actually want to. I want to feel Josh's hands on my waist, want Josh's fingers brushing back strands of my wet hair.

I want to talk with him more, find out more about him. Tell him more about me. And that, more than anything else, scares me.

"Family stuff?" Shane asks. "Can't you ditch it? It's not like you guys are doing the Grillmaster Championship right n—"

"It's not family stuff. It's Josh. My—" there's that word again "—the agent guy I'm dating. He's here."

Shane's blue eyes widen. "Really? You didn't tell me he was going to be here."

"I didn't know. It was a surprise."

"Huh," Shane says, and I can tell he's keeping something in that he wants to say, but I'm not sure I want to hear it anyway.

"So you really need to go before he—"

"But he's not your boyfriend, right?"

I pause. "No. But—"

"And I don't see him here right now." Shane's hands go back to my waist, pulling me closer. "We could lock the door, or we could get out of here and be back before—"

"No," I say, more forcefully, taking a step back. "Josh is a great guy, and I'm not going to be like that. Not with him."

Shane frowns and opens his mouth, but before he can say anything, my bedroom door opens.

"You should know there's a big mountain of fur I think is a dog parked right outside your—" Josh says as he walks in, cutting off as he sees me standing there with Shane.

His gaze flicks back and forth between us, and I have to

restrain myself from stepping even further away from Shane, which would make me look even more guilty than I undoubtedly already appear.

Shane, however, takes his opportunity to sling his arm around my shoulders. He grins at Josh. "Hey, man," he says.

Josh smiles back, though I can see the uncertainty in his expression. "Hey. I thought I'd met all the family already downstairs, but I guess not. So which one are you?"

Oh god. I can see Shane's grin getting wider and know that I can not let him answer that.

"He's not—" I blurt out, already regretting that I have no idea what to say. "He's my—Shane."

I cringe the second those words leave my lips—the same words I stupidly said about *him*—and hate myself when I see Josh's smile vanish, when I see the flicker of hurt in his eyes. He blinks. Then he's got an expression on his face I've seen before when he's talking to people he doesn't particularly like, but has to be polite to. Professional Agent Josh gives a curt smile and nod. "Hey. Nice to meet you." He looks at me with that same expression and I feel it like a knife in my gut. "I can leave if you—"

"No," I say quickly, not sure if he just means leave the room or leave my life and terrified of risking the latter. "No, I just—"

"It's okay," Shane says smoothly. "I can take off." He tightens his grip around my shoulder just enough to lean in and plant a kiss on my head. Then he extends his hand to Josh. "Nice to meet you, too." Instead of his usual slouch, Shane has drawn himself up to his full height, which puts him an inch or so taller than Josh, who stands right around six feet.

Josh shakes his hand, and his smile back is coolly pleasant. Then Shane gives us one last smirk, and a wink to me. "Later, babe," he says, and climbs back out the window.

There's a stretch of heavy silence after Shane slides the window shut behind him.

Josh leans back against my dresser, his gaze trailing over the various things left there from years ago—old bottles of Clinique Happy perfume and lotion, a framed photo of me as a little kid with my dad, a stack of CDs. It's like he's trying to look at anything but me, and that knife in my gut twists deeper. "He climbs in the window, huh?" he finally says. "Too cool for doors?"

"It's just—it's a thing." I curl and uncurl my bare toes on my carpeting.

"Yeah," he says, like he gets it, though I'm not really sure what it is he gets. He looks over at me, and while I'm relieved the Professional Agent Josh veneer is gone, there's still this distance between us. Physically, because he's over by the dresser with his arms folded across his chest, and I'm by the end of my bed in a similar pose. But it's more than that; it's like there's this vast gulf between us instead of mere feet. After how connected I'd felt to him the last time he'd been in this room, I feel hollowed out.

Judging from his expression, I think he feels the same.

"So is he why you left me hanging before?" Josh asks. "About the girlfriend thing, I mean."

I swallow past a lump that has formed in my throat. "Part of it." I know it's not in the way he's thinking, but I'm not sure how to explain that. "Definitely not all of it. I'm sorry, Josh," I say, and my voice breaks on his name. "I didn't mean to—"

"Hey, no," he says, his expression softening. "You have nothing to apologize for. I knew you weren't really inviting me out here. I knew you were just joking around. I was the one who intruded on your life, and I can leave, and you can call me when you get back to LA, and . . ." He trails off and studies the carpet. Maybe because he doesn't know how that sentence should end any more than I do.

But I do know this.

"I don't want you to leave," I say. "You're not intruding on anything. I-I missed you."

Saying those words out loud makes the blood rush in my ears. But the panic of that admission is drowned out by the even worse panic that I've already screwed up this thing Josh and I have, this thing that had just taken on entirely new meaning and depth.

He looks up from under the locks of dark hair hanging over his eyes. "Yeah?"

I bite my lips together and nod. "Yeah. And yeah, maybe I was joking around, but I am really happy you came all the way out here. If I'd had any idea you would, then when Shane came over last night, I wouldn't have—"

"Last night?" Josh drops his gaze to the carpet again.

Guilt pools in my veins. "Yeah. I'm sorry."

"You don't have to be. We aren't in a committed relationship," he says gently. "You have every right to be with whoever you want."

He's right, of course. This is the point of not being serious, isn't it? So there's no jealousy and hurt feelings and betrayal.

Except I'm suddenly not sure I've avoided any of these things.

"You too," I say, and I immediately picture Macy in that dress cut down to her well-toned belly. Ugh.

He nods, but his lips twist in a strange way.

"You've been with other people, haven't you?" I can't help but ask. "Since we've been dating, I mean."

He cringes, looking adorably abashed. "No, I actually haven't. It's cool, though. Really."

I gape at him. Is that possible? This is Josh Rios. Not that he's known to be a Ryan Lansing-level player, but there's no way the guy hasn't had plenty of opportunity to be with other women—incredibly beautiful women—in the two months we've been seeing each other.

Then again . . .

"I haven't either," I admit. "Until . . . well."

Josh glances over at the window. He unfolds his arms, but then stuffs his hands in the pockets of his cargo shorts. "So is Shane—?" He cuts himself off, shaking his head. "Never mind. It's not my business."

"No, ask me. I'll tell you anything you want to know. It's

okay." And it is. I don't want to hurt him anymore, but I find that I don't want to keep anything from him, either. I decide to sit down on the floor rather than keep standing. Partially because my legs are trembling, but mainly because I think that if he sees me sit, he will. And then he might not be as likely to walk out that door and into his car and away from me.

He seems to consider this, and I pat the carpet beside me.

A small smile creeps onto his face and he comes and joins me in sitting cross-legged at the foot of my bed. "Okay," he says. "So is Shane—do you guys have some kind of long-distance thing going on?"

"No." I have to tamp down my own smile, one forming out of sheer relief to just have Josh close to me again, at least physically for now. "Before yesterday I hadn't even talked to him in five years. He was my high school boyfriend. We broke up for good about a year after we graduated."

"For good?"

I shrug. "We broke up a lot in high school, too, usually not longer than a couple of weeks at a time. But yeah, the last time stuck."

There's a flicker of him looking tempted to contradict this, or at least question it—which would be fair, given that I just slept with the guy last night. But he doesn't, and I appreciate that.

"Shane came over last night, a few hours after I got off the phone with you," I continue. I figure if he stops wanting to know, he can tell me. Otherwise, I'm not going to make him ask. "I wasn't planning on getting together with him when I was here, but he just came over and we started catching up, you know—talking about my job, and he was telling me about how his band is doing—"

"He's in a band." Josh rakes a hand through his hair.

"Yeah," I say, not sure how that detail is incredibly relevant. "And then, I don't know, we just decided to take off and go to these hot springs we used to hang out in. And then these Boy Scouts showed up and they all saw me totally naked and—"

"What?" His brow knits together in confusion.

"I heard a van coming and I tried to get out to put on clothes before people showed up but my shorts got caught in this scrub-brush, and ahhhhh, it was so horrifying." I bury my face in my hands. I'd shoved the humiliation away, but talking about it again, I can remember that moment, caught in the headlights, bare to all the world. Or at least the world of Everett's impressionable youth.

I feel Josh's arm around my shoulders—not possessive, like Shane's, but comforting. "I'm sorry that happened to you," he says.

"It's okay to laugh," I mutter through my fingers. "Shane sure did. And I get it, it's funny. I flashed an entire troop of Boy Scouts."

"It's not funny if you don't actually think it's funny. Other people seeing you naked when you didn't want them to isn't funny. Trust me, I deal with that kind of thing pretty often in my job." He smiles. "Not people being seen by *Boy Scouts*, so much . . . but still. It's violating, even if it was an accident."

"It felt violating." I lean into his side, closing my eyes. The humiliation lessens, like somehow knowing I'm allowed to feel that way makes it better. Then I remember the panic in the troop leader's voice as he's begging the boys to stay in the van, and I let out a little giggle. "And, okay, I do think it's a tiny bit funny."

I look up at him, and he's still smiling down at me. Not quite the full-on happy grins from our previous conversation, but we're closer.

It makes me hate that I need to continue the story.

"So then Shane and I came back here and we . . ." I trail off, wrinkling my nose.

"I really don't need to hear details." Josh rolls his eyes up to the ceiling, leaning his head back against the bed frame.

"Fair enough. But you should know, it didn't go well. We got attacked by a bat."

This time he does laugh, in surprise. "A bat? Like—"

"Yeah. Like a giant flying rodent from hell. And I screamed and before I knew it, my whole family was in here and my dad and Shane had to get rid of it, and that pretty much ended that."

And maybe the thought of me being caught naked against my will isn't something Josh finds funny, but something about the bat story makes him chuckle. "Ah, yes. My attack bat."

I raise my eyebrows. "Your what?"

"You haven't noticed? I've had him circling around you for weeks, ready to swoop down and attack any guy who got too close to you." That mischievous gleam is back in his eyes, and I love seeing it again.

I grin up at him. "What took him so long? He should have attacked back at the hot springs."

"I don't know. Maybe he got lost on the way. Like your aunt's UPS driver."

I laugh, and his arm tightens around me, his fingers trailing along my skin. There's hope, maybe, that we can get back to where we were less than an hour before.

Hope warring with fear, because I don't know if that's a good thing. Not really.

"When he came back tonight, I was telling him to leave," I say. "I was telling him you were here, and that I wasn't going to—you know."

Josh pauses, and I feel this tension stretching out between us—not in a bad way, necessarily, but like a cord pulled taut. It could either pull us back together or snap entirely. "But if I wasn't here," he says. "If I was still back in LA."

He leaves that hanging, like it's a complete thought, and I wince. "If you were still back in LA, I would be missing you, and worrying about whether you're finding anyone you like better in my absence."

He smiles. "So, did you want to be my girlfriend?"

There it is, the thing I've avoided like the plague for years: girlfriend. Commitment. The beginning of the road to pain and distrust and bitter public tabloid breakups (for the Hollywood set, at least). All things I never want in general, and really really don't want with Josh. I should just tell him I'm just not looking for anything serious right now. I've said that to plenty of guys over the years. But he's different than all those other guys. He was different even before today, and he's sure as hell different now, but I can't bring myself to say the words.

"I don't know yet," I finally say. "Is that okay?'

"Yeah, of course," he says, but I can see the flicker of hurt in his eyes again, even as he squeezes my arm and holds me close.

It doesn't feel okay. It feels like shit. It feels like my chest aching and my insides twisting. It feels like fear and frustration. "I'm just not good at this kind of thing," I blurt out, more forcefully than I mean to, and he looks kind of startled. But he doesn't say anything, just waits.

"Relationships, you know? It's like the damn trophies." I gesture at the shelf. "You have to come in first place or it's nothing. Second or third doesn't count. And even if you think you've gotten that first place, you think you have the one, and then, you know, it all falls apart and it turns out you had nothing. Worse than nothing."

He's looking at me with a mix of confusion and possibly concern, and I realize I sound like I'm having some kind of mental breakdown, and hell, maybe I am. But I feel like I have to keep going. For myself, if not for him.

"I'm just not sure how to do it. I'm not sure that I even believe in love, like the forever kind. I want to believe sometimes, but then I think of my mom, or all of my stepmoms. They believed, you know? And look where it got them. Look where it gets pretty much everyone." Tears are forming now, burning at the edges of my vision, and I blink them away, looking up at the ceiling. "I just—I don't know how to do it, and I don't want to mess this up."

His mouth is gaping open a bit, and for a panicked moment I think he's going to decide that there's no amount of pretty that makes up for this level of crazy and walk out the door. But he swallows and pulls me in closer, so he's resting his cheek against my head. "You haven't messed anything up," he says. "It's okay."

I let out a breath. My heart is still pounding and I can feel his through both our shirts, pounding in a similarly fast rhythm. "Okay," I say.

There's a beat of silence. Then he says, "So tell me, fellow geek Anna-Marie. Which episode of *Buffy* is your favorite and why?"

I smile. "I actually have two favorites. And the why could keep you here all night."

He laces his fingers through mine. "Sounds good to me."

ELEVEN

Josh

I leave Anna-Marie's room after telling her I'm going to get some sleep. She was beginning to droop against my shoulder, and after the long drive and the Boy Scouts and me showing up out of the blue, she probably needs sleep, too. I'm not sure how much she's had since she's been here, because of, you know.

Shane.

I'm tired, too, and I haven't even checked out this store room bed, which is definitely not how I imagined spending my nights here. I'm tempted to go get a hotel, but my phone isn't finding one for thirty miles, and I'm not driving that far tonight.

Or that far from Anna-Marie. I wanted to stay with her tonight, but at the same time, I was glad she didn't seem too certain it's what she wanted. I'm lightheaded and things have changed so much in the last few hours that I feel like I have whiplash from trying to keep up.

So I amble quietly through the empty house and out to my car, where I call Ben.

"Hey," he says. "Do you know what time it is?"

"I think it's midnight here. Are we still in the same timezone?"

"We are not. But now telling you this is the second night you've called me past eleven seems anti-climactic."

"Be glad you don't live in New York," I say. "There it must be two in the morning."

"Hang on," Ben says. "No, of course I'm going to ask him. Give me a minute."

I gather none of this is to me. "You haven't, though. Asked how it's going."

"I know! Jeez. How am I supposed to with the two of you pestering me?"

I can hear Wyatt talking on the other end, but I can't tell what he's saying. After a long silence, Ben sighs. "So you made it to Wyoming? How's it going?"

I take a deep breath. This is what I called to talk about, but I'm still not sure how to answer. I decide to start from the beginning.

"Well, I showed up and sat in my car down her street for thirty minutes wondering what the hell I was doing here."

"Ha," Ben says. "You drove away without talking to her, didn't you? After all the hell you gave me about not talking to Wyatt."

It had actually been the thought of this moment that had finally gotten me out of the car. "No. I knocked on the door and her aunt showed me down to the basement where Anna-Marie was doing a one-woman fashion show in what looked like an Ice Capades costume and makeup that had been done by her ten-year-old future stepsister."

"Wow," Ben says. "I bet that's not what you were expecting."

I smile. "I wasn't what she was expecting either. Her embarrassment was kind of adorable."

"Okay," Ben says. "But Wyatt notices that you're not in bed with her right now, and he makes a good point." He pauses for a second. "That was me asking why not. No, I didn't ask it as a question, but I'm pretty sure he understood."

We'll get to that, but since he didn't ask a question, I don't answer. "She likes *Buffy*," I say. "And *Full Metal Alchemist*. And *Death Arsenal*."

"Wait, whaaaat? How do you know?"

I close my eyes, and I'm back on Anna-Marie's bed, holding her in my arms with her legs wrapped around me, kissing her and kissing her and feeling things I've never felt before in my life. "Because she told me. I'm not sure if it's because I drove all this way or just because it came up, but I told her about my crush on Leia and she told me about her fan fiction and, god, it was the hottest conversation I've ever had in my life."

"Huh," Ben says. "I didn't see that coming."

"Yeah, me neither." It all feels a little bit surreal, like maybe I'm still back in LA in my recliner having the most fantastic dream. I'd already been wanting more with Anna-Marie, but the idea that I could let her in the basement and she might still kiss me like *that* . . .

If I'm dreaming, I wish my subconscious hadn't conjured Shane.

"I told her my lobster joke," I say.

"That joke is not funny."

The memory of the look on her face when she heard it makes me smile. "She thought it was. And she snort-laughed and then died of embarrassment, and I'm pretty sure that's the moment I fell in love with her."

"Yeah," Ben says. "Diva Josh *would* fall in love when a girl laughs at his jokes." I hear a squeal that can only be Wyatt. Ben sounds a little stunned, which is reasonable, because I've never been in love before, not even back in college, and Sandy and I dated for two years. "I figured you were already in love with her when you drove all that way."

"Maybe I was. Or getting there, anyway. But that's when I knew."

"Damn," Ben says. "Did you tell her?"

"No. I'd already said something earlier suggesting that maybe she could be my girlfriend and she kind of blew me off."

Ben groans. "So she doesn't feel the same?"

I think maybe she does—I wasn't the only one grinning like

an idiot through that entire conversation—but there's an elephant in this conversation and the elephant's name is Shane. "I don't know. Because then her high school boyfriend showed up."

"Her what?" Ben asks.

I hear Wyatt say something in the background that sounds suspiciously like *plot twist* and I realize my love life has now turned into a soap opera.

Fitting. "Her high school boyfriend. Who is six-one and in a band and dresses like Jared Leto and is probably hotter than me."

"Wyatt says nobody's hotter than you," Ben says. "Hey, what do you mean? Damn right besides me. And Ryan Lansing. And—"

"Yeah," I say. "Anna-Marie apparently slept with him, too."

"Who?" Ben asks. "Ryan Lansing? Yes, he says she slept with him. No. No, Wyatt, I doubt he knows the details." Then, to me: "Wyatt is texting you a list of questions to ask Anna-Marie about Ryan Lansing in bed."

I don't see how this could make the situation *more* awkward. "Great. I'll see what I can do."

"But this Shane guy. Are they together?"

"No. But they did sleep together last night."

Ben lets out a low whistle. "Bet you regret not calling her first."

I do. God, I do. If she'd known I was actually serious about driving out here, the whole thing with Shane last night might not have happened at all. "So once that became clear, I asked her if I should leave, and she basically begged me to stay, and then got tears in her eyes and said that she's not sure she can be my girlfriend because she's scared to believe in love that lasts forever, but she's terrified that she's messed things up with me. And something about trophies and how she doesn't know if she can get first place and even if she does that someday I might cheat on her . . ." I sigh. "It made more sense when she said it."

Ben is quiet. "Do you think she's playing you?"

"I don't think so. She's never seemed like she's into me just to be seen with me, and she didn't seem like she was putting on a show of being upset. But she is an actress."

It's that last part that haunts me. I like to think I'm pretty good at sniffing out women who feel like I'm just a rung in a ladder, or a nice ride. But it's my job to spot good acting, and she's got it. I can't rule out that she might be using it on me.

"But for what?" I ask. "She's already been seen with me. She's probably got what mileage she's going to get out of that."

"Maybe she wants you to rep her," Ben offers.

"Yeah, I already offered. She turned me down."

"Really?" Ben says. "Wait, Wyatt, are you on the forum? No, you definitely can't say anything about *Buffy*. Because she'll know exactly where it came from, that's why."

"I don't know what to do," I say. "They've got me staying in the storage room, apparently, and I don't think this Shane guy is totally gone. And he seems like an asshole but Anna-Marie obviously likes him, and shit, I'm the nice guy, right? I'm the nice guy who's hanging around wishing that she'd give me the time of day while she'd rather be with the hot drummer. Or singer. Or whatever he is."

"Dude. You're jealous."

"I am." It hits me then, how much, and not just because of last night. "He knows her in ways I don't. I bet he got to hang out with her through *Buffy* marathons and play *Death Arsenal*. He probably wrote songs for her and she sat in front of the stage and swooned while he sang them. God, how am I supposed to compete with that?"

"Um, dude," Ben says. "You know I don't follow your public life that closely, but aren't you some kind of celebrity?" There's muffled talking in the background. "Wyatt tells me you are. And he's Googling this Shane guy. Wait, I think he found him. Is his band called . . . Accidental Erotica?"

"Probably," I say. "Are they from Everett, Wyoming?"

"Yeah, this is them. I don't know, I think he's hotter than Josh. What? Josh, are you offended that I think he's hotter than you?"

Ben is not the kind of guy who can rate other men on their

objective attractiveness, only on how attracted he is to them. He's not exactly *Queer Eye*. "I'm basically your brother. You think all men are hotter than me."

"This is true," Ben says. "Wyatt says you're hotter."

"Thanks, Wyatt."

"Josh says thanks. Wyatt says you're welcome, and also that Shane looks like an asshole and Wyatt's totally Team Joshamarie. Ouch, what? Oh, and I am too, but not because I think you're hot."

I lay my seat back and stare at the roof of my car. "Are you sure? You think I should stay?"

"Do you want to?" Ben asks.

I want to be close to her. If I missed her before, I can't imagine how much worse it would be to tear myself away from her now. "Yes. But I'm scared."

"I know," Ben says. "Being in love is scary as hell."

"God, why did you never tell me?"

"Dude. I'm pretty sure I did. You didn't listen. And if you're in love with her, you better stay where you are and see how it plays out, or you're always going to wonder."

He's right. I know he's right. "Yeah, I'm going to. I was thinking I might leave, but then she seemed so scared, like she couldn't stand the idea that I might not want to be with her."

"But you do."

"Yeah, I do. And I told her about Dothraki and she seemed to think that was kind of cool."

"Seriously, dude," Ben says. "Hold on to *that*. No, Wyatt, I seriously don't think he wants to ask about Ryan Lansing's penis size."

"I'll ask her," I tell him. "Anything for Team Joshamarie."

"Thanks, man," Ben says. "Good luck."

And when we hang up, I stand outside my car for a moment, staring up at the stars, thousands of them, unlike the twelve you can see from my place in LA. I want to wish for luck on every single one of them that I get to keep this girl, because I'm in this so deep with her that I'm drowning, and I don't know if she's ever going to throw me a ring.

TWELVE

Anna-Marie

The next morning, when I pad downstairs to start making some coffee to bring to Josh in the storage room, I'm shocked to find him already awake and sitting at the kitchen table, flipping through Everett's local newspaper, *The Ranchlands Record*.

I am not, however, shocked to find Lily in the seat next to him, leaning close to him—ostensibly to read from the newspaper as well, but really just to show off the boobs that are all but spilling from her tube top.

"You can have the paper if you want," Josh offers. "I'm fine waiting."

"Oh, I'm perfectly comfortable right here," Lily purrs. "No need for either of us to wait. We can finish together."

Good god. She couldn't be more obvious if she started giving him a lap dance. And I think the only reason she isn't going for that tactic is because Uncle Joe is in the kitchen as well, making french toast at the stove.

Josh has been hit on enough—and in similarly unsubtle ways, I'm sure—that he doesn't look particularly alarmed, but I'm happy to see his expression is one of mild disgust rather than temptation.

"How about you go finish your eyebrows, Lily?" I ask, leaning against the kitchen door frame. "Or should I help you?"

Lily glares at me, but she sits back in her chair and pretends to examine her fingernails.

"Anna-Marie, hey," Josh says, clearly happy to see me, and hopefully for more than just extricating him from uncomfortable Lily situations.

"There's our girl," Uncle Joe says, looking back over his shoulder. "Up for some breakfast? Or have they got you on some kind of hoity-toity all-grass diet on that show of yours?"

"All-grass? Like pot? No, they let me have meth too, if I really nail my scenes." I slide out the chair on the other side of Josh and sit down. He grins at me and puts his hand on my knee and squeezes. My insides flutter happily.

"Very funny." Uncle Joe sets a plate in front of me with two slices of french toast. My stomach grumbles at the heavenly smell. "Well, we'll make sure you eat some real food while you're out here. There's more toast ready on the counter if anyone comes in wanting more. And after you eat, you and your friend here can do the dishes."

"Thanks, Uncle Joe." I nod at him, and Joe heads out into the living room. I wish Lily would join, but she just sits at the table. Looking all too innocent.

I decide the best course is just to ignore her completely. I run my fingers up Josh's arm. It's surreal, having him here in my kitchen, the local paper spread out on the table, one of my dad's coffee mugs sitting in front of him, nearly empty. "You're up early," I say.

"I guess I started to get used to your insane call times," he says. But I can see the dark circles under his eyes, and I wonder if the reason isn't more that he never really got to sleep at all. I get that—I didn't sleep all that great either, and I wasn't trying to do so on an air mattress on top of a bunch of canned peaches.

Guilt gnaws at me. He said I wasn't messing this up, that he wasn't mad about the Shane thing, but clearly this is stressful for him. And I'm still not sure he's going to think I'm worth that for much longer.

Josh folds the paper back and slides it my direction. "The Halsey family reunion is a bigger deal than I thought—you guys got a mention in the paper."

I look down to see it there, a small blurb about our yearly reunion, right there between Pearl's Gardening Corner and the Weekly Cattle Count. "This is Everett. Anything happening is a big deal."

"There's also an obituary for an Ida Halsey." Josh frowns. "I'm guessing she was related?"

"To Satan, maybe." I glance up to make sure Patrice didn't hear. Lily appears like she's about to genuinely laugh, but then catches me looking at her and purses her lips.

"That bad, huh?"

"Depends on who you ask. But I'm fairly certain there was a celebratory tailgating party held outside the funeral home." I smile. I should feel bad talking about the dead this way, but honestly, part of me thinks Ida would approve.

Josh is clearly going to ask another question, but Lily leans forward again.

"I bet Shane went to that party," she says, pressing her boobs against the table so her cleavage is practically spilling into the maple syrup on Josh's plate. "He's always up for a good time, isn't he, Anna-Marie? Josh, have you met Shane?"

And there it is. I can see that little bit of hurt again on Josh's face, and it makes my chest tighten.

I'm about to snap at her, but Josh squeezes my knee. "I have," he says, and I see that Professional Agent is back, all cool charm and Teflon-like resistance to anyone's shit. One thing about Josh is, he knows when someone's trying to mess with him or his clients, and I can see he's not oblivious to mean girl tactics. "Nice guy. We're all thinking about going to get drinks later."

Lily blinks, completely taken aback. "Oh. Well, then. That's . . . nice." Then she scoots back the chair and leaves the room.

I groan as soon as she's out of sight. "I'm sorry. For her to bring that up—"

"Hey, it's okay," he says, and he's back to being my Josh again, all caring and—

Did I just think of him as *my* Josh? My nerves skitter, even as my heart seems to swell. Regardless of whether I can or should call him that, I don't want to keep hurting him.

"Thanks for shutting her up." I squeeze his hand, and feel my skin prickle as his thumb rubs gently over my knuckle.

"Not that you don't seem capable of that on your own, but I *really* didn't like that she tried to play me against you like that. Does she do that often?"

"Not as often as she tries to sleep with whoever I'm dating. Or did you not notice her incredibly subtle come-ons?"

Josh laughs and is about to respond when Patrice comes in from the backyard. The screen door bangs shut behind her. The strong scent of her perfume—which today I assume is called "Mugged by an Entire Field of Wildflowers"—hits us with an almost visible wave. Josh coughs into his fist.

"Well, hello you two!" she says. "I hope you slept well last night, Joe's Way?"

I groan again. This has to stop. "His name is Josh, Aunt Patrice."

Patrice clucks at me, but doesn't otherwise address what I said. "I called UPS, and they said they had a little problem with their driver in Lander. He had a heart attack or something. Big fellow, I suppose. Drove the truck into some fencing, let a whole bunch of goats out of a pasture. But they assured me the reunion shirts were not among the boxes the goats started eating, and will be here before the competition tomorrow!"

"Oh good," I say. "For a second there, I thought this man's heart attack was actually going to inconvenience us." Patrice ignores my heavy sarcasm.

Josh just gapes. It's almost like he's not accustomed to goats breaking into crashed delivery trucks for a snack.

"Speaking of the competition," Patrice says, opening the fridge and peering in. "I need to go to the store today and pick up some supplies for Joe." She pulls out a bottle of honey Dijon and pulls off the lid, sniffing at it. "Should I pick anything up for you, Joe's Way? Something that will make you feel at home here?"

"I'm fine, thanks," he says.

"Nonsense." Patrice shuts the refrigerator door like she's punctuating with it. "Why don't you enter the Halsey Grillmaster Competition?"

"He doesn't grill," I say quickly. Then I pause and look at him. I suppose after yesterday, I'm realizing there's lots I didn't know about him. "Right?"

"Right," he says with a smile. "I don't cook much."

Patrice clucks again. "No need to be humble with us. You're a man. You can grill."

"Hey, are you saying I can't because I'm a woman?" I frown.

"No, you can't because the one time we let you make the stuffing for Thanksgiving, you turned it into a solid black brick. We had to air out the house for three days." She looks at Josh. "And it wasn't like she was cooking from scratch, either. This was out of the box."

She's not wrong. I blame our faulty stove. And maybe Stouffers, just because.

"Anyway, Joe's Way, it would mean so much to us if you could introduce us to the food of your people," Patrice says, then taps her finger on the counter. "I did a quick search online for Bel-Airia, but I must have spelled it wrong, because I couldn't find anything on that region. But Puerto Rico sounds like it has a rich culinary history. I read all about it on Wikipedia."

"I don't really—" Josh starts, but Patrice grips his shoulder and squeezes it.

"Then it's settled! I'll let you know when I'm going to the store, and you can join me to pick up whatever ingredients you need. Foster's Food and Feed has a whole shelf full of ethnic foods."

"A whole shelf, huh?" he says weakly.

I shake my head. "Josh, you don't have to do this. Patrice, he doesn't have to—"

"No, it's okay," he says. He smiles up at Patrice. "I'd be happy to grill . . . something."

"I like this boy, Anna-Marie," Patrice says to me. "Hold on to him. Have either of you seen Grandpa? Dad!" she shouts out towards the living room. "Dad, have you eaten breakfast yet?"

And without a backward glance, she sweeps out.

"You'd be happy to grill something?" I raise my eyebrow. "A food of your *people*?"

He holds up his phone. "There's recipes on here. I'm sure I can find something. It's not like my parents will be here to tell me if it's authentic or not. Besides it sounds fun. Maybe I'll take home the Big Weiner. You know, start my own trophy shelf to compete with yours."

I laugh. "The Golden Weiner. But I'm all up for watching you try." I stand up, and pick up my plate of french toast, which I've only eaten a single slice of. My director will be pissed if I come back to LA and can't wiggle my way into Maeve's skin-tight cocktail dresses.

Josh swipes his phone and opens his text messages. "By the way, I'm going to forward you some very invasive questions from Wyatt about Ryan Lansing's penis. You don't have to answer them if you don't want to, but if you do, you'll make his day. Or maybe his whole month." He cringes. "And you should know that I tell Ben and by extension Wyatt an unhealthy amount about my sex life, and I know an unhealthy amount about theirs. Is that, like, a problem?"

I shrug. "Gabby knows a frightening number of details about my sex life. And you should know I own an unhealthy number of shoes."

Josh laughs. "That sounds like an even trade, then."

I scrape off my plate, breathing through a brief panic that we're somehow talking about deal breakers as if there's some kind of *deal.* I start filling the sink, and without me even saying anything, Josh is at my side, pulling a drying towel out of a nearby drawer. And I start washing the dishes, and handing them to him to dry, and we're smiling at each other and I'm taken aback by how *normal* this all feels—even though I've never so much as loaded the dishwasher at Josh's place.

As I'm scrubbing a spatula, I flick some soap bubbles at him. They land squarely on his cheek and stick there, and I giggle.

Josh shakes his head. "So immature, Halsey."

Then he takes one of the spoons he's just dried and puts it under the running faucet at just the right angle. Water sprays all down the front of my shirt and I shriek and start laughing even harder, and grab the faucet hose to spray him, which he only partially blocks with his hand. We both get blasted in the face with water, and we're both laughing and dripping wet.

And then I can't resist, and I step in to kiss him—or maybe he steps in to kiss me, but somehow we're pressed together in our wet clothes and making out and his hands are in my hair, and mine are up his shirt, pressed against the tight muscles of his back, and—

A throat clears. Loudly.

We jump apart to see my dad standing there with Tanya. I hastily fold my arms across my chest, even though it's clearly too late to hide that I appear to have just come from a wet t-shirt contest. "Hey, Daddy," I say.

He blinks. "Hey, Pumpkin. Interesting way you have of doing dishes."

Tanya makes a snorting noise. "Come on, Bill. It's not like you and I haven't done our share of dishes that way."

I stifle my gag reflex. I appreciate her defense and all, but I really don't need to picture my dad and her engaged in dish-washing-related foreplay.

"Josh," Dad says, nodding to him.

Josh dries his hands off on the dishtowel and reaches out to shake his hand. "Mr. Halsey. I didn't get a chance to talk with you yesterday, but it's really nice to meet you."

If I didn't know better—that Josh interacts with movie producers and huge A-list stars and directors on a first name basis—I would say that Josh sounded . . . nervous.

My dad shakes Josh's hand, and then returns to folding his arms across his chest. Which I notice is covered with a too-tight t-shirt, in addition to yesterday's skinny jeans.

I do not agree with Tanya's choice of fashion for him.

"So Josh, that's a nice car you're driving out there."

"Thanks," Josh says.

"You must do well to afford that kind of thing. You're an agent, right?"

"That's right."

I'm used to Josh responding to people in more than one or two words, so I'm starting to think my guess about his nervousness was actually right. I put my hand on the small of Josh's back, so he doesn't feel like he's some high school kid, going up against the big scary dad (who would be scarier in looser clothes, I imagine) alone. "He's one of the best. Really highly respected in the industry."

Dad frowns. "So how come you're not representing Anna-Marie, then?"

I choke and cover it with a cough, but my dad plows ahead.

"If you're the best and all. Seems like you'd be able to recognize talent. She's going to win an Oscar one of these days."

Josh opens his mouth, but I beat him to it. "I have an agent already, Daddy. Brent. He's pretty good."

Now my dad turns his frown to me. "Pretty good? Why aren't you with the best? I mean, if you're in this, you want to be—"

"Bill," Tanya says. "I'm sure Anna-Marie knows how to manage her career without your help."

I smile at her, but I can feel how weak it is. The truth is, he's not wrong. If I want to really succeed, I should be with the best. I should, like Josh said back when he first offered to rep me, be out auditioning, putting myself out there for more and better roles.

But I don't honestly know if I have what it takes to do better than *Southern Heat*. I love what I do, and I know I'm attractive and at least reasonably talented, but there's a shit-ton of girls in LA that fit that description. And now I really don't want Josh to take that kind of chance on me and watch me fail, over and over and over again.

I can't help but wonder if he'd regret all the other chances he's taken on me.

Dad's expression softens. "Well, she has been doing pretty well at that. We'll get one of those Oscars on that trophy shelf yet."

I don't have the heart to tell him that if I were ever to win an Oscar, I am sure as hell not keeping it with my pie-eating medal in Everett. That sucker's going to have its own shelf and dedicated lighting system with fanfare sound effects. Probably along with some of my more prized designer shoes. "Sure thing, Daddy."

Josh eyes me, and there's an awkward pause where my dad just stands there, in which we are thankfully saved by Patrice. Whose arrival I am generally not so grateful for.

"I'm about to go to the grocery store. Joe's Way and Anna-Marie, are you coming with? Have you decided what you're grilling for us?"

"It's going to be a surprise. I just need a few minutes to . . . look something up real quick." Josh squeezes my hand and then nods to my dad and Tanya before fleeing the room to frantically Google recipes.

"Fantastic," Patrice says, beaming, and heads out the front door.

Tanya and Dad start to head into the living room. And I know I shouldn't involve myself any more with her, but I can't help it.

I like Tanya.

"Tanya," I say. "Do you mind talking with me for a minute?"

She looks justifiably surprised. "Sure."

Dad smiles at me before he leaves the room, probably happy

I'm taking the time to get to know Tanya a little better. He wouldn't be as happy if he knew what I want to say to her.

But first. "You've been sticking up for me a lot," I say. "My family's a little crazy, as you well know, and—anyway, I just wanted to let you know I appreciate that."

Tanya cocks her head to the side. She's wearing a different pair of dangly feather earrings today. "Of course. But I have the feeling there's more you wanted to talk to me about."

And there's part of the reason I like her. She picks up on stuff quick, and she doesn't seem inclined to hold back what she thinks.

"I love my dad," I start. "Like I really love him. And I want him to be happy. But—"

She narrows her eyes, and I can tell that I'm not saying this right.

Screw the preamble. "You know his track record, right? How many times he's been married? How those marriages have ended?"

She looks down at the floor, scuffs her sandal along a crack in the linoleum. "I do. So is that it, then? Is that why you're avoiding me?"

Honestly, I don't know that I've had time to avoid her, what with all the Shane and the Josh of the last two days.

Except that I have avoided her, and for a lot longer than two days.

"Yeah. The thing is, you're awesome. And that's great, you know, for my dad. But I don't want to see you or your kids get hurt." And now I'm staring at the floor too. "Because I've seen that a lot."

"I'm scared, too," Tanya says, and I look up in surprise. "Terrified, some days. But he's a good man, and I love him. And I think that's worth the risk. Don't you?"

I blink at her, stunned.

Do I? Could I ever?

I hear myself talking to Josh last night, his arm warm around my shoulders. *Sometimes I want to believe . . .*

"Anyway, I appreciate your concern," she says. "I think you're awesome, too. And clearly, you have your own romantic concerns to worry about."

I really, really do.

THIRTEEN

Anna-Marie

Patrice takes Josh and me—and unfortunately, Lily, who hops in at the last minute—to Foster's Food and Feed in her extended cab pickup truck, where we park in the lot next to a half dozen other, similar trucks. Josh spends most of the car ride texting with his assistant—he's cleared his week of things that require him to be in LA and apparently has some fellow agents covering for him, but he still has a lot of work to do.

"So what did you decide on?" I ask as we get our own cart and head down a separate aisle from my aunt and cousin.

"Carne asada. This recipe has like five hundred reviews and looks easy enough." He eyes the aisle around us. "Why are there so many different exhaust pipes for sale in a grocery store?"

"What, you've never been at Trader Joe's and felt a desperate need for a new muffler?" I gesture to the other side of the aisle. "Or farming equipment?"

"Can't say that I have."

"Such a city boy, Rios." I shake my head in mock sadness.

He grins. "Says the girl with a designer purse and the world's most unstable-looking sandals."

I laugh and look down at my Tory Burch wedges. "What? They make my legs look good."

"Well, I'm not arguing with *that*." We've made our way into an actual food aisle and Josh picks up a can of chiles, eyeing it thoughtfully. I'm wondering if he has ever cooked anything before when he says, "So your dad was pretty intense."

I grimace. "Oh, god, I'm sorry about that. I think he was trying to make up for years of not being able to grill the guys I'm dating—"

"No, I didn't mean to me. I meant, you know, with the whole Oscars thing." He puts the can in the cart and turns his gaze to me. "Did he really mean that?"

I shrug. "I told you before, he and my mom are both kind of intense. They're really proud when I succeed."

"Yeah, but there's *succeeding* and there's winning an award that statistically an incredibly small number of actors will ever even be nominated for."

I can almost hear Brent in my head. *Soaps are a good place for a girl like you, Anna-Marie.*

"You don't think I ever could," I say, and maybe that's true, because I find I'm not able to keep the hurt from my voice.

"That's not what I mean," he says quickly. "It's just—that's a lot of pressure, don't you think?"

"Maybe. But that's just the nature of my career, you know?" He should know that more than anyone, what the industry expects of actresses—stay young, stay thin, have perfect skin and hair and teeth. Be compliant and simultaneously ballsy. Ambitious yet appropriately reserved. Be the best, always, because you're forever on a precipice with a row of beautiful women behind you, ready to push you off and take your place.

A chill runs through my veins. Maybe Brent is right. Maybe I should just be happy with what I have.

The wheels on the cart squeak as he pushes it a few steps forward. "Is that even what you want, though? To win an Oscar?"

"Isn't that something every actor wants?"

"It's just not healthy to have your success determined by something you have no control over," he says. "And I don't think it's fair of your father to put that on you."

"He just wants me to be the best. He thinks I *will* be the best. Is that so wrong?" The chill has become a flush of anger I feel all the way to my fingertips, and I stop walking and fold my arms across my chest. I'm not sure if it's the dig on my father or just more hurt that Josh clearly doesn't see an Oscar in my future—though if I'm honest, I know how unlikely it really is.

Josh stops walking, too, and the front of the cart turns a few inches to the side. "Is that why you told him I'm the best? Because otherwise I'm not good enough for you?" He looks back at me, his dark eyes haunted. "Because I'm good, but I'm not the best. And you know that."

His words are like a punch in my gut. I gape, not even sure how to respond.

"I didn't—that's not—" I start, but I find myself staring down at my feet. I can't bring myself to tell him how terrified I am of failing, *especially* failing in front of Josh—because that leads to all the other things I can't bring myself to tell him.

There's a silence that sits like lead in my stomach. The tinny country muzak piping over the store sound system buzzes in my ears.

Josh clears his throat. "The recipe says I need flank steak. It looks like the meat counter is over there?"

I nod and we start walking again. But I feel numb, even as we pick up the rest of the ingredients we need. Even as we start talking again, both of us clearly trying to pretend that whole Oscar discussion never happened.

Even as we pass Lily, and she picks up the nearest phallic-shaped grocery item—which happens to be a raw sausage she peels from its plastic wrapping—and seductively sucks on the end of it while winking at Josh.

Okay, maybe the numbness cracks a bit then, but mainly because I'm so disgusted. Too disgusted to even be *angry* with Lily about her increasingly bold seduction attempts. Josh looks like he's about to start dry heaving as we turn the corner into another aisle.

"Did she really just do that with raw meat?" He shudders.

"That girl's going to pick up mad cow disease. She should really stick to pickles."

He laughs, but there's still something holding him back. And I don't think it's the fact I'm related to the girl who performs sex acts on uncooked meats, or even that he really thinks I—a soap opera actress, for crying out loud—would only be his client if he was the very best agent in Hollywood.

When he referred to what I said to my father, I wonder if he wasn't thinking about me refusing to be his girlfriend. Him not being good enough for me isn't even close to the problem there . . . but there's no way to explain that without telling him all the things I'm afraid to say and think and want.

And because I'm afraid to say those things—and now to ride home with Lily, because who knows what she'll try next—I suggest we take a tour of Everett. Josh seems relieved, and agrees, and for once, Lily seems too ashamed of herself to interfere, and heads back to my dad's house with her mother.

We spend the afternoon walking around town. I show him the convenience store where the teenagers hang out, especially when it's too cold to do anything outside. We chat with the old knitting ladies in front of the post office, who are eager to tell us all the gossip about how Pearl Marmon (of Pearl's Gardening Corner fame) has been "getting her dirt tilled" by Ted Hess, which I assume is a metaphor for sex, but these ladies have a combined age of about two hundred and might actually be scandalized by Pearl outsourcing her tilling, so who knows. We stop in at Sheila's Bakery and eat thick slices of banana bread and I try not to imagine Sheila—who is significantly thinner than the last time I saw her, thanks to the gastric bypass surgery Patrice mentioned—taping down her skin flaps. We pass Everett's movie theater, which only has one screen and plays mostly John Wayne movies and, weirdly, anything by Pixar. There's the high school and various friends' houses, and I tell him stories about growing up here, and he laughs and shares his own stories.

But there's still this weird tension, and it doesn't help that walking around town is bringing back all these memories of Shane—memories I can't tell Josh, because I don't want to hurt him any more than I already have, or make things even more awkward.

If I were here with Shane instead, this would be easier. Uncomplicated. Shane doesn't make me feel like Josh does—like I've found this piece of myself I didn't even know I was missing. But being with Shane doesn't make me panic. It doesn't make me feel like I have everything in the world to lose.

I need to talk to Gabby, I realize. Too much has happened in the past couple of days, and my brain feels like it's spinning but going nowhere, like tires in a patch of mud. And all I'm doing is messing up everything around me the more I try to get myself free. Gabby is really good for this sort of thing.

Even though Everett's a minuscule town, we still manage to kill enough time wandering around there that it's dark by the time we get back to my house. Josh has work calls to make, so that gives me an opportunity to text Gabby.

I need to talk to you. Are you free?

About ten seconds after I hit send, she calls me.

"Anna-Marie, I'm so sorry," Gabby gushes as I pick up. "Did the landlord call you? I told him not to call you until I'd checked on your shoes."

And now I have an entirely different kind of panic. "My *shoes*? What happened?"

She makes a verbal cringing sound. "Unnggh. It's my brother. Felix. He broke into our apartment earlier today when I was at work."

"Oh my god. How do you know it was him?"

"Mrs. Villanova from down the hall saw him leaving and described him to me. It was definitely Felix. Plus, from what I can tell, he didn't actually steal anything, he just tore the place apart. He must have been looking for his cello."

She sounds completely heartbroken, and I wish I could reach through the phone and give her a hug. Or better yet, give her junkie brother a swift ass-kicking for doing this to her. The last stint at rehab didn't take any more than the first one, and he's been back on heroin for months now. Before he completely slipped off the radar, he gave her his cello for safekeeping—a job she takes as seriously as if she was keeping the country's nuclear codes from Russian spies, rather than pawn bait from some strung-out kid. I don't have the faintest clue where that cello is, and I doubt Will does, either.

I know she'd desperately hoped that Felix wouldn't ever get so low as to test her on this. But it appears that he has.

I groan. "Gabby, that sucks. I'm sorry."

"Yeah. It sucks." There's a pause where she draws in an uneven breath. "I really don't think he took anything. I haven't checked everything yet, but your Xbox is still here. As well as the Holy Trinity."

The Holy Trinity is the semi-joking term for my three most beloved—and ridiculously expensive—pairs of Louboutins. If he was looking for something to sell for drug money, he would have done well to take those, so the fact that he didn't speaks well for the safety of the rest of my collection.

"Good. But I'm not worried about that. I'm just worried about you." If I'm being honest, this is much easier to say now that I know my Louboutins aren't currently sitting in some seedy pawn shop.

I shudder.

She sighs. "I'm okay. I just—I don't know what to do anymore. Of course he's not answering my texts."

"I think you're doing everything you can. He knows you love him. He knows you'll help him when he's ready for it. That's why he gave you the cello in the first place."

"Right. Right." But there's the unspoken worry—that he'll never be ready for help. That maybe he won't get the chance to get help before the drugs kill him.

Now I feel like a total dick for worrying at all about my shoes in the face of *that*.

"But you didn't know about that when you texted, right?" Gabby says. "So clearly there's something going on in Wyoming I need to hear about."

Boy, is there ever.

"Yeah, but you don't need to listen to me whine about dating stuff when you've got this with Felix."

"Oh god, *please* let me hear about your dating stuff," Gabby says. "It'll give me something else to think about while I put our apartment back together."

I can see her point. And really, if she needs a distraction, the tale of my last couple days will certainly provide that.

"And anyway, you have dating stuff to talk about?" Gabby continues. "In Everett, Wyoming? The place you once referred to as 'the town where dreams go to die a long cowboy-boot-wearing death?'"

I may be a bit melodramatic at times.

"Yeah, well, the past couple days have been crazy," I say, "so you'd better settle in."

"I can't settle in, I've got to hang up all the clothes he pulled out of your closet and—"

"Metaphorically, Gabs."

"Right. Got it." She sighs and I hear the clatter of what sounds like my plastic hangers. I wince at the thought of all my clothes strewn all over, and start spilling all that has happened since I arrived in Everett.

Gabby may have started out a bit distracted, but it only takes until I'm telling her about Shane climbing through my window (the first time) before I'm pretty certain she's abandoned her cleaning entirely and has settled in (literally) on the couch with a bag of Doritos.

"Shane? Ex-boyfriend Shane?" she asks, between crunching sounds.

"The very same. But wait, it gets better. Or worse. I'm not sure." I launch into our adventure at the hot springs. She actually chokes on her chips when I tell her about the Boy Scouts and I have to wait to make sure she's not actually dying.

Then there's the bat attack.

"Oh my god, Anna," she says, laughing, after I describe my dad ordering Shane to put on pants and help him. "This all sounds like something that would happen to me."

It's true. Somehow Everett has turned me into Gabby. Which, if we were talking about her generosity or sense of humor or ability to perform CPR on dying soap opera stars—as she actually did once, saving the life of the legendary Bridget Messler—that would be a good thing. But we are not.

I sit on my bed and continue. "Then, yesterday evening, just as I'm doing this ridiculous fashion show for my future stepsister, Josh shows up."

"Josh? He drove all the way to *Wyoming?* After a conversation about *hot dogs*?"

I flop onto my back, staring up at my ceiling, and I can't keep myself from smiling. "Yeah. He did. And get this, Gabs. We talked for—I don't know, a long time. And he's a total geek." I tell her about our conversation, about Carrie Fisher and *Death Arsenal* and Dothraki and anime, about how we were one-upping each other and his lobster joke that made me snort-laugh, and his reaction to *that* and—

"Wait a minute. He said your snort-laugh is his favorite sound ever?" Gabby says, taking a break from the little squeeing sounds she'd been making at every revelation before.

I grin. "He thinks it's adorable."

"You need to lock this down, Anna-Marie. Because your snort-laugh is not adorable."

Lock this down.

So much of me wants to. Wants to be with him right now rather than just talking about being with him.

"Yeah, okay, but there's more," I say. And then I tell her about

Shane, and our little snit about my dad and the Oscars and the walk through town and all the stuff I didn't want to bring up because I didn't want to make things weird anymore or, worse, hurt him.

"I don't know what to do," I say when I'm finally caught up. "There's Josh and there's Shane, and . . . I don't know. Maybe I shouldn't sleep with either of them until I've decided what I want, you know?" I try to imagine myself telling this to Josh, and my chest aches. He'd leave for sure, then.

Wouldn't he?

"What? Why would you do *that*?" Gabby's practically shouting, and I can picture her, leaning forward all intensely on the couch, pointing a Dorito at where I would normally be sitting there next to her.

"Isn't that, like, the responsible thing to do?" It feels like it is, but being responsible has never really been my forte.

"Maybe, if you were actually choosing between two guys. But that's not what's happening here."

I pause. "It isn't?"

"This entire time, you've been either gushing about Josh or worried about how he's feeling. You haven't done either of those about Shane. You don't care about Shane."

"I care about Shane," I say defensively. But I know what she means.

"Not like you do about Josh. Josh is the one you actually want to be with. You're just scared of that, so you're using Shane as an excuse not to get serious."

Damn. She's right. I know she's right. I knew it before I even called her, on some level.

I let out a shaky breath. "So what do I do?"

"Well, first, drop any stupid ideas about not having sex with Josh. You're totally crazy about him, and, dude, the guy drove out to Wyoming for you, is putting up with your family, loves your snort-laugh, and is sleeping on an air mattress in your dad's storage room. He deserves at least a little action."

I laugh. "Yeah, okay. Probably more than a little." And I'm certainly not opposed to that. "But what about being his . . . you know."

I trail off. I can't even seem to say the word "girlfriend" any more. God, am I messed up.

She sighs. "I know you don't do serious. I know you're scared, even though I'm not sure I totally get why. And I'm not saying you should commit to anything you're not ready for. But I've heard you talk about lots of the guys you've dated. Lots and *lots* of guys—"

"God, you make it sound like I personally sponsor fleet week or something."

"My point is, I've never heard you talk about a guy like this. Not even close. You're already in this, Anna-Marie. And Josh sounds perfect for you. Like the kind of guy worth taking a chance on."

My throat feels like it's closing up. He is the kind of guy worth that.

But I'm not sure I'm the kind of girl capable of it, no matter how much I may want to.

I think of Tanya, who knows about my dad's past, who is scared—wisely—he'll hurt her like he's hurt so many others before. *I think it's worth the risk*, she said.

Is she right? Is anything worth that risk?

But then I think of how it felt to have Josh hold me and talk me down from my tears, how it felt hearing him admit to geeky thing after geeky thing, how it feels to laugh with him and kiss him and . . . well, *everything* with him.

"Okay," I say, though I'm not really sure what I'm agreeing to. "Thanks, Gabby." I pause, as another fear, another kind of sadness, hits me. "When you move out . . . we're still going to talk like this, right? And hang out a ton?"

"We'd better. Or I'm just going to have to move back in with you and bring Will with me. And then you can say goodbye to your precious mango shampoo."

"Good. And Gabby, I'm really sorry about Felix."

"Me too," she says.

We talk for a few more minutes and then hang up. And though I'm still not sure what to do about all my fears and issues, I have at least figured out one thing.

I grab a bag of some things and walk to the storage room and open the door. Josh is sitting on the air mattress with his back against a five-foot stack of number ten cans of beans and flour. He's wearing a plain white t-shirt and pair of plaid flannel pajama pants, and scrolling through something on his phone. He looks up in surprise when I enter, and then gives me a tentative smile.

"Hey," he says.

"Hey," I say back. I lean against the door frame in a casually sexy pose and smile. "Don't get too comfortable here. You're sleeping with me tonight."

He raises an eyebrow. "Yeah? Won't your aunt freak out if she finds me in your bed?"

I grin at him. "Probably. But we're not sleeping there, either. I have a better idea."

FOURTEEN

Anna-Marie

We get in Josh's Porsche with the two sleeping bags I've requisitioned and some pillows, and I direct Josh to a spot about ten minutes outside of town. There's some trees and brush to walk through from where we park the car, but not much, and we end up in a large clearing ringed with mostly pine trees. In the day, you can see the mountains in the distance to the west. In the dark, though, it's like this perfect circle from which to view a sight that's way better than anything nature provides in LA (Josh's naked ass in the shower being a lone notable exception).

Josh lets out a low whistle as he takes in the vast night sky. Not that this same night sky can't be seen from, say, my house—Everett doesn't exactly offer much light pollution—but there's something magical about this place, like you emerge from trees into a dome of millions of stars.

"Pretty nice, huh?" It makes me happy that he feels that same kind of magic here that I do.

"God. Yes."

"It's the only thing I miss about Wyoming, most of the time."

He looks at me, and I wonder if he's thinking about whether or not Shane is the thing I miss occasionally. But Gabby was right, I don't have feelings for Shane, at least not beyond general friendship and shared history. I wonder if Josh will believe me if I tell him that.

I'm about to when I see him about to trip over a rock. I swing the flashlight beam downward and grab his hand. "Careful," I say.

"Yeah, I'm clearly not an outdoorsman."

I smile. "I'm not either. But I think we can manage to stay alive out here for one night, at least. We might need to stay pretty close to each other, though. For safety."

He squeezes my hand. "I think I can handle that."

Me too.

I find us a spot near the center of the clearing, someplace with enough room to stretch out both sleeping bags side by side and not have any rocks jabbing us in the back. I'm happy to see we're alone in the clearing—I had a back-up place in mind in case we happened upon other campers, or god forbid, another Boy Scout troop, but it's just Josh and me and all the stars, and though it's not as cold as last night, it's chilly enough out that we'll definitely want to help heat each other up. I zip the sleeping bags together so they form one bigger bag, and we crawl inside. I turn off the flashlight, and he puts out his arm, and I curl up into his side, my head resting on his shoulder, while his fingers gently stroke my waist, just under my t-shirt.

We both stare up at the stars for a long moment, breathing in the clear night air and each other. A few shooting stars streak across our view, and it's beautiful—meteor showers are common this time of year in Wyoming, but they never stop being awesome.

I just want to enjoy this with him without the shadow of our spat hanging over us.

"I'm sorry," I say quietly. "About earlier, at the grocery store."

"About the nightmares I'm going to have from seeing Lily debase a raw sausage? Because that wasn't your fault."

I laugh. "Well, yeah, I'm definitely sorry about that. For both our sakes. But . . . you know what I mean."

"Yeah, I do," he says, his tone more serious. "And I'm sorry, too. I don't want you to think I don't believe in your talent. Because I do. You're incredible." He squeezes me closer. "I just worry about you putting too much pressure on yourself."

I sigh. "That may be something I have a tendency of doing. And I probably let my parents goad me on too much." I roll to the side and look up at him. "But when I told my dad you were the best, I didn't mean to make you think I needed you to be the best agent ever, or that I doubt your skills, or that—"

"Hey, it's okay," he says, and I realize I had started babbling. He frowns. "I wasn't really upset about that." He pauses, then lets out a small breath. "I think it was really about Shane."

He looks down, then back up, like he's forcing himself to meet my eyes, and my heart constricts. I'm hurting him, and I can't seem to stop it.

But I want to, desperately.

I reach over and grab his free hand, entwining my fingers with his. "I don't want to be with Shane. I didn't really want to be with him before, I just—I think I was afraid of what I was feeling for you. Like, um. How *much* I was feeling for you."

I'm afraid now, saying even that much. I don't do this, I don't talk about my feelings with guys, because I don't generally have feelings for guys. Never like this.

His eyebrows draw together, his thumb rubbing gently over my knuckle. "Yeah?" he says, cautiously. I'm not sure whether he's having a hard time believing me, or whether he's just afraid to do so.

I nod. "I don't do this, normally. You know, feelings and commitment, it's all—it scares the hell out of me. And Shane . . . he doesn't scare me like you do." Josh flinches, and I know I'm screwing this up and oh my god, I wish I had a scriptwriter right now, because no matter how terrible my *Southern Heat* dialogue can be, Maeve would surely handle this better than Anna-Marie is.

"I scare you," Josh says.

"How I *feel* about you scares me," I say quickly. Maybe I should just have Gabby tell him how I feel about him; she doesn't seem to have any problems getting the point across. "Because I want to be with you, and I'm . . . terrified. And Shane—it's not like that with him. His band is talking about moving to LA, and probably he was just trying to reconnect so he'd have a place to land—one I have no intention of giving him, by the way." Josh doesn't look comforted by this revelation, and I can hardly blame him. "The point is, I don't have feelings for him, not anymore, and that makes him safe."

He studies me, and even in the dark, with our sight adjusted to the light of the moon and stars, I can see his face, the slight downturn to his lips. And even though he's holding me, and our faces are mere inches apart, there's this distance I can't seem to get across.

Maybe because I'm too scared to.

"What exactly are you afraid of?" Josh asks, after a long moment.

I could bring up any number of tabloid reports of bitter Hollywood breakups—hell, Watterpless's public meltdown was just this week. But it's more than Hollywood and what the industry does to relationships.

It's what relationships do to relationships.

"I'm afraid it will end badly. I'm afraid one day you'll find someone else, and you'll leave me for her. Or just cheat on me with her, but either way, this thing that was so great will have become nothing but bitterness and resentment and pain, and I . . ." I pull in a ragged breath. "I decided at some point that I didn't ever want that. I never wanted to be my mom, or any of my stepmoms. And the thought of something like that happening with you, of losing you that way—" Hot tears prick at the corners of my eyes, and I try to blink them away, looking down at our bodies curled up next to one another.

And maybe I'm just imagining it, just desperately wishing for it, but I think I feel that distance between us shrink, even though neither of us actually moves closer.

"It is just what happened with your dad?" He runs his hand through the ends of my hair, his fingers gentle along my back. "Not that that isn't enough to give someone a jaded view of relationships, but . . ." He trails off.

I shrug. "I guess it was my dad, and then it felt like everything confirmed it, you know? Joe and Patrice are still married, but it's not like I think they're actually happy. I don't know if Shane ever technically cheated on me, but he would flirt so much with other girls, and there were always rumors—and really, we broke up enough whenever he wanted to sleep with someone else that it didn't take long to see a pattern there." I roll my eyes, remembering some of our more ridiculous fights. "And then there was this guy, Reid."

Josh's fingers freeze on my back, and I hope I'm not giving him even more reason to feel insecure—though god, how could a guy like Josh Rios be insecure about me?—but he needs to know how deeply messed up I am.

He deserves to know.

"A while after Shane and I broke up for good, I was working at this bar over in Riverton, and I met Reid. We dated for about three months, but we weren't serious, even though he kept wanting to be. But I already had, you know . . . issues with that kind of thing."

I say that last part lightly, but Josh doesn't smile. Probably because it's not funny, not even a little bit. And what happened next is even less so.

"But he was a good guy, or at least I thought he was. And then I found out he was married."

Josh's eyes widen. "Oh god. I'm sorry, Anna-Marie. That's—ugh."

"Yeah. It was the worst. I mean, I liked him, but that wasn't the bad part. It was knowing that I'd become the other woman, you know? It wasn't my fault. I get that. But he'd used me, and he'd betrayed his wife, and god, I was just *done*.

I packed up my stuff and drove out to LA the next day." I smile then, but it's a bitter one. "I'd thought about trying to be an actress—I'd loved being in plays and musicals in high school—but I guess I have Reid being a total dick to thank for pushing me into actually doing it."

"You do want to be an actress, though, yeah? Because you're great at it."

My smile becomes more genuine. "I love it. Like an insane amount."

And now his lips twitch into a smile, too. "Yeah, that's kind of how I feel about my job, too."

I want to end all the serious talk right there and ease into joking and laughing and kissing and making love here under the stars, but something compels me further.

"It doesn't help, though," I say. "Being in the industry. Seeing people use each other and hurt each other, and it's all so public and . . . and here's the thing. I get that I'm good-looking. I get that I'm good at what I do. But there are a thousand other gorgeous girls who could also do my job, and I can't ever forget that." There's a lump building in my throat, and I clear it. "And I guess that's what scares me the most in relationships, too. That I'm replaceable." I feel a rogue tear drop down my cheek and I brush it away, angry and embarrassed.

I've always thought of myself as strong, as resilient and brave. But it turns out I'm just an insecure mess. And I don't think I can blame this on Wyoming.

Josh's expression softens, and he leans in and kisses the top of my head, pressing me closer against him, and I just breathe in the scent of his neck, feel his pulse against my cheek.

He pulls back, just enough to look me in the eyes. "You are not replaceable. There's only one Anna-Marie Halsey. Trust me. I've spent years looking." He lets out a breath. "I didn't know what I was looking for, but you're it."

My heart swells in my chest, warmth flooding through me, even as my own pulse picks up. Because I can tell he doesn't mean what he was looking for in a client, or a girl to have great casual sex with.

"And I know you're scared," he says. "I get that. But I'm not going to cheat on you. I wouldn't do that. I've had girlfriends before—I dated my college girlfriend for over two years—and I never cheated on them, and I wasn't even in love with them, not like—"

My breath catches, and he stops, as if he just realized what he said. Or implied, I suppose.

He cringes. "Can we pretend I didn't say that?"

I can't. More surprisingly, I don't want to. "Not like me?"

He closes his eyes. "Yeah. Not like you." Then he looks at me again, and I think he might be as terrified as I am. "You don't have to say it back—it's okay. But it's true. I'm in love with you."

I've had guys say those words to me—and some guys who I think actually may have meant it, or at least thought they did. But I've never felt so lightning-struck by those words before—like I can feel the current of them coursing through my veins, lighting up every part of me.

"How do you know?" My voice is barely above a whisper.

He shrugs one shoulder. "I was already falling in love with you before this, but . . . it was the lobster joke. That was when I *knew*. Like how you laughed and it was like . . ." He shakes his head, then smiles. "It was like you get me. I knew you were what I've been looking for, maybe my whole life."

I feel like I should be hardcore panicking, but strangely, something else is happening. It's like my body is exhaling, slowly, sinking into the unexpected bliss of this realization:

Josh is in love with me.

He's *in love* with me.

And maybe I can't say it back, because I have no idea how you just know something like that and I'm not sure my panic wouldn't flare so much that I'd have some kind of love-admission-induced stroke.

But I can do something else. I lean in and bring my lips to

his and press my body fully against his and work my hand under the cotton of his t-shirt, along the muscles of his back and—

And something's off.

He's kissing me back, and his body is giving some pretty definite signals that he wants to rip my clothes off as badly I want him to. But there's a hesitance to his movements, an uncertainty that I've never felt before from him in all the (many many) times we've been together.

I pull back. "There's something wrong still, isn't there?" Now the panic is creeping in, tugging at my nerves. Whispering to me that he may be in love with me, but that doesn't make me any less of a commitment-phobe and a romantic disaster waiting to happen. It doesn't mean he can put up with that for very long.

Maybe he's wishing he could have fallen in love with someone else.

Josh sighs and runs a hand through his hair, which flops right back over his eye. I want to brush it back, but I'm suddenly feeling all kinds of exposed and touching him even more than I already am doesn't feel like a smart idea.

Maybe none of this is a smart idea.

"I seriously don't want to admit to this," he says, which doesn't help my nerves any. I chew on my lips, waiting for him to just get it over with:

I can't do this. I don't want to do this. You're too much of a mess, Anna-Marie, and even love isn't worth this.

"I meant it when I said it's okay if you can't say it back," he says slowly. "But it's—it scares me, being in this deeper than you are. And Ben, he told me once that sex is different when you're in love with someone. Like it means more." He rolls his eyes up to the sky. "God, this is not something I'm supposed to worry about as a guy. Which is probably sexist to even say. But whatever." He blurts out the next bit as if he's confessing to burning passion for knitting and wishes he could spend his life outside of the post office with the two old ladies and their eternally-growing scarves: "I'm worried it's going to be different for me, like even better, but it won't be for you."

Well, *that* was not what I expected.

I'm not sure exactly what he reads on my face, but he groans and flops onto his back, his head on the pillow. "It's ridiculous, right? Feel free to mock me. In fact, I think I'd feel better if you did."

I get the feeling he's actually serious about that last part. "Well, I believe you now that Ben doesn't watch *Southern Heat*. Because no regular viewer of my soap opera actually believes that sex in love is better than sex with your boyfriend's evil twin brother."

Josh laughs, and tugs me closer again, and my heart flutters like I've possibly done something right.

"Yeah, okay," he says. "Evil twin sex sounds pretty hard to beat."

I decide to continue in the teasing vein. I think we both need a little of that, after all the heavy emotions of today. "Or maybe all that agent and client sex you mentioned before? Does that generally happen right there on the conference table, on top of contracts about volumizer?"

Josh laughs and groans simultaneously. "I knew saying that was going to bite me in the ass one day."

I raise my eyebrows and smile wickedly. "Is ass-biting also involved?"

"How many clients do you think I've actually slept with?"

"I don't know, Mr. 'It's No Big Deal'," I say, and I find it really doesn't feel like so much of a big deal. Now I know that since we've been dating, he wasn't banging Macy or Asia or anyone else. "Maybe all the hot, straight, twenty-something female ones? How many of those do you have?"

He groans again. "You make me sound like a real stand-up guy, Halsey." But he's still smiling. "Do you want to know the number?"

"I kind of think I need to, now."

"Zero. I don't sleep with my clients, as a general rule."

"What?" I laugh and pinch his side, and he pinches my ass

in retribution, making me squeal and laugh even harder. "Then why did you—"

"Because I wanted to sign you. Because you're good. And I also wanted to keep sleeping with you. Because you're *very, very* good." Now his smile is the wicked one, and I want to lean down and kiss him and show him how even better than very, very good I can be when I put my mind to it.

But I can't help but ask something instead.

"Would it be a problem, then? If I were to be your client someday?"

And I know I don't just mean the sleeping together part. But all the feelings and the possible falling apart—and I also realize suddenly that was why I really turned him down the first time. Yes, I wanted to avoid awkwardness after some future expiration date on our dating, but it was so much more than that.

I already had feelings for him, even then. Before I knew about his geeky side. Before I knew how much I'd miss him after being in a different state from him for even a day.

And now . . .

"You've made it clear *that's* not going to happen," he says, interrupting whatever conclusion I might have drawn from that.

A conclusion I don't think I'm ready for. But this . . .

I suck my lips inward. "Maybe it could. If you still want it."

He sits up so fast I almost roll out of his arms. "You want to be my client?"

"Well, I did tell my dad you're the best," I say, with a teasing tone. "And I know Brent sure as hell isn't. He would never fight my hair-care battles. So yeah. I would love it if you'd represent me, Josh Rios, super-agent."

Josh grins, and kisses me deeply enough I'm left breathless. "I'd be happy to be your agent, Anna-Marie Halsey, super-actress." Then he raises an eyebrow. "Clearly, that was your end goal all along, wasn't it?"

"No way." I lean in, lowering my voice seductively. "My end goal is to see what's in your basement."

"I wouldn't be surprised if you got that secret out of me soon, at the rate I've been confessing everything else." He tucks a strand of my hair back behind my ear, his fingers lingering there. "What kind of magic power do you have over me, Halsey?"

"It's not magic. It's the shadows," I say in this mysterious voice. And then before I can talk myself out of this—or before the Gabby voice in my head can do so, because she sure as hell would try—I put my hand over my mouth and do my truly terrible (but in my mind hilarious) impression of Bane from *The Dark Knight Rises*. "The shadows betray you, because they belong to me!"

His mouth drops open. He blinks. "Is that Bane? Did you just do a *Bane* impression?" He turns his head back and forth, looking from one side of the clearing to the other. "Am I on TV? Are you real? Oh my god, you are the perfect woman. Did you hear that, Wyoming?" he shouts, and I start giggling, despite myself. "Anna-Marie Halsey is the perfect woman!"

God, the thought that Josh Rios would think I'm the perfect woman because of my Bane impression . . . It's like he said about the lobster joke, this feeling that he *gets* me in a way no one else does. But part of me still needs to make sure he really does.

"Even though I'm kind of a geek, I'm not *just* a geek, you know?" I say. "I'm still the girl who has too many shoes and reads fashion blogs and probably cares way too much about what kind of hair products I use—though clearly not as much as some of your other clients, and—"

"I know." He presses his forehead against mine. "And I'm a geek, but I'm also the guy who actually likes the industry parties and clubs, and only wears suits by my three favorite designers, and who hired a decorator to put together my living room, which means I paid like six hundred dollars for a set of mason jars full of beans. So yeah. I get it. And I never thought I'd find someone who would get both sides of me like you do."

I never thought I'd find that either. I'd so carefully compartmentalized my life, keeping certain guys in one part and certain guys in the other, and it never really occurred to me that one day I could have a guy who fit it all.

"We are a bit ridiculously perfect for each other, aren't we?" I say softly. And before he can answer, because I just can't take being so close to those lips anymore without doing something about it, I kiss him with all the longing that's been building ever since we crawled into these sleeping bags.

And I don't know if it's that he's no longer worried about whether or not the sex will mean more to him than to me, or whether my Bane impression was just so hot it pushed him over the edge of caring, but the hesitance from before is long gone. His hands are under my clothes, burning along my skin, making me gasp and arch against him.

We kiss like we need each other's breath to survive, and I think maybe we do. Even with him, I've never felt this kind of raw need to have his skin pressed against mine, to feel him all around me and inside me. My hands betray my desperation, tugging off his shirt, and then his pants, digging my fingers into his back. He moans, even as his lips work their way down my neck, past my collarbone, and further and further south.

My legs spread and my hands are in his hair and the world is all heat and the most delicious aching I've ever felt. And though I've had lots and lots of *really* incredible sex with Josh, being with him now is somehow different than anything before and better than everything I've ever known. And I think he's feeling the same intensity I am, because we barely remember the condom in time—thankfully I brought several of those with the camping supplies—and then we're together again, our bodies moving in this perfect, delirious tandem. He whispers in my ear that he loves me, god how he loves me, and I'm lost in the pure ecstatic sensation of those words, of just being with *him*.

We shudder apart against each other, gasping, clinging tight, and I wish I never, never had to leave these arms.

And that's when I know.

This is different. It means more.

We lie there, after, still pressed together in the sleeping bag. I press my forehead into the curve of his neck, and before my fears can take over, I say, "I love you, Josh."

He pulls back enough to search my eyes. "You don't have to—"

"I do, because it's true. I'm in love with you." I let out a small, shaky breath. "I'm still scared, and I don't think I'm ready for the girlfriend thing yet, and not because I want to be with anyone else, but just because. I know it doesn't make sense. But I love you."

Josh smiles in an adorably stunned way, and then kisses my forehead, his lips lingering on my skin. "It doesn't have to make sense. I'll wait until you're ready."

Our breathing grows slower as we lie there in each other's arms, watching the stars above. A handful more slide across the sky.

"You know," he says. "If it's just the word 'girlfriend' that's the problem, we can always skip that part."

And even though there's a definite teasing note in his voice, my heart squeezes tight, in a combination of pure happiness and panic that seems to be all too common around Josh of late.

I look up at him, and even though I'm scared—terrified—of everything that has changed in just this night alone, I can't help but grin. Because Josh is in love with me, and I'm in love with him, and that's reason enough to spend the rest of my life smiling.

"Don't push your luck, Rios," I say.

FIFTEEN

Anna-Marie

The next morning when we get back to my house, and after we take showers and get dressed—separately, sadly, because Patrice is eyeing us judgmentally—I go outside to call Brent and tell him the bad news. I've got a whole speech prepared, in which I thank him for all he's done for me as an agent, for taking a chance on me, blah blah blah. It's important not to burn bridges, and really, I am grateful.

I don't get a chance to deliver it, because I've barely gotten out the words "I've decided to sign with Josh Rios," when Brent cuts off the rest with a harsh laugh.

"Yeah, I saw that coming." He sounds like he's eating something, his lips smacking wetly together. This is not new—during my first meeting with him, he ate two foot-long meatball sandwiches and left marinara-smudged fingerprints on my contract.

"Oh," I say, not sure how to respond. "That's good, I suppose. And Brent, I want you to know I'm so grateful—"

"I figured it'd happen as soon as I saw that picture of you two in that club. He's a slick one, Rios. Knows how to use what the good lord gave him."

I bristle. "Josh isn't dating me to sign me." I'm actually surprised Brent doesn't think it went the other way around—everyone else in Hollywood will, no doubt.

"Whatever you need to tell yourself to sleep at night, sweetheart," Brent says. "Just remember who was here for you from the beginning. When he's done screwing you, and is working on his next poach, I'd be happy to—"

I don't bother hearing what he'd be happy to do. I hang up on his pompous ass and stand there fuming on the front lawn.

When he's done screwing you . . .

It sounds so much like something my mom would say that I can practically hear her echo the words in my head.

I'm spared from reliving a full memory of my mom's litany of reasons to distrust men by a UPS truck pulling up in the driveway. A heavyset woman in the brown uniform emerges with a large, battered-looking package in hand.

"Are you Patrice?" the delivery woman asks. "Because we at UPS are officially sorry about the lateness of the package, but really, we'd appreciate it if you'd stop leaving long messages threatening to report us to the Bureau of Land Management, and even if your brother does work there, I don't think they—"

"Oh my god, did she seriously . . . never mind." I shake my head. "I'll make sure she gets the package. And the message. I'm sorry. On behalf of . . . humanity."

The UPS driver gives me a look, and has me sign for the package. Then she peels off down the street, probably vowing never to return to Everett again.

I should follow the woman's stellar example. Instead, I heft the package, wondering briefly if that tear on the bottom is from being chewed on by a goat, and bring it in the house.

"Patrice, your t-shirts are here," I call.

My aunt pops out of the kitchen to snatch the package from my hands with the speed and aggressiveness of a blazer zombie in *Death Arsenal.* I might have reflexively punched her if I hadn't smelled her cloud of perfume a second before. I'd think we'd be back to the lilacs in the rotation by now, but this one could only be called "Suffocation by Tangerine."

"Thank heavens!" Patrice says. "And not a moment too soon! I have your dad and Tanya already getting the grills set up for the competition." She lowers her voice and leans in conspiratorially. "Did you know *Tanya* is entering this year?"

"Really? That's . . . kind of cool, actually."

"Is it?" Patrice twists her lips. "I'm not one to put stock in traditional gender roles, but grilling really is a man's domain."

"So true. I can't count the number of times I've wanted to make a burger but remembered I didn't have a penis."

Patrice frowns at me. "Why don't you go downstairs and tell everyone the shirts are here," she suggests. "And tell Joe and Joe's Way they need to get started prepping their food."

I don't bother reminding her that really, he wants to be called Josh; it's wasted air once Patrice has her mind set on something. Instead I head down to the basement, where I see Grandpa in his usual armchair, and Joe and Josh on opposite ends of the couch. Uncle Joe appears to be sleeping. Byron is sunk low into an old red bean bag chair that lost half its beans when Shane and I had sex on it back in high school and it popped. Ginnie is splayed out on her stomach on the floor, petting Buckley, who is lying on his back, his long mop-like hair spread out in every direction.

They're all staring at the TV—except Josh, who gives me a wide grin when I enter the room. I think maybe he's just happy to see me. And then I see what they're all watching.

It's on old episode of *Southern Heat*, from like three or four months ago. And there I am on screen, in a bright blue bikini, making out with Matt Kearn, the actor who plays Bruce, on the deck chair of his backyard pool set.

I remember that shoot—I'd gotten a spray tan specially for it, and seeing how long my legs look wrapped around Matt's torso, I decide it was definitely worth it.

"Turn this off," my grandpa says, gesturing at snoring Uncle Joe. "I don't need to see my granddaughter gyrating around on national television."

Both Byron and Ginnie protest, though Byron catches my

eye as he does so and flushes the shade of the bean bag chair. Josh just raises an eyebrow, and pats the seat next to him, which I gladly take, happy to curl up with him. He puts his arm over my shoulders, and we smile at each other and I know we're both thinking of last night.

Which is something I'd much rather be thinking of than what that asshole Brent said.

Josh doesn't get the mental memo on that, though, because he says, "So, did you call Brent?"

I sigh. "Yeah, I did. And he was kind of a jerk about it, but whatever. It just makes me feel better about—"

"Shhhh!" Ginnie says, glaring at us. "They're talking now."

"Does your mom know you're watching this?" I ask. "And how did you find this old episode, anyway?"

"SoapNet's running an all-day marathon," Josh says, with a little shrug.

"Great. Just what I want to watch with my family for twenty-four hours." But I find myself watching anyway, even though I'm supposed to be telling them about t-shirts and food prep.

Here's the thing about watching myself on TV. I don't know if this is how most actors feel or if it's just me, but even though I know before we shot that scene, Matt probably told me some story about his two-year-old son stress-vomiting at Disneyland, and also Matt kisses like he's trying to run my tongue through the spin-cycle at a cheap laundromat, I forget about that when I'm watching. It's not Matt and me; it's Bruce and Maeve up there.

"I can't, Bruce," Maeve says, pushing him away. "I told you before, I—"

"You told me you love me." Bruce takes her hand and presses it to his chest. "And I know you mean it. So why can't you be with me?"

My throat goes dry. Damn, couldn't they be watching one of the stolen baby episodes?

Josh gives me a look, his eyebrows raised. Like, *yeah, why,*

Maeve? He's clearly teasing me, but I know there's still some hurt under there.

We can skip that step, he'd said last night.

I'd brushed it aside, hadn't let myself think overmuch about it. But did he mean living together? Engagement? *Marriage*?

I'm afraid to ask, because if I can't even give him—who I'm crazy in love with, I know that much—the commitment level of girlfriend, I think my head might explode to consider the steps after.

"You know why," Maeve says, glaring at him. "You're sleeping with my sister."

Ha, that's right. Things are a little more cut and dry for Maeve.

Now Josh gives a shrug like, *yeah, okay, that makes sense.* His fingers trace along my upper arm, and I let out a breath, trying to calm my pulse, which has picked up considerably. I need to just not think about the future. I need to not pay attention to Brent, and my mom's past warnings, and my past experiences, and hell, even my own damn TV show, and—

"Only because you won't follow your heart," Bruce says.

Maeve's eyes grow teary. "You didn't wait very long to follow yours, did you, Bruce?"

Bruce pulls Maeve towards him. "I thought I could be happy with her. She's beautiful and she's, you know, really flexible since she's a yoga instructor—"

"Okay," I say, jumping up and grabbing the remote from Joe, who startles awake with a snort. I turn the TV off. "Aunt Patrice sent me down to tell you all that the shirts are in, so you'd better get upstairs and put them on. And that it's food prep time for the Grillmaster Championship contenders."

This wakes Joe up for real—he takes the Grillmaster Championship as seriously as if he's Everett's Gordon Ramsey, fervent swearing and all. He heads upstairs, followed by a slumped-shouldered Byron and a pouting Ginnie, who still sweetly helps my grandpa up the stairs, which makes me like the girl even more. Buckley snuffles at my feet and then follows after them.

"You okay?" Josh asks. He looks hesitant, and suddenly all I want is to go back to last night, to us making love under the stars and hearing him tell me how much he loves me and me saying the words back to him and all of that being so much more powerful than the fear.

"I'm okay. Brent was an ass, but I don't have to deal with him anymore. I've got a much better—and dare I say hotter—agent now." I step up to Josh and wrap my arms around his waist. "Though," I say, as if considering, "you should see the sexy way that man takes down a meatball sub."

Josh laughs. "I can only imagine." He presses his forehead against mine. "I love you," he says quietly.

"I love you, too," I say back, and he closes his eyes briefly, like he just needed to hear it again. I wish I could say even more. My hands work their way up the back of his shirt, though, because I can't seem to keep my hands off him when he's this close, and his fingers inch below the waist of my jean cut-offs, and—

"Anna-Marie! Joe's Way!" Aunt Patrice calls down, and both of us groan, as if on cue, which makes us grin at each other.

"You ready to cook them the food of your people?" I ask.

"I think Bel-Airia is going to represent really well this year," he says with a smile.

When we get upstairs, Patrice thrusts a shockingly neon pink shirt at me. "Here's yours, dear."

I hold it up. There, emblazoned across the front in large, equally bright lime green letters, backed by a glittery gold star, are the words "Halsey Reunion Superstars." It's like the early nineties came and threw a huge neon orgy and these were the discards picked off the floor the morning after.

I'm embarrassed that I actually kind of like it.

"Now Joe's Way," Patrice says, "we didn't know you were coming, unfortunately,"—here she gives me a pointed look—"so I didn't have a shirt made for you."

Josh smiles. "That's really okay, I'm just fine in my own—"

"But," Patrice steamrolls over him, "we do have Aunt Ida's shirt, rest her soul. And I think she would be honored to have you wear it. Don't you, Anna-Marie?"

"Ohhhh, yes. Absolutely." I'm unable to contain my delight at this idea.

Josh shakes his head and gives me a mock glare when Patrice turns around to grab another pink shirt, and I widen my eyes in innocence. Patrice hands him the shirt.

"Thanks," he says. "I'll try to make Aunt Ida proud."

I'll have to tell him later that doing so would require body-shaming overweight teenage girls to tears, or publicly slandering Israel, so that's probably not a good life goal.

He heads to the storage room to put on his shirt, and I change in the bathroom. When I come out, I head over to the "deck"—which is really just a big slab of concrete jutting out into the backyard—where everyone is milling around in their bright pink shirts. Normally, the deck has a hammock and a grill and not much else. For the Grillmaster Championship, there are separate grills for each entrant—four this year, set up in a circle—and even separate prep tables. The grills are stored in my dad's garage all year long, because while we used to borrow the extras, there were so many accusations of sabotage that my dad finally bought up the used grills from Jeb's Grill Shack when it closed.

The hammock is still there, and folding chairs are set up, enough for the handful of neighbors that inevitably stop by when they smell the grilling. On one small stand in the middle of the ring of grills is the coveted Golden Weiner. It's a big hot dog made of foam pieces from a craft store—bun included—that's about as long as my forearm and spray-painted bright gold and then mounted to a block of stained wood.

It's hideous and huge, and has been in our family ever since I can remember.

"So that's the Big Weiner," Josh says from behind me.

"The Golden—" I start, and then gape openly when I see him.

Aunt Ida's tiny shirt is stretched so tightly across his chest it looks like we're running a test on the fabric strength. The words are deformed by the stretching, and his toned, tan midriff is bare above his cargo shorts.

"Oh my god," I say.

"Pretty hot, huh?" Josh does some flexing poses. "You like this, Halsey?"

"So. Very. Much." I laugh. "I think you should start wearing tiny old ladies' clothes more often."

"Don't tempt me. I've been thinking I owe the world more exposure to my bare stomach."

I sling my arm around his bare waist, and we head to his prep table, where Patrice has already set out the steak Josh started marinating yesterday when we got home from our tour of the town. And for the next hour or so—after my family sees Josh and whistles and teases him about the shirt, laughing and clapping when he plays it up—we're cooking, and music is blaring from my old stereo system, and we're having a surprisingly fun time with my family.

After the initial prep, the contestants aren't allowed any assistant help, so Josh has to grill his own carne asada, alongside Joe with his multi-championship-winning hot dogs, my dad with his sea bass—really, Dad? You think you're winning this with fish?—and Tanya making burgers I'm a little worried are made out of soy.

I make my way over by my cousin Cherstie to watch the actual grilling portion of the competition. Just before I settle into the chair next to her, I catch a glimpse of a photo on her phone that she's looking at intently, with a smile tugging at her lips.

The pic is of Cherstie, with her arms around a cute girl with a spiky blond pixie-cut and a silver nose ring. Their hands are linked, and I've never seen my cousin beam so brightly as in that picture.

I'm happy for her, and a little surprised. I had no idea

Cherstie is gay, and I definitely thought I would have heard about that from Aunt Patrice by now if—

Cherstie tucks the phone away quickly and with a flash of a nervous expression, and I have a feeling she hasn't exactly shown that picture—or that girl—to anyone in the family yet.

I decide not to say anything about it, since it doesn't seem like she's ready to share that part of her life. And I get it—if Cherstie's gay, I'm sure she's got her own share of awkward family reunions in the future, full of Aunt Patrice talking condescendingly about supporting her daughter's "lifestyle choice" and Grandpa trying to show Cherstie's girlfriend his "netherregions," because he once met a lesbian who was a doctor.

No way I'm going to be the one to foist *that* on her before she's ready. Which might understandly be never.

"Sooo . . ." Cherstie says, waggling her eyebrows at me as I sit down. "He's hot. And funny. And super nice."

I grin at her, looking bck over at Josh, his brow adorably furrowed as he studies the recipe on his phone. He pokes at the slab of meat on the grill with a pair of tongs. "He is," I agree. "All of that." And so much more.

"And willing to put up with all of *this*." She gestures at my family in their matching pink shirts. Her dad, Uncle Joe, swears loudly at the grill, as if punctuating that statement. Ginnie is running around the yard with a hot dog she snatched from the prep table, being chased by a barking Buckley. Byron has an iPad out and is huddled into a chair by the back door, while Grandpa is muttering something to him about the Korean War. Patrice is flitting from station to station like she's some kind of show host, cheering them on individually (though her cheers to Tanya, are, I notice, less impassioned than the others). And Lily . . . Lily is splayed across the hammock wearing what looks like nothing but the reunion shirt. She's facing Josh, and keeps crossing and uncrossing her legs. Slowly.

I groan. "Is she trying to *Basic Instinct* my—?" I cut off, flushing.

Cherstie doesn't miss it. "Your boyfriend?" she goads, her dark eyes flashing.

I swallow. "No. Just . . . we're dating."

"Uh-huh. Well, that boy wants more than just dating, that much is clear."

We can skip that step. My nerves skitter under my skin. But Josh chooses that moment to look up at me and grin, and my heart pounds in all the best ways at seeing that incredible smile.

The smile of the man I'm in love with.

I give a knowing look to Cherstie, who laughs, and then I walk over to Josh.

"I don't know if it's the grilling or the shirt or what," I say. "But this is doing it for me."

"I don't need to be hearing this," My dad calls from the next grill over.

"Too bad," I call back, and Tanya laughs. Joe yells for a beer, and Patrice scrambles to bring him one, like a nurse handing a doctor an important surgical instrument. She even wipes his brow with a dishcloth.

Josh grins. "I'm glad." He lowers his voice. "Your uncle Joe has been casting some aspersions on my sexuality, and frankly, I'm tempted to encourage those, if only to get Lily to stop flashing me."

"Ugggghhhh. My *family*," is all I can say.

"Well, it's not the first time."

"That you've been flashed at a barbecue, or accused of being gay by a man whose goal in life is to go home with the Golden Weiner?"

"Well, when you put it that way, I guess it is my first time. For both." He smiles and shakes some more seasoning onto the meat, which smells seriously amazing. "But growing up with Ben, and us being so close—people always thought I was gay, too. It pissed Ben off, like I was stealing his coming-out glory."

I laugh. Mentioning Ben's coming out makes me want to tell Josh what I suspect about Cherstie, but definitely not with her parents hovering nearby. "How did Ben come out, anyway?" I ask instead. "Was that weird at first, with you guys being so close?"

I'd love to meet Ben someday, but it scares me a bit, too. Ben is more like a brother to Josh than Josh's actual brothers, and I know how much he values Ben's opinion.

"Ben was definitely worried it would be weird." Josh pushes the meat around on the grill, though I'm not sure that's accomplishing anything. "But I'd known for a long time before he actually admitted it. Like, you remember my, uh . . . Leia thing?"

"Oh yeah. I remember." And I definitely need to get myself one of those costume gold bikinis.

"Well, Ben used to pretend to like that too, but it was pretty clear he was paying far more attention to any scene with Han Solo."

"I don't blame him for *that.*"

"But I never brought it up, because, you know. Whatever. He was Ben, no matter what, and it didn't matter to me that he was a Han Solo man." Josh shrugs. "But I finally told him I knew when we were fourteen. We were at the mall, and Ben was totally checking out this guy at one of those sunglass kiosks, and kept making us walk past it until finally I was like 'dude, just go talk to him.' And he had this freak-out moment, and then realized that he and I were good. And then he went and chatted up the guy and totally got shot down." Josh grins, shaking his head.

"Awwww, that's cute. Less the getting shot down part."

"Yeah, well, I think he's much happier with Wyatt than he would have been with frosted-tips guy at the Sunglass Hutch, so I'd say it worked out for him."

I can't argue with that.

Shortly after, Patrice calls out that it's ten minutes until the tasting and voting. About a dozen neighbors have arrived and I answer question after question about what it's like working on a soap opera—which, admittedly, is a line of conversation I enjoy basking in—and introduce everyone to Josh, who I just refer to as "my agent." It's Everett, so people don't seem to think it's strange that my agent would come out for my family reunion. But more than a couple of them make sure to "casually" mention their own talent for the stage, or their son's love of ventriloquism, or their cousin who can yodel the National Anthem, as if Josh will sign them as soon as he's done flipping the beef. He handles it all with his trademark charm, and I imagine he's used to this kind of thing.

Then one of them, a girl named Beth who is two years older than me and already has four kids, turns to me with a wide grin. "So where's Shane? I don't think I ever saw you much without seeing him right there too."

I try to stifle a wince, and glance over at Josh. He's staring fixedly at the grill, and I can tell he heard.

The truth is, I don't know where Shane is. He's no doubt heard about the barbecue, and I'm surprised he hasn't used it as an opportunity to show up and taunt Josh again.

Though I suppose I'm giving myself too much credit. Not everything in Shane's life is about me.

"Shane and I broke up," I say quickly. "Like five years ago."

"Pfft," Beth says dismissively. "You two are never really broken up, not for good. You two are like—"

But I'm spared hearing what Shane and I are like by Aunt Patrice, bless the woman, who rings the end-of-grilling cowbell. "Line up for tasting and voting!" she calls. "And no double votes! I'm watching you, Hal!"

Everyone laughs, even our neighbor Hal, who did indeed get caught trying to stuff the ballot box one year. We form a line and grab a plate, putting a few bites of each contestant's entry on it. I want to stand by Josh and hold his hand and reassure him that Shane and I really are broken up and will stay that way. Josh, though, has to stand away from the voting, along with Joe and my dad and Tanya.

He won't meet my eyes.

I take a bite of carne asada, barely paying attention to the competition itself, and nearly drop the plate in surprise. It's fantastic. Like unbelievably good. Even better than Joe's hot dog, which hasn't wavered from its usual deliciousness.

Apparently Josh Rios can add "great cook" to his long list

of qualities that make him the perfect man. I can't wait to tell him this. And that he really shouldn't be worried about Shane.

From the murmurs around me, I can tell everyone else is suitably impressed too. We file up to the table where Patrice has set out slips of paper and pens, and write down our vote and stick it into an old rusted coffee can that probably predates World War II. Then Patrice takes a few minutes to tally the votes, and grimaces at her husband briefly before announcing, "And the winner is Joe's Way Rios, and his carne asada"—the 'r' she rolls dramatically—"from Bel-Airia!"

Everyone claps and cheers, and even Uncle Joe shakes his hand like a man conceding defeat to a respected opponent. Patrice hands over the Golden Weiner to Josh, who holds it up proudly and grins at me. I grin back, and realize I don't have my phone on me to take what feels like a necessary picture. I look behind me to see if I left my phone on my chair, when I notice Byron staring at me, his eyes wide. Wider, even, than when he first met me, if that's possible.

He glances down at his iPad, and then back up at me, his cheeks flushed. Even the tips of his ears are red.

I suddenly have a very bad feeling. Especially when Grandpa looks down at the iPad and says, "I told you, I don't want to see my granddaughter naked on TV. I don't care what young people think is normal these days."

Did he say *naked*?

I am over there and grabbing the iPad from Byron's hands in two long strides.

"Wait," Byron yelps, "I didn't—a friend sent it to me, I swear, I wasn't looking for—"

But I'm not paying attention to him. Because on the screen I see myself at the edge of the hot springs, naked and standing in a van's spotlights, my expression horrified.

Probably similar to the expression on my face right now.

Not just a picture. A video.

Online, for the whole world to see.

SIXTEEN

Josh

I hate leaving Anna-Marie while she's freaking out about the video—especially in the middle of a crowd of neighbors and family and . . . Patrice. But I'm her agent, and I have to figure out what the reach of this thing is so we can be fully informed and get ahead of it if necessary. After Tanya confiscates the iPad and fends off the few nosy neighbors who were gathering around to see what nudity Grandpa was so loudly advertising, I squeeze Anna-Marie's hand and tell her I'll find out how bad it is. Then I walk around the side of the house so I can make phone calls without being overheard by half of Everett. I'm about to call my office and ask one of the publicity specialists to do a workup for me of everywhere that's posting the video and what kind of traffic they're seeing, when I notice I have a text from Ben.

Have you seen this? it says, followed by a link.

I'm pretty certain what the link leads to. Instead of clicking, I call him. "Hey," I say when he answers. "You guys have seen the video?"

"Yeah," Ben says. "Wyatt found it. Someone posted it to the forums."

"Do you know how many people have viewed it?"

"Um," Ben says, "how many people do you think want to see Anna-Marie Halsey naked?"

"Shit. How bad is it?"

"You haven't seen it?"

"Not yet." I'm hoping I won't have to. I really don't love the idea of seeing her with Shane. "And I'm not super thrilled to have to crawl the internet looking at everything people are saying about her, but as of this morning it's my job to know."

Ben pauses for a second. "You signed her?"

"I did. And I told her I'm in love with her, and she said it back." I close my eyes, remembering what it had felt like to hear her say those words. She loves me. I'd had no idea how much I'd needed to hear that until I did.

"No shit," he says. "Really? Wyatt, they're in love."

I hear squealing, and damn it, I want to join in. "Look, have Wyatt send me the link to the forum post. And if he wants to keep an eye on where else it gets posted and how many views it's getting—"

"Oh, say no more. Wyatt's already on it."

I cringe. "How's the reaction?"

"Wyatt says it's about how you'd expect. Some say good for her, a lot of wow she's hot, an unhealthy dose of slut-shaming."

I nod. That is what I expected. "So nothing out of the ordinary."

"No," Ben says. "How's she taking it?"

"We just found out about it. Not well."

"Damn. Shane is—"

"Her boyfriend from high school," I say.

"Yeah, I know. Dude. He's good looking with his clothes on, but without them, he's—"

I groan, and on the other end I hear Ben fending off Wyatt as he smacks Ben for saying that. Which I appreciate. I really don't want to hear how sexy Shane is, any more than I wanted to hear he was *safe*. "No, really!" Ben shouts. "Did you see the size of his—"

I hold the phone away from my face and close my eyes. "Dude," I say when I lift it back up. "Can we focus?"

"Right," Ben says. "On your girlfriend's reaction to having her breasts bared to the world. I still don't get your fascination with those."

"I remember. And she's not my girlfriend."

"Whaaaaat? Wyatt, he says she's not his girlfriend." On the other end I hear Wyatt echoing Ben's whaaaaat.

I sigh. "It's complicated, okay?"

"Complicated like she's still into Shane?"

"No," I say. "Complicated like she has commitment issues, but she loves me, so she's working on them."

Ben is quiet for a moment. "Dude. Is this girl jerking you around?"

I close my eyes again. She said she loves me, and I believe her. I just wish that gave me more confidence things were going to work out. "No. She's not into Shane. And apparently her best friend talked some sense into her, and she's doing better with the commitment thing. She's just not ready for the label."

Ben hesitates, and I know what he's thinking. That sounds like what a girl would say when she's jerking me around. "It's not like that," I say. "She's got all this stuff in her past. Her dad's been married three times, and her ex-boyfriends are assholes. She's apparently been avoiding relationships that involve actual feelings for years, but now she's in love with me and she's scared I'm going to hurt her."

"Really? She's afraid of *you*?"

"Of what she feels for me," I repeat, leaning against the house. I suddenly feel so tired, I'm not sure I can continue to stay upright. In the heat of last night—god, the heat, I have never had sex like that in my life—this had all seemed okay, but today something she said keeps bothering me. "I think she feels safer with guys who are assholes because there's no real attachment, so it won't hurt when it ends. And this is all going so fast, I have no idea if she's going to change her mind and back out, but I'm in love with her and I don't want to leave until I know for sure."

Ben's quiet again, and I hear Wyatt pestering him for details on the other end. "Yeah, man. That's a tough call."

I take a deep breath. "I get why she's hesitant, but it's driving me a little bit crazy knowing that at any minute she might rightly decide I'm not worth the stress."

"You are," Ben says. "But I get it."

"Does this ever get less scary?"

"Yeah. Like, after you're married."

I wince. "I may have told her if she wanted she could skip the girlfriend stage."

"Whaaaaat?" Ben says again. "And like, what? Get married?"

"I wasn't specific," I knock my head back against the wall of the house. I probably shouldn't have said that, which is basically the theme of the week. "Be my fiancée, I guess?"

"Wow," Ben says, and I can tell he doesn't entirely approve. I can't blame him. If he was talking about getting engaged to some guy I'd never met, I'd be terrified. "Are you sure about this?" he says finally.

"No." The words had felt so true when I said them, and they still do. I want to be with Anna-Marie more than anything, and if I have to commit long-term to make that happen, I'd do it in an instant. Happily. But even if that wasn't a really stupid thing to say to a girl I'm already crowding, there's no reason to think she couldn't panic and leave me just because we skipped a damn step. If she did, it might hurt even more. "I'm scared as hell. But right now I need you to send me those links, and I want a text immediately if it hits any major news outlets, or if the story changes to anything out of the ordinary, okay?"

"We're on it," Ben says, and I nod. This is miles better than using the publicity people at work. Wyatt's going to be glued to this story anyway, doubly so because I'm involved.

"Thanks," I say. "You guys are the best."

"We know. And hey, you said Anna-Marie has a best friend

who's on your side, right?"

"Gabby. They're roommates."

"Get me Gabby's number," he says. "I want to make sure Anna-Marie checks out."

I smile. I should probably think that's an invasion of my privacy, but if the situation was reversed, I'd want to do the same thing.

"I'll ask," I say.

"Okay. And you better call me when things calm down. I need all the details."

"Done." And I hang up the phone, but it immediately rings in my hand. It's an unfamiliar LA number, and I answer.

"Josh Rios," I say.

"Josh!" a man's voice says. "Glad I could reach you. This is Brent Farthing. How are you doing?"

I grit my teeth. Brent is Anna-Marie's agent. Or he was, until this morning. "Great!" I say, faking my tone. "Hey, I'm glad you called. I was just about to contact you." This is a lie, but I should have been on top of this. If it had been a client I was less involved with, I would have been. "I'm sure you're getting inquiries about the video, and I'm going to need each and every one forwarded to me. You got it?" The last thing I need is Anna-Marie's bitter ex-agent handling media comments.

"That's what I'm calling about," Brent says. "You couldn't have known about this when you made her that offer, and you and I both know what you're in this for isn't worth this kind of trouble. Send her back my way, and we can just forget it ever happened."

I want to chew him out for suggesting I only signed her to sleep with her. "Actually, I'm thrilled to be working with her. She's a really promising actress, as I'm sure you know, and definitely worth any *trouble*. So send me those inquiries, Brent, and I'll take care of it."

Brent drops the polite act. "Really, Rios? There aren't enough other starlets you can bang? You have to poach mine?"

I hold back a laundry list of objections to that accusation, but my anger seeps into my tone. "The inquiries," I say firmly. "Now."

"Fine, whatever. But don't say I didn't give you the out. Word is there's more coming, but if you want to be the one to mop up the mess, be my guest."

And, somehow, that asshole manages to be the one who hangs up on me.

I groan and bump my head against the wall again, and then head off to find Anna-Marie. Because whatever Brent thinks, I mean it. She's worth all this trouble—the drive to Wyoming, her interesting family and their strange obsession with my cultural origins, the fear and the uncertainty, and definitely whatever problems are going to arise from the fallout of this video. She's not the first actress to end up naked on the internet.

But it's the first time for her, and even though I'm her agent, I'm mostly worried about whether or not the girl I love is going to be okay.

SEVENTEEN

Anna-Marie

I can't handle watching the full video with my family and half of Everett looking on, so while Josh makes his phone calls, I take my phone into the house. I run upstairs and realize my room doesn't have a lock, and damn it, I need to lock out the rest of the world right now. So I hide out in the bathroom.

Before I can even play the video, I see that I have several texts—a few from concerned friends and co-stars (Matt/Bruce is especially worried about how I'm handling this, if the long string of emoji-faces is any indication) and, more concerningly, one from my director.

Hey Anna-Marie. Give me a call.

Shit.

Am I going to lose my job? I'm on a soap opera, not freaking *Sesame Street*. But even if I manage to stay on *Southern Heat*, this could follow me into all my future auditions—I can forget about scoring the Jessica Biel role in the *Seventh Heaven* reboot (that, okay, isn't a real thing, but totally should be).

But the pit in my gut has less to do with my career than the sheer dread of watching the video. I clench my teeth and click play.

It's everything I feared from that brief snippet I saw outside—thirty-three seconds total, over fifteen of which are me being totally nude, inept at putting on shorts, and even worse, all filmed in terribly unflattering lighting. It ends with Shane, who is laughing the entire time, pulling himself out of the pool. So he's naked, too, but unlike me, he appears completely unfazed. Totally confident in his skin. Whereas I look like Gabby the time I took her to that new sauna and it turned out to have a co-ed changing room. Thankfully Mr. Dart isn't in the shot, so at the very least I don't appear to have been sexing it up in a really unbalanced three-way.

I shouldn't care. I shouldn't. Hell, I work my ass off—literally—to have a body I should be *proud* of displaying to the world. But as I play the video a second time, and then a third, I find that my hands are shaking, and it's getting harder to breathe. I pace the small bathroom, each sharp clip of my Zara sandals on the tile floor pinging against my nerves, but I can't stop moving in circles.

"Anna-Marie?"

It's Josh, calling from the kitchen. A beat, and then I hear his footsteps climbing the stairs. I hug the phone to my chest. The video is playing again, and even though I can't see the screen anymore, I can hear Shane's laugh. Hear one of the Boy Scouts say "Awesome," and others murmur their agreement.

He calls my name again, just down the hall, and my pulse beats in my ears. Surely he's seen it by now. He's my agent. It's his damn job, now, to watch me naked in this video with Shane and figure out how to spin it. Even though it's going to hurt him.

I'm afraid to face him.

I also need him, in this primal, visceral way.

This latter instinct wins out. I open the door and see him half in the doorway to my room, peering in. He turns and sees me there in the bathroom door. I haven't been crying, but I must look a wreck, judging by the look Josh gives me, his expression softening.

"Hey," he says, stepping up to me close enough that I can smell the smoke from the grilling and the spices from his carne asada. He puts his hands on my arms. "So I've made some calls, and I've got my people keeping track of—"

I don't let him finish. I grab him by his shirt front and pull him into the bathroom with me, only pausing for the barest second to slam and lock the door before I'm pressed against him, my mouth on his and my hands already tugging at the waistband of his shorts.

He responds without much more prompting. Before long, my jean shorts are off and he's boosted me up onto the sink. The ceramic is cold on my ass, and I'm guessing this sink hasn't been sanitized in months, but I need this, and judging by the returned intensity, I think maybe he does too.

It's not the same experience of last night, under the stars, buoyed by his whispers of love and long, lingering touches. But it's raw and powerful and more than enough to keep me from having to think, which is what I really want right now more than anything else.

And it feels *so* good.

After, he holds me pressed against him, and kisses the top of my head. The whirling rage of emotions from before are still there, but muted now. At least I feel like I can breathe again.

"So was the drive worth it?" I ask. "Now that you've tasted the hot dogs?"

"Mmmm," Josh says against my hair. "Yeah, definitely. For the hot dogs."

He sounds pretty blissed out for a guy who just became aware of a sex tape with me and another man, though I suppose he's just had the real-life thing. "I think I just used you for your body," I mumble into his neck.

"I'm never going to complain about *that*."

I hop down from the sink, but my legs don't quite feel up to supporting me. I slide down so that I'm sitting on the fuzzy mat. He pulls up his shorts and sits down next to me, his dark eyes taking me in. "Are you really worried about that? Because it's fine. I get it."

I'm not sure I do. It's not like I haven't handled a stressful situation or two in my life with some quickie-therapy, and that was certainly part of it. But I didn't just need sex; I needed *Josh.*

Is this part of being in love? I draw my legs up to my chest, my hands trembling again.

"No," I say. "It's not that. It's just the video." If this is a lie, it's only partly so. "It's got me all messed up. Which is ridiculous. It's not like I'm one of those actresses who swore I'd never do nude scenes."

Josh shakes his head. "That would be you consenting to be filmed nude under carefully controlled conditions. This is totally different. And you have every right to be upset about it."

"I like that you think about it that way." I squeeze his hand. "I'm guessing I have your mother and her women's studies to thank?"

He hangs his head, like he's *embarrassed* of not being a dismissive asshole. "Probably. But my little brother Adrian grew up with the same lectures I did, and he still left his wife last year to party and sleep around and snort cocaine, so I might have to take some of the credit."

I try not to wince as I think that even Josh, aware as he is of all these issues, could still slip into something like that. I don't want to believe that, but I don't know how not to. I rest my head back against the cabinet under the sink. "I've got like a dozen emotions happening right now, and upset may be one of them. I'm not even sure. I don't know if you've noticed, but I've generally spent my life being emotionally . . . avoidant."

"I may have noticed," he says drolly. Which almost, *almost* teases a smile out of me. Then he runs his hand gently along my bare calf. "Why don't you try to separate out the emotions. Name them for me."

I give him a look. "And afterward, are you going to bring out some crayons and have me draw my feelings?"

His lips quirk upward. "Let's try this first. I left my feelings crayons back in LA."

I sigh. I'm not sure this will help, but the guy is sitting

half-naked on a bathroom floor mat with me, so I probably owe him an attempt. "Well, I'm angry. Like seriously pissed at whatever little turd in a merit-badge sash posted this."

"Me too. Are you mad at anyone else?"

I think about this, and then shift, uncomfortably. "At myself."

His eyebrows draw together. "Really? Why?"

"Because I shouldn't have even been with Shane that night!" The words burst out of me. "Let alone skinny-dipping with him in a place that is apparently a favorite Everett camping spot."

"You didn't do anything wrong."

I can feel my face flush. "Yeah, maybe not technically. But if I hadn't been the kind of idiot that had to go sleep with my ex-boyfriend to try to prove to myself I didn't have *feelings* for someone else—"

"Anna-Marie," he says softly, putting his other hand on my other calf, turning me slightly so I'm facing him. "Maybe you made a decision you aren't proud of, but so has everyone else in the whole damn world. It doesn't mean you deserve *this*."

He's right. I know he is. But not everyone will agree with him. "The gossip sites are going to say I'm cheating on you."

He pauses, then nods. "Maybe. But you weren't, and it's none of their business anyway, so they can fuck off."

This time, a surprised laugh bubbles out. Josh doesn't swear all that much, unlike pretty much everyone else in the industry. So it's like a lovely little obscene gem whenever he does. "Is that going to be your official statement to the press, Mr. Rios?"

He smiles. "I may massage the wording a bit."

I let out a breath, feeling the tightness in my chest as I do so. I reach for his hand and thread my fingers through his. "I'm worried, too."

"About what?"

"The effect this will have on my career. I mean, I know some actresses have benefited from sex tapes getting out, but those are generally more sexy and involving far fewer pervy Boy Scouts."

He squeezes my hand. "This won't hurt your career. It's clear you were caught by surprise, and doing something totally legal."

"Well, it *was* on private property," I say, mostly to be difficult. No one's going to care about that, least of all Ken Randall, who I'm sure is not the least bit surprised about what goes on in his hot springs.

Josh makes a dismissive gesture. "Look. We're going to get lots of inquiries for awhile. And we may get questions about this when I send you out on auditions. But I'll handle all that. It's going to be fine. If anything, you'll probably just get a boost in name recognition."

"For *this*." I glare at my phone, which is balanced precariously on the edge of the sink above us where I had set it before jumping Josh.

"For a little while," he acknowledges, and I appreciate that he doesn't pretend otherwise. "And then you'll keep killing it on your soap, and book more and more roles, and show everyone how talented and incredible Anna-Marie Halsey is. This will become nothing more than some internet footnote."

His confidence is contagious; even though I'm fully aware that it could—and probably will—take years to get to that point, I believe him that I will. That I *am* talented and incredible, damn it, and will one day have a whole legion of fans ready to troll the hell out of anyone who won't let this video disappear into the internet garbage heap where it belongs.

I also realize that my worry wasn't solely for my career.

I can't look him in the eyes as I say this next part. I pick at a long fiber of the shaggy floor mat. "What about the effect it will have on us?"

"You and me?" He sounds surprised.

"I mean, you had to see me and Shane like . . . that, and it couldn't have been great. And all the extra publicity this'll bring, and complications, and . . ." *And maybe you won't want to do this anymore,* I mentally finish, because the words get lodged somewhere in my throat.

And I know, though I hate myself for it a little bit, that this was part of why I needed Josh so badly. I needed the reassurance that everything we felt last night under the stars wasn't some fluke, and it isn't over.

"Come here," he says, pulling me into his arms—at least as much as he's able, with my legs still tucked up against me. "It's not easy seeing you with him, I'll admit it. But this doesn't change anything for me. I love you." I find myself relaxing into him—at least until he pauses, and I see a little bit of tension around his eyes. "Does it . . . change anything for you?"

I shake my head. "No," I say, then give him a small smile. "I'm so glad you're here right now." I mean here in this bathroom, but also here in Wyoming. Here in my life. And I think he gets all those meanings, because he smiles and presses his forehead against mine.

"Me too."

"Also, I'm actually feeling a bit better. I think your little 'talk about your emotions' thing helped."

He grins. "It's called labeling, and it's pretty much the only thing I remember from the one college psychology class I took. You'd be surprised how useful it is in my career."

I'm actually not surprised. I can see him talking like this—okay, maybe not like *this* exactly, but still—with his clients, helping them through whatever professional crises come up, and I know it's one of the things that makes him an incredible agent. He cares about his clients. They aren't just dollar signs with flawless skin and excellent bone structure, not to him.

And I'm so glad he's mine now.

Agent, that is.

"So," he says, like he's broaching a topic he's not too thrilled about. "You aren't mad at Shane? He was kind of a dick to you in that video."

I frown. "I don't know. I was at the time, but really, it's just the way he is, you know?"

Josh eyes me for a moment, but then he just nods. "Yeah. Okay."

"And it's not like I'm going to be doing *that* again with him. Ever." I shake my head. "I should probably call him, though. See if he's heard about this yet. I don't think he'll be that upset about it, but—" I shrug.

Josh smiles, but it's not quite genuine. I hate having to bring Shane into this at all, but there he is in that damn video with me, captured for all of internet eternity. "Yeah, definitely. And I need to make some more calls myself, make sure Brent has sent over those inquiries."

He stands, and I want to reach out for him, but he slips out the door and I'm still half-naked, and everyone in the world has already seen enough of me naked.

"Congratulations on the Golden Weiner," I say at the door. But Josh is already gone.

EIGHTEEN

Anna-Marie

Josh and I both make phone calls for hours, me shut in my bedroom and him pacing up and down the hallway outside. I call my director (who is supportive) and then Gabby (who sounds like she's having trouble breathing on my behalf), all the while hearing snippets of his conversations about reach and spin and phenoxyethanol, the latter of which I hope is not about me.

Josh's voice is faint at the other end of the hallway when I finally call Shane. I haven't talked to him since he left through the window the night before last, and I'm realizing now I probably should have at least texted him.

I don't have any idea what I would have said. But he's still my friend, and the least I can do is to give him a heads up that he's naked on the internet.

"Anna!" Shane says. "Nice of you to call." His voice sounds fake-cheerful in that sarcastic way of his that tells me he noticed I haven't called him.

"I just wanted to let you know that one of the Boy Scouts got some video the other night. We're both—"

Shane laughs. "Yeah, I saw it. I think everyone in our graduating class has emailed me the link over the last few hours. I had no idea you were such a popular search term."

My chest tightens and I try to breathe. "Yeah," I say, my voice sounding strangled. "So there's that." I want to sarcastically thank him for calling to let me know about the video, but I'm not sure I have a huge amount of moral high ground there.

"Aww, Anna, are you upset about it? You know it's not a big deal, right? It's not like it's the first time this has happened."

"Yeah, I know." I wonder if Josh was just being nice by not telling me I was being dramatic. Maybe Shane's right. This isn't a big deal. It happens all the time. "But I didn't want it to happen to me."

Shane's voice grows serious. "Yeah, I know. Look, I've been meaning to call you. I'm sorry about how awkward things were with you and your friend the other night."

I don't love Shane calling Josh my friend, but really, what else is he supposed to call him? I'm the one who made such a point of him not being my boyfriend. "Josh," I say.

"Yeah, Josh. Why don't you guys come over tonight and hang out? We'll play some *Death Arsenal*, him and me can get to know each other. It'll be fun, and it'll get your mind off all the fourteen-year-olds jacking off to your wardrobe malfunction."

"I could have lived without the image." I close my eyes. "But I'll talk to Josh."

"Sweet. See you tonight."

It's not until after he's hung up that I realize he acted like I agreed to going over there when in fact I didn't. I roll my eyes up at the small holes in my ceiling where my poster of Nathan Fillion used to be.

Shane is still Shane, even when he's naked on the internet. Hell, it might not even be his first time.

I open my door and find Josh standing in the hall, leaning against the wall, looking like he hasn't slept in a week. "How'd it go?" I ask.

He gives me a weak smile. "I now know more than I ever wanted to know about the volumizing properties of filloxane. But I talked to the people at *Southern Heat*, and they have a positive attitude about the video."

"By which you mean they're looking forward to my small boost in popularity?"

"Mmmm," Josh says. "I can't keep any secrets from you, can I? This may be problematic for our professional relationship."

I join him leaning against the wall. "I talked to my director. He expressed his support and tried to sound sorry, but really. Why should he be? All publicity is good publicity, right?"

A bitter edge has crept into my voice, and Josh wraps his arm around me. "We don't know how big this is going to get," he says. "Hopefully it settles in the dark recesses of 4chan and never breaks any bigger."

I cringe. Of course it's on 4chan. And Reddit. And every other corner of the internet.

"Hey," he says, "I know this is a little weird, but could I have Gabby's number for Ben? I think he wants to get together with someone and gossip about us. He's pretty much dying back home."

I would think this is weird, but I'm sure Gabby would have asked for the same thing, if she'd thought of it. "Is he worried I'm playing you?"

Josh meets my eyes. He looks nervous, and he doesn't deny it.

I don't ask the question that hangs between us. Does *Josh* think I'm playing him?

I'm not sure I could blame him if he did. "Of course you can have Gabby's number," I say. "I'll text it to you, and you can forward it to Ben."

Josh takes a deep breath, as if steeling himself. "And how's Shane?"

"He's . . . *Shane*. He already knew, and is taking it all in stride even though he's as naked as I was." I wince. Josh doesn't need the replay. Especially before I ask him—"He wants us to come over tonight and play *Death Arsenal*, to get my mind off it, and so you guys can get to know each other."

Josh gives me a skeptical look, and I hold up my hands. "I

know, I know. Given your first impression, you probably don't want to get to know him. But it would be nice to do something tonight other than be harassed by my family, and I only got in six solid hours of DA before I had to leave it and my console behind." I poke him in the side. "Plus, you said you play, right?"

"Yeah," Josh says. "So you want to do this?"

I lean my head against his shoulder. I've been so worried about what Josh would think about Shane, but I feel like what he really needs is to see the guy again and realize he's not actually a threat.

"I do," I say. "I think it would be good for both of us."

Josh folds his arms. "You could go without me, you know. It's not like you're glued to me."

He's back to not meeting my eyes, and my chest aches. "I could," I say. "But I'm not going to. I want you there with me."

He looks at me out of the corner of his eye, and then nods. "Okay. All right. We'll go."

I step away and lean against the opposite wall, our feet side by side at the middle of the hall. I cross my arms and stare at him, but he's looking studiously down at our shoes. Which, granted, mine are adorable, but I really don't think he cares deeply about foot fashion.

"What's wrong, Josh?"

He looks up at me in surprise. "What? Nothing. I—"

"You're obviously upset. Come on, Rios. Label those feelings for me. If I have to dig through all this emotional crap, I'm dragging you right along with me."

Josh smiles briefly, and then his smile drops. "You want to know how I feel about Shane?"

"Yes," I say, even though that knot in my chest is tightening, and I'm starting to worry again that he's realizing no girl is worth this trouble.

"Jealous," Josh says. "Like crazy, irrationally jealous. And also angry, like I want to reach right through my phone screen and punch him in the face for laughing at you when you were in that situation."

He takes a breath, like he's getting worked up about this, and he wants to shake it off. I reach across and take his hands in mine. "You wouldn't have laughed."

He glares at the wall next to me. "Hell, no, I wouldn't have."

I squeeze his hands. "You would have protected me."

He closes his eyes briefly, and when he looks at me again, there's pain in his eyes. "You know I would, right? From all of this, if I could."

My heart melts. I've been so worried about what I'm putting him through, and here he is, wishing he could do more. "I know. It's not your fault either, you know."

He shrugs that off, but I can tell that somehow it's part of it. And while I get why the whole thing makes him jealous—imagining the situation reversed with Macy or Asia makes me want to sharpen my nails and get back to my high-school catfight roots—I want him to know he has no reason to be. "I'm not in love with Shane," I say.

Josh bites his lip and nods, but I can tell this doesn't fix it. Not really. I'm about to ask him again to talk to me about it when he looks right into my eyes. "So how come he gets to be the one you feel safe with?"

My throat closes. When I'd said that last night, I'd only been trying to explain to him why I was still attracted to Shane at all, not to justify wanting to be with him. But here's Josh, doing everything he can personally and professionally to support me, to protect me, to help me be okay through this situation that most definitely *isn't*.

After all that, I can see why it hurts him that I used the word "safe" to describe the guy who laughed at me while I was being violated.

But Shane doesn't make me promises—at least not ones I'm tempted to believe. He doesn't ask me for anything, much less an emotional connection.

"I believe you'd never hurt me," I say. "And that's what scares me. Because if you did, it would hurt so damn much more."

Josh squeezes my hands, and then runs his up my arms, drawing me toward him. "You really want me to come with you to see Shane?"

"I do. Shane's an old friend, nothing more, and I think it would be good for you to actually *see* that, you know?" Especially after the things he unfortunately had to see on that video—though I'm not going to add *that* part to my argument. "Plus, it would be nice to de-stress by shooting up a bunch of zombies. But if it makes you too uncomfortable, we don't have to. Really."

Josh doesn't look thrilled about the idea, but he kisses my forehead and nods. "Okay. We'll go."

And while I hate myself for putting him through all of this, I'm also terrified at how deeply I need him to stay.

We arrive at Shane's place—the basement apartment to his dad's house where he's been crashing while the band builds up. I'm glad I don't have to knock on the door to the main part of the house. Shane's dad is an alcoholic and also a class-A asshole whose favorite hobby is to criticize Shane. Shane got into a lot of trouble when we were younger, mostly, I think, because he could never please his dad anyway, so he did his best to stop giving a shit.

He hadn't fully succeeded by the last time we broke up, but I hope for his sake that he has by now.

Since the last time I stood at the door to the basement, Shane has acquired a door knocker that is an actual pair of brass balls, which I ignore and rap with my knuckles instead.

"Come in!" Shane yells through the door, and Josh gives me a look.

"That's Shane," I say. "The picture of class."

I shove open the door and find Shane sitting on an enormous

Love Sac, next to which he's propped a folding chair. The game system is already on, muted, with the DA menu emblazoned across his big screen. There's a controller sitting on the folding chair, and another on the other half of the Love Sac—not the old white controller I used to play with, but a newer one of the same color.

Shane grins up at us from the Sac, which he is clearly not vacating for fear that Josh and I will claim it and ruin his carefully arranged seating trap. I force myself not to roll my eyes at him. "Anna!" he calls. "Welcome. And Josh, was it?"

Josh has his professional face on again, and while I suppose that's preferable to him punching Shane in the face, it's still hard to watch.

Shane's grin is wide—too wide, in fact. He's up to something beyond the seating arrangements. Even Shane can't be this pleased with himself over that. "Have a seat," he says, waving his phone at me. "I have a surprise for you."

Oh, god. Please do not let this be a slide show of all of our couple photos from high school. I move toward the folding chair to sit in it, but Shane waves at the spot next to him. "You don't mind, do you, Josh?" he says. "Anna-Marie always gets the best seat in the house."

Josh doesn't respond, but he takes the folding chair and sits down on it, his spine uncomfortably straight. He bends down to move something under a bent leg of the chair. It's a book, and Josh stares at it.

"Allen Ginsberg," he says. "Is this poetry?"

Shane looks over at it skeptically. "Maybe? It's Kevin's. I told him if he left that shit here I was going to put it to good use evening out the legs of my chair."

"Sounds like a good use for a Beatnik." Josh's tone is sarcastic, and I think he may just be trying to emphasize to Shane—and possibly to me—that he knows who Allen Ginsberg is.

This is off to a fantastic start. I settle into the spot next to Shane—as far from him as I can get on a cushion that is bent on tipping me into the middle, and give Josh an apologetic glance.

And then I catch a glimpse of what's on Shane's phone, and I freeze.

It's me—or it *was* me, at about sixteen, sitting on Shane's lap in Rainie Lawrence's hot tub, one of my knees sticking up out of the water.

Completely and totally naked.

"Shane," I say. "What the hell—"

"This," Shane says, gesturing toward his phone with gusto, "is a special presentation I prepared just for you. I call it 'naked photos of Anna-Marie Halsey that are *not* on the internet.' I've gathered quite a collection over the years. Watch, Josh. You might learn something."

Shane holds the phone out so both of us can see, and Josh and I stare in frozen horror as he scrolls through pictures—ones I had forgotten even existed. There's me in Shane's bed, posing for him twisted in the classic T&A shot so you can see both my boobs and ass. A topless photo I don't remember taking on some camping trip, and it's no wonder given the startling number of shots I'm downing. An assortment of selfies I do vaguely now remember, mostly of me in my bedroom, featuring various boob shots, and oh god, there's one of full genitalia.

"Sh-Shane—" I finally manage past my shock. "I don't think—"

I shoot a panicked look up at Josh who has averted his eyes and looks like he's given up on punching Shane and is now thinking about strangling him.

I'm ready to join in.

"Shane, stop being such an asshole, and—"

"Hey, this is a good one!" Shane says, arriving at a picture of him and me in bed together. I had completely forgotten about that time he talked me into propping the phone up and set it to shoot continuously while we did it in my bedroom.

It's a freaking miracle he hasn't plastered these all over the internet. Knowing Shane, he would somehow dodge the child pornography charges.

"Stop it," I say more firmly. "*Now.*"

Shane's grin only widens. "I will, but you have to see this next set. Brings new meaning to the words 'money shot'—"

Josh leans forward in his chair, damn close to getting in Shane's face. "She said *stop.*" His hands inch forward, and I'm pretty sure he's about to grab the phone right out of Shane's hands.

I beat him to it, taking his phone and flipping it over the back of the Love Sac. It smacks against the kitchen lineoleum, and I hope I managed to at least crack the screen. Not that even a fully broken phone would keep the pictures from existing.

God, I was an idiot as a teenager.

"That's it, Shane." I scramble off the Love Sac. "We're leaving."

Josh stands to go, moving immediately to my side, but Shane waves his hands in surrender. "Hey, wait," he says. "I'm sorry. I just wanted to make you laugh. Relieve the tension a little, all right? I didn't mean for you to take it like that."

I look up at Josh, and he still looks like he wants to punch Shane in the face, and I do too, but this is exactly the kind of punk thing Shane's always done to make me laugh. He's a dick, but he means well by it.

"I'm not laughing," I say, and he makes a pouting face at me.

"Fair enough," Shane says. "Slideshow over. Now can we please kick some futuristic zombie ass?"

Josh gives me another skeptical look, but now that Shane has his bright idea to be an ass out of his system, it'll be fine. "Is that okay?" I ask Josh.

Josh shrugs. "Sure, fine. Whatever you want."

It's clearly not fine, and I waver, thinking about just telling Shane he's out at one strike, but I don't think that walking out at this moment is going to be the best way to convince Josh I don't have complete shit taste in men.

"All right," I say, "let's play already."

Shane glances up at Josh's tense face and then eases back

onto the Love Sac, the self-satisfied smile returning to his face. "And really," he says. "It's nothing Josh here hasn't seen before, amiright?"

I freeze, looking from Shane to Josh. Because while Josh has certainly seen me naked plenty of times, he doesn't have any pictures like that. And not for any reason Josh should be jealous of.

He's never *asked* me for any. Josh respects me. He's never done anything to make me uncomfortable, and any time he thought he might—like when he showed up in Everett uninvited—he's given me ample opportunity to tell him it's not what I want. Josh pushes me just the right amount, asking me for things that terrify me, but always leaving me an exit, never boxing me in.

And then I realize what bothered me so much that night at the hot springs. Shane says he wants me to laugh, but he's always laughing *at me*, and he goads me when I don't join in.

Shane's smile fades as he looks up at the expression on my face. I realize I *am* still mad at him, but for more than just being a jerk that night at the hot springs, for more than inviting us here with the intention of making us both uncomfortable. I'm mad at him for being such a shitty boyfriend to me over the years. For being a shitty *friend*.

Josh is watching me, following my lead, because he respects me enough to let me call the shots in my own life. Shane may want me to laugh, but really he only wants a reaction out of me. Josh is the one who wants me to be happy.

"What?" Shane asks.

"Shane," I say. "You're a dick."

Shane laughs at this, but it's an uncomfortable laugh. "Yeah. But you love it."

I shake my head. "No, I don't. I don't love that you laughed at me while people took pictures of me naked. I don't love that you expected *me* to laugh about it, too. I don't love that you saw it on the internet and didn't even bother to give me a heads up about it. I don't love that you asked us over here just to mess with us. After all these years, you don't give a shit about me or my feelings."

I look up at Josh, who doesn't have even a trace of a self-satisfied look. There's a smile playing at his lips, which he's clearly trying to smother, but it's not a smug one.

He's proud of me.

"Um, *okay*," Shane says. His tone hardens, and he gestures at Josh. "Is that what this guy has been filling your head with? That I'm some asshole who doesn't care about you? And you *believe* that shit?"

I shake my head at him. It's because I've known him so long that it was so hard to figure it out. I wouldn't take this from any other guy.

And I'm sure as hell not going to take it from him. Not anymore.

I point a finger at him. "Don't talk about my boyfriend like that. In fact, don't talk to either of us anymore. We're done, Shane."

And I turn and walk out of the apartment, up the crumbling concrete stairs, and out to Josh's car, with Josh following tentatively along behind me.

My boyfriend, I said.

And I'm startled to realize that I like the way it sounds.

NINETEEN

Anna-Marie

I get as far as Josh's car before I spin around and grab him by the waist, pulling myself into him. Josh offers no resistance, holding me tight.

"You okay?" he asks.

I want to cry, mostly because after everything I've put him through, he's still concerned about whether or not *I'm* okay. "I'm sorry about that. You were right. It was a bad idea."

"Hey," Josh says, rubbing my shoulder. "I think that was good, actually. It sounded like something you needed to say."

I smile. "You mean the part about you being my boyfriend?"

Josh lets out a little sigh, like the words make him unspeakably happy, but he's afraid to lean into it.

I know exactly how he feels.

"I meant the part where you called Shane a dick, but I like the other part, too."

"I meant it," I say. "The boyfriend part. If you still want to be."

Josh's arms tighten around me. "Hell, yes, I do."

I wrap my arms around his neck, and his hands draw me in by the waist, and now we're kissing up against his car like people do at the end of movies right before the credits start to roll. But this doesn't feel like the end. It feels like the beginning. Our bodies are hungry—I want to tear his clothes off right here, and I can tell by the way his hands press at my back that he's feeling the same. I look up at him, breathless. "Let's get out of here."

Josh groans. "This is petty, but I kind of want to make out in front of Shane's house for a little bit longer."

This makes me laugh, but genuinely, not like Shane's ridiculous stunts. "Rios," I say, "I'm not sure how much longer I can control myself, and I'd rather not face the release of a second sex tape."

Josh looks over his shoulder, and for a moment I think the jealous part of him is going to want to have sex right here on his Porsche in front of Shane's house, neighbors with smart phones notwithstanding. Then he sighs. "Yeah, okay," he says, and he opens the passenger door for me.

The thought of going home where we could—and likely would—be interrupted by any number of family members doesn't sound great, so I direct him to a grove of trees not far off the highway, and we pull the sleeping bag out of the trunk. We find the first soft patch of ground and attack each other, working off the stress of the last few days, dissolving into each other like there's nothing in the world but the two of us. Josh must need this as much as I do, because we're up late into the night, and then we wake up in the early morning still wrapped tight in each other and do it all over again.

I'm stretched out beneath him, head thrown back, eyes filled with stars, when something moves in the trees a few feet away. Josh might have mistaken my scream of surprise for one of pleasure, but when I shove him off me, he jerks back in alarm.

"What?" he says.

A jumble of words come out of my mouth that aren't even close to forming a sentence, and the only coherent thing I can do is point and say "that!" because I'm staring up into the wide eyes of a moose that from this angle looks like it might be seven feet tall at the shoulder.

It lowers its head, ears pointed back, and licks its lips at us.

This moose is either channeling Lily or it's identified us as a threat and is about to charge.

"Whoa," Josh says, with a kind of hushed awe in his voice that is entirely inappropriate to the situation. Moose kill more people in Wyoming every year than bears and wolves combined. You're not supposed to be within twenty yards of a moose, and here we are mere feet away.

All the hair rises down the moose's back like a cat.

"Run," I say.

Josh looks at me in surprise. "Won't that startle—"

There isn't time for this. I shove Josh off me and haul him toward the nearest tree. He fumbles for our clothes but I don't care if there's a whole jamboree of Boy Scouts in these woods, I would rather run past them all naked than be trampled by the woodland equivalent of a steam engine. I pull Josh by the arm behind the tree, just as the moose takes off through the clearing, hooves pounding over the soft ground and right over the open sleeping bag, flipping it upward in a cloud of dirt. One of my fake Uggs goes flying, along with a piece of silver that catches the first rays of sunlight filtering down through the leaves.

It's my phone case. Oh, god, there's my phone, the screen shattered, the case nearly broken in half.

Shit. Shit shit shit.

The moose makes a low moaning sound and pauses, and I pull Josh around the tree to keep it between us and the moose while he sorts through the clothes he has in his hands. Pine needles poke the arches of my feet, and I scuff my toe on a rough tree root.

"Here." Josh hands me his shirt. The morning air is bitingly cold and my breasts are all kinds of articulate. I pull it over my head, feeling decidedly less sexy in it than the times I've lounged around his place wearing his shirt.

Josh puts on his pants, and leans around the tree, but I pull him back at another moaning noise from the moose. I look down and see that he doesn't have any more clothes. This is it—his shirt and pants, no shoes. He reaches into his pocket and takes out his phone—at least he has that, and his wallet, and I left my purse in his car—but neither of us has what resembles clothes that are fit to be wandering back into town in.

The moose shuffles through the brush and noses around our sleeping bag again. And while I can replace my fake Uggs and am obviously going to have to replace my phone, I can't help but feel like this moose has taken something more important from me. I'd say it was my dignity but I'm not sure there's a scrap of that left after the past few days.

Josh swears, and I realize the moose is relaxing, its ears no longer drawn back like an angry dog, its hair no longer standing on end.

It's also lying down on top of our sleeping bag, as if we'd occupied its favorite morning napping spot, and it's pleased to discover we've left behind extra cushioning in the form of our bag, shoes, and clothes.

Josh takes my hand. "What do we do?"

"I think the universe might be trying to kill us." I swallow the other thought, which is that the fates are clearly against me and Josh having anything resembling a normal relationship, even if I were miraculously capable of such a thing.

"Okay," Josh says slowly. "But what do we do about the moose on your clothes?"

There's really only one thing we can do. "We're going to move very slowly around to the car, keeping trees between us and the moose as much as possible. And then we're going to get in your car and drive back into town and find something that actually covers my butt cheeks for me to wear while we sneak back into my house for regular clothes."

Josh glances down at my ass. "You do look good in my shirt."

I squeeze his hand. "And I'll wear it for you whenever you want, but I'm not going to be caught pants-less during the family reunion. Again." Turns out I do have one small scrap of dignity left, and damn it, I'm going to guard that sucker with my life.

After long, painful minutes (literally, because neither Josh nor I are accustomed to walking barefoot through the forest) we finally circle back to the Porsche. It actually surprises me the car hasn't been inhabited by a family of rabid raccoons in our absence, but it's blessedly empty and we get in and pull slowly back onto the road.

The damn moose doesn't even stir, which furthers my theory that the universe—or at least Wyoming—has some kind of score to settle with me. I didn't know when I came back for the reunion that I was entering some sort of death match, and I'm incredibly outmatched.

Josh rests his hand on my knee as we drive back into town. "You okay?"

He's been asking that a lot lately, and while I'm thrilled he cares, I'm less excited about being the one in this very new relationship who needs constant tending. "Yeah. I just need a shower. And to never come back to Wyoming again."

"I can support that."

When we get into town it's still too early in the morning for the grocery store to be open. Not that they carry many clothes, but they do have a selection of t-shirts with steer horns or a pair of pistols with the words "got guns?" across the chest, and occasionally these gems come with matching shorts to complete the set.

"Is there anywhere else that carries clothes in town?" Josh asks.

I sigh. "The only thing open at this time is the bait shop, but unless I'm going to wear a fly-fishing vest, I don't think they'll be able to help."

Josh shrugs. "It doesn't hurt to try."

I direct him to the right part of town, and Josh parks on the far end of the lot so fishermen don't randomly pass by and see me tugging down the hem of his shirt. Josh saunters up to the bait shop like this is something he does every day, and it occurs to me that I don't know if Josh has ever been fishing in his life.

I can't picture it, but I couldn't picture him learning Dothraki either, so who knows.

Josh comes back with a plastic bag with a vaguely clothing-shaped lump in the bottom, which would give me hope if it weren't for the look on his face, which rests somewhere between shame and glee. He opens the door, and passes me the bag.

"What is it?" I ask. It comes out in my flat voice, which is the one I use to address Will after he's used the last of my mango shampoo, but Josh doesn't seem put off.

"It will definitely cover your butt cheeks."

I snatch the bag and peer inside. He's bought a pair of those plastic overalls fly fishermen wear when they wade out into rivers, and from the amount of material there, it looks like these could fit a very large man.

I glare up at Josh, and he holds up his hands. "You don't have to wear them. But they're pants. We could also sit here in the car until the grocery store opens and see if we could find you—"

"No," I say, more snappishly than I mean to. I soften my tone. "Thank you. Really. I'll wear these. At least I won't be flashing my ass at my uncle Joe and revealing to him that I had the Millipede Corporation tattoo he gave me removed."

Josh has just settled into his seat, and he pauses and stares at me. "I have so many questions about this."

Despite everything, I laugh. "I bet you do."

"Your uncle Joe does tattoos?" Before I can tell him about Joe's brief stint as a tattoo artist, Josh continues on. "And most importantly, you *seriously* had a *Death Arsenal* tattoo? Which you had *removed*? *Why?*"

Josh looks as if I'm telling him I turned down a starring role in Spielberg's next film, and I laugh harder.

"Was it a tramp stamp?" he asks. "Please tell me you did not remove a geeky tramp stamp. My heart will never recover."

Now we're both laughing, and it feels so good I never want to stop. "Sadly, Rios, I did exactly that."

He groans like this kills him, and I pull him in for a kiss

before unwrapping and shimmying into the waders, which bunch around my waist like they are one hula-hoop away from being clown pants.

"There it goes," I say. "My last shred of dignity." And yet somehow, Josh and I both laugh our way to my house.

"Okay," Josh says. "Do you want me to scout ahead? Make sure Patrice isn't waiting to ambush us with family pictures?"

"No way. You're just trying to get first dibs at the shower."

Josh puts his finger to his lips and we both smother our laughter as we slip into the house via the kitchen. For a moment it seems as if the coast is clear. I don't hear anyone moving around in the house, even on the floor above.

And then Josh stops in his tracks, and I realize this is because my entire family is sitting in the adjoining den in a circle around a cheese platter, staring right at us.

Maybe I'm just growing paranoid, but I have a sinking feeling they've been lying in wait.

TWENTY

Anna-Marie

I blink, trying to make sense of why my entire family is sitting in the living room waiting for me at an hour when most of them should still be asleep. And they, likewise, study me, probably trying to piece together why I'm wearing a men's shirt and a large pair of rubber waders.

"What's going on?" I direct this at my dad, but he avoids my eyes, staring at the cracker and cheese platter sitting on the coffee table. Speaking of which . . . "Why is there one of those grocery store party platters? And is that a banner?"

Strung across the top of the large bay window is a whole bunch of pieces of printer paper, with large glittery letters drawn on—by Ginnie, I'm guessing—that all together spell "WE'RE HERE FOR YOU."

"Anna-Marie," Aunt Patrice says, trying to project an essence of calm it's clear she doesn't actually feel. She gestures to an empty armchair with the deliberate air of one of those game show models on *The Price Is Right*. "Please. Have a seat."

This is the absolute last thing I want to do right now, with all of them crunched together on the couch and loveseat, watching me—or the party platter—with varying expressions, all of which are weirdly intense. Joe, next to Patrice, is clearly uncomfortable, his lips pursed under his moustache like some selfie girl doing duckface before a badly needed wax. Next to him is Lily, who is dressed shockingly modestly in a pair of jeans—without holes in the crotch!—and shirt that can't be seen through. She looks altogether too pleased with whatever is going on for my comfort. On the other side of her, Cherstie sits crammed up against the couch arm, biting her lip and tying the ends of her dark hair into nervous knots with her glitter-nailed fingers. Grandpa is on an armchair beside the couch, eyeing my waders with narrowed eyes, like he's trying to figure out if this is the latest youth trend.

On the loveseat is my dad, drumming his fingers on his knees, and next to him Tanya, who is clutching his arm and watching me with wide eyes. Next to her is Buckley, who is the only one not acting weird, because, well, he's a dog and possibly has even less idea of what is happening than I do.

I don't see Ginnie or Byron anywhere. This worries me more than anything else, oddly.

What is happening that they don't want the kids around for? Kids who have already seen the Boy Scout video, so it can't be about that, can it?

"I think I need to change first," I say, then glance over at Josh, who is folding his arms across his bare chest self-consciously, probably because of Lily's hungry gaze. "We both do. There was this moose, and I lost my pants, and—"

"I think *this*," Patrice says, gesturing at us in a way that somehow encompasses both our current state of dress and possibly who we are as people, "is exactly why you need to take a seat, right here with your family. Who loves you." She presses her lips together. "And Joe's Way, it would probably be best if you joined us for this."

Josh and I exchange a look, and I can tell he's going to follow my lead. Which is good. Whatever is going on, I have a feeling I'm going to need him at my side.

"Fine," I say. "But can we make it quick? Because these

waders are . . . well, like wearing giant rubber clown pants."

I sit at the very edge of the armchair, and Josh sits on a folding chair that has been set up next it.

"She's here now, can I finally have a damn cracker?" Grandpa says, and Patrice glares at him.

"Not now, Dad."

"You dragged me out of bed, and I haven't even had a decent breakfast, and I've been sitting in front of this cheese plate for the last twenty minutes—"

"Anna-Marie," Patrice says, steamrolling over Grandpa's complaints. "You know we love you."

"Yes. I do," I say carefully. "And according to the banner, you are also here for me. Which is great, I guess. Is this about the video? I'm sorry you guys had to see that, but, really, it's going to be fine. Josh is handling all the press stuff for it, and—"

"It's not just the video," Patrice says. "We know now, and everything makes so much sense. The video, you . . . servicing Shane in your room—"

"*Servicing* him? I was on my knees because of the bat! Not that it's any of your—"

"—And then sneaking out with Joe's Way the very next night, and now, returning home half-clothed—"

As she rattles off every indiscretion of the past several days, I hear the chime of Josh's phone turning on. It starts buzzing like it's having a seizure, as text after text pops up. Josh's eyes widen, and my stomach turns in dread.

"What do you mean, you 'know now'?" I ask, cutting off Patrice. "Dad? What is she talking about?"

My dad looks up at me then, and it's almost like he can't bear to do so, and I feel like I've been slapped.

My dad has never looked at me like that, like he's *ashamed* of me.

"Bill . . ." Tanya says softly, squeezing his arm.

"This is nonsense," he says gruffly, and then stands up and leaves the room.

"Bill, get back here!" Patrice yells. "This is your daughter and she needs your support!"

I don't know what they think I need support for, but that look on his face lingers in my mind, cutting through me.

"Anna-Marie, darlin', I think this is just a little much for him right now," Uncle Joe says, and Patrice nods along with him.

"What is?" I realize my voice is starting to sound squeaky in my growing panic.

"*Shit*," Josh says, with the utmost feeling, and he hands me his phone. Then he run his hand through his hair because he looks like otherwise he might punch a wall instead.

I look down at the article he's got pulled up on the phone, at the top of which is a picture of . . . Ryan Lansing? My ex-costar beams at the camera, posing at some charity event, and it takes me a long beat of even greater confusion before I read the pull quote at the top of the article.

"Our time together was brief, but long enough for me to see a pattern of out-of-control and deviant sexual behavior . . . I just want Anna-Marie to get help."

And in bold, the article title: Soap Star Ryan Lansing Dishes on Former Co-Star's Sex Addiction.

Oh. Hell. No.

"He said I'm a *sex addict*?" I jump to my feet, my voice well past hysterical. "That mother-fu—"

"And we're here for you," Patrice says. "Even your dad, despite his refusal to acknowledge your problem."

Uncle Joe grimaces. "Go easy on him, Patty. I can't imagine what it would be like to know your little girl is giving more rides than Disney World."

Really Joe? You can't imagine?

But Lily just nods, her face the picture of innocence, and Cherstie glares at both of them. "Dad, that's not fair. We haven't even given Anna-Marie the chance to say anything."

"I don't care what *anyone* says. I'm eating a cracker," Grandpa says, reaching for the cheese platter.

I'm only partially paying any attention to them, my eyes scanning over the article, though the pull quote captured the essence of it. Ryan Lansing—Ryan Man-Whore Lansing!—is giving his reaction to the video, talking about how he's not surprised I would jump from Josh Rios to some guy in my hometown, how he guesses there are dozens more men—*dozens*, he says—that we don't even know about. He calls our series of hook-ups while I was on *Passion Medical* a "lovely, passionate affair," which is giving it considerable more romance than either of us did at the time. And how my "increasingly apparent addiction" led not only to him regretfully needing to end things—as if he dumped me!—but ultimately to . . .

"He says it was *my* sexual problems that got me fired? *Mine*?" I feel like my brain is going to explode all over the cheese platter. "He was the one who broke Bridget's Bubble Time Award! *He* was! While having sex with Sarah! Who framed me! Who—"

"It sounds like your work environment isn't helping your problem." Patrice oozes sympathy. "All those sex parties. And cocaine."

"Anna-Marie isn't on cocaine," Tanya snaps at her. "We're not talking about drugs."

"I'm just saying they go hand in hand. I saw a documentary once."

Grandpa swears, glaring down at his pants covered in cracker dust. "The damn cracker broke! It can't even support the cheese! What kind of platter is this?"

Patrice ignores him. "Even if cocaine isn't involved"—and here she sounds incredibly doubtful, like she thinks if she broke into my trunk she'd find enough blow to film the sequel to *Wolf of Wall Street*— "we've certainly seen the behavior to support Mr. Lansing's claims, behavior that is out of control. I have some information here that I was recommended by Doctor Wagner—"

"Don't listen to him!" Grandpa says. "He's a quack."

Lyle Wagner is our neighbor, and also, I'm fairly certain, a proctologist. Probably the one Grandpa should be seeing for his netherregions. I'm about to say this when Patrice holds up a sheet of paper she's clearly printed from the internet. "Some of the symptoms," she says with an air of authority, "include having sex in public, an excessive number of partners, the impairment of family relationships, the loss of jobs because of sexual behavior—"

"It was *Ryan Lansing's* sexual behavior that lost me the job," I snap.

"Still," Patrice continues. "The behavior we've all seen since you've arrived is definitely excessive."

"Don't forget deviant," Lily chimes in brightly.

"You! How dare you, with your flashing my boyfriend and . . . and your sausage!" I shriek incoherently, because language itself is failing me in my rage.

Lily shakes her head sadly. "I'm glad Josh finally knows the extent of the problem. He deserves a woman of class."

She reaches for a piece of cheese from the platter, but Patrice shoos her away. "You don't want to upset your stomach again, dear. Not after how sick you were last night."

I smirk at her, not caring that I'm probably a thick layer of facepaint away from looking like an evil clown. "Wonder what upset your stomach. Have any ideas, Lily? Any raw meat products find their way into your mouth?"

"Clearly not as many as have been in yours," Lily says.

I can't take it anymore. I lunge forward, I'm not sure what I'm actually going to do to Lily, but it sure as hell isn't going to be classy. Josh reaches his hand across me, blocking me from leaping across the coffee table.

"Anna-Marie." His voice is calm, too calm, like he's forcing himself along a very thin line. He grips my arm. "Who is Ryan Lansing's agent?"

I'm shaking, but I manage to calm down enough to answer this. Mainly because it's an easy question. "Brent. He has—*had*—the same agent as me."

"Brent." Josh's dark eyes gleam with a look that is vicious and almost . . . eager. "Fantastic."

He takes his phone back out of my hand.

"Anna, honey," Patrice says. "Maybe you should sit down, and we can go around the room and talk about our concerns. And you'll see that we don't want to *judge* you, we want to *help* you. Dad, why don't you start?"

"Because I'm finally eating!" Grandpa grouses around a mouthful of cheese.

"Fine." Patrice sighs. "I'll begin. I'm concerned about what kind of strange sex-play you've been engaged in wearing fly-fishing gear and—"

"Brent!" Josh says loudly into the phone, making it clear he's going to make this call right here and now. I can hear Patrice's teeth click together as she shuts her mouth. "Josh Rios here. When you said there'd be more coming, I didn't think you meant a lawsuit for one of your biggest clients. But I'm reading the baseless and defamatory accusations Ryan Lansing is making against Anna-Marie, and I have to say, I'm itching to get lawyers involved."

There's a silence in the room as pretty much everyone—including myself—strains to hear what Brent is saying back, but all I can make out is the reedy quality of his voice. I wonder if I'm imagining it, but I do think I can hear him eating something. Probably another meatball sub, even at like seven in the morning.

"Yeah, maybe you're right," Josh says, in a tone which implies everything but that. "A lawsuit is a lot of hassle, and though I'd love to make Anna-Marie rich off of whatever settlement Mr. Lansing would beg us to take, I think it would be even more satisfying for some of Mr. Lansing's sexual proclivities to make the news. How long do think it would take us to find some jilted lovers willing to spill all the details? And since he likes to toss the word 'deviant' around so freely, how much do you want to bet we can find a few stories of his sex life that would make

Hugh Hefner blush?"

Having slept with Ryan, I'm fairly certain he's not actually creative enough in bed to have stories like that, but I have to admit, it's thrilling—and vindicating—seeing Josh go full agent beast-mode on Brent's ass.

And judging by the wide-eyed way everyone in my family is looking at him—with the exception of Grandpa, who is poking at the cubes of swiss and grumbling about "uppity foreign cheeses"—they're seeing a new side of him as well.

Brent's tone sounds a bit frantic. I can't make out the words, but I can almost feel the breeze from all the back-peddling.

"No, Brent, we're well past what I *want*," Josh says. "What I demand is that Ryan Lansing issues a full and complete retraction of his accusations concerning my client's personal life. One in which he acknowledges that though he plays a doctor on television, he is in fact not a medical professional capable of making a mental health diagnosis."

Brent speaks again, his tinny voice wheedling, but Josh cuts him off.

"I don't care what you have to do to make that happen. I only care that it does. And that there is equal or greater coverage on this retraction. And I promise you, Brent, if this doesn't happen, you will regret ever having signed that lying piece of shit you call a client."

And then he hangs up before Brent can say anything back.

Part of me wants to fling my arms around Josh and another part wants to sit back and admire the sexiness of his (shirtless) protective wrath. But most of me knows that even if Ryan issues this retraction, it won't solve everything.

People think I'm a sex addict, with a proclivity for flashing Boy Scouts at hot springs.

My own *dad* thinks I'm a sex addict. That expression on his face, the clear shame that made it so he couldn't even look at me—

Tears well up in my eyes, and Josh sees it, his cold fury

softening. He squeezes my hand, but before I can follow my instincts and melt into his arms and just let him hold me, Patrice clears her throat.

"Well, that was . . . very forceful." Patrice sounds a little out of breath, and her cheeks have spots of pink in them. "But back to sharing our concerns about Anna-Mar—"

"That's enough," Josh says, standing in front of me and shielding me from my hounding family members the way I did for him the first day he showed up at my house. "Anna-Marie isn't doing this right now, and maybe not ever. She's not a sex addict, and beyond that, any details about her sex life are up to her to decide if she wants to discuss with you."

He looks back at me, and there's a hint of uncertainty about whether he should have dressed down my family like that. But I'm glad he did, because at this moment—and maybe always, because it's Josh—he's far more capable of handling this like a calm and rational adult than I am, and after dealing with Shane and then a murderous moose, I'm likely to either beat my cousin to death with a cheese platter or just start crying in front of my whole family.

The first of those options is far more appealing, but I don't think either will help my situation.

I squeeze his hand back, just as Patrice tries one last time.

"But Joe's Way," she starts, in this placating voice, "If we just—

"*No*," I say to my family, with a special glare at Patrice. "Josh and I don't want to hear another word about this." And even though this may not be the best time to do so, I can't help but also blurt out, "And the name he wants to be called is Josh. Not Joe's Way. *Josh*. Respect that, and him, or you don't get to talk to him *at all*. Got it?"

I'm not sure I'm able to police this threat as long as we're staying in the same house as her, and honestly, I don't think Josh cares about her butchering his given name nearly as much as my tone implies, but it sure feels good to call her out.

Patrice's mouth slams shut in response, which is also gratifying.

I pause, and then turn to Tanya. "Tell Ginnie she did a great job with the banner. I like the glitter."

Tanya smiles at me. And I find myself hoping she doesn't believe a word of these crazy accusations. That maybe she'll be my stepmom, for good, and more than that—maybe someday she'll be my friend, too.

Then I turn and lead Josh upstairs, where I can change out of my bait-store clothing and maybe, just maybe, get some sort of grip on my life.

TWENTY-ONE

Josh

I want to think that the day can't get any worse, but somehow it does. By noon, Anna-Marie's mother has her on the phone, pacing up and down her dad's patio. I can't hear what she's saying, but from the look on Anna-Marie's face, I gather it isn't good. More than anything, she just looks tired.

I can't blame her. I feel it, too. It felt good to yell at Brent, but in the end, even if Ryan prints a retraction, it won't change what's been done. Even if this doesn't reach national awareness, everyone in her part of the industry is going to read it. It's going to change the way they think about her, irrevocably. Possibly forever.

It has to hurt that her family believes these things, too. I want to fix it, partly as her agent, and partly as her boyfriend. I can't shield her from this, and it eats at me.

And then Ben calls.

"Dude," he says. "Wyatt found something on TMZ you need to see. He's sending you a link."

I want to say that I've seen quite enough, but if there's something else, I clearly do need to know about it. "Something worse than an accusation of a sex addiction?"

"Possibly," Ben says. My phone alerts me to a text message,

probably from Wyatt. "It's her ex, Shane."

My stomach drops. Shane. "What did he do?"

"He called the press with some sob story about how they've been in love since they were kids, and how they've been doing the long distance thing while she was in LA, and he had no idea she was cheating on him with you."

I swear. Loudly. In the next room, I hear Patrice clear her throat with equal force, but I can't bring myself to care. "That's not true."

"I know. But he claims he doesn't care that she cheated. He just wants her back, and apparently he's working on a song to prove it."

I swear again, and this time Patrice comes out into the hall. "Joe's W—" she starts, and then flushes. "Josh. There are children in this house."

I appreciate her effort with my name enough that I manage not to snap at her and instead nod in acknowledgement and turn my back on her. "He's just doing this for the attention. He's trying to get press for his band."

"Probably," Ben says. "Gabby confirms that Anna-Marie hasn't been with Shane for years. But if that's what he's doing, it's working. Well. The story is spreading, and the views on that video are shooting through the roof."

Damn it. I knew Shane was an asshole. I thought it was brave (or naive) of Anna-Marie to tell him off when he had a phone full of naked pictures of her, and I wouldn't have been surprised if the news was that those had hit the web. But no. Instead of just humiliating her, he's decided to use her as a stepping stone, like Ryan did.

This time, there's no agent for me to call. Even if Shane has one, no one in music gives a damn about me.

"Okay," I say. "Thanks for keeping tabs on this."

"Yeah, of course. But dude, are you okay? This is a really big mess you're caught up in."

I sigh. "Honestly? I'm just worried about her."

"Yeah, I know," Ben says. "That's what I'm worried about."

I lean against the hallway wall. Patrice has retreated, but I'm sure she's lurking, waiting to pounce if I use another epithet. "We'll be back in LA in a few days," I say. "Then you can meet her."

"I'd better. I'm tempted to drive to Wyoming and do it right now."

In his position, I'd probably already have done it. "Stay put. I need you on media duty. Cell service between here and there is spotty at best."

"Fine," Ben says. "But you be careful. I really don't want you to get hurt."

I take a deep breath. I don't want to get hurt either. But. "The person getting hurt here is her."

Ben grunts, but he doesn't agree. When we get off the phone, I hear the back door slamming, and head down to the kitchen as Anna-Marie stalks through.

"How'd that go?" I ask.

She waves a hand at me dismissively. "Oh, you know. She may not trust men in the slightest, but she sure is *thrilled* I'm dating you. She thinks it'll be good for my *career*."

I wince. "Ouch."

"Yeah. *Don't screw this up, Anna-Marie.* Thanks, Mom." Her voice is pure bitterness.

"It isn't like that."

She nods. "Tell that to her."

I glance down at my phone. There's the text from Wyatt, with the link I don't want to click on. "There's something else."

She gives me an exhausted look. "What now?"

"Apparently Shane talked. To TMZ."

Her mouth drops open. "*What*?"

We stand in the kitchen and read the article, Anna-Marie making a series of strangled noises that sound like tortured cats. The article is pretty much as Ben said, though he glossed over Shane's effusive descriptions of how Anna-Marie is the light of his life, and he's always known they're soul mates. There's an updated link to a song, "I'll Take You Back," which he's apparently posted on YouTube just minutes ago. Anna-Marie clicks the link, and there he is, sitting on a stool with an electric guitar in front of a poster for his band.

Shane's hair is tousled and he's barefoot and shirtless, wearing only a pair of tight jeans. He looks like he's been up all night, and no doubt he has been, as he's apparently found time to contact the press *and* write the nightmare that begins to play, a hard rock song about how Anna-Marie has wounded him. He doesn't name me, but both my job and my car make an appearance. As he sings the chorus—*I'll take you back, baby, I'll take you back, you're the dawn to my darkness, the sun to my sky, you're the lightning to my thunder, baby, I'll take you back*—his face scrunches like he's passing a kidney stone. He's clearly not a singer, but his voice is raw and gets the message across, and from my limited knowledge, he seems to be pretty good with a guitar.

I wish I could say people were going to listen to this and laugh, but I know the truth.

Girls across the country are going to eat this up.

"Oh, god," Anna-Marie says when it finishes. "I can't believe he would . . . No, of course he would." She buries her face in her hands. "I'm in hell."

I shove my phone in my pocket and put my arms around her. Her body is limp, and I can only imagine what she's feeling. Shane might be a dick, but he's been in her life a long time. To be used by someone you once loved—it's everything she's so afraid I'm going to do to her, and none of the men in her past are helping me convince her otherwise.

There's only one thing I can think of to do.

"Hey, look," I say. "This is clearly getting out of control. When it was just the tape, I think it was good to ignore it. But this time, we could strike back. Make a statement, you know?"

Anna-Marie turns her head to look at me. "What would I even say?"

I shrug. "That Shane is full of shit, and you've been broken up for years. If you want to respond to the tape, you could take a look at the statement Jennifer Lawrence made when her phone was hacked. She killed it addressing what was wrong with everyone looking at pictures she didn't give them permission to see. Or . . ." A plan is forming in my head, a way I can help, even if I can't stop any of this from happening. "Or we make a statement and say we're together, that we're in a relationship, and Shane isn't part of the picture. When we get back to LA, I can get us on some daytime talk show and we laugh and we tell the whole story—the parts we're comfortable telling, at least. And then you're with me, and we're stable, and people will realize you're not careening down some path to celebrity implosion. The story will probably still roll for a while, but then it'll die down and it'll be over."

Anna-Marie bites her lower lip. "Are we?"

I freeze for a second. "In a relationship?"

She shakes her head. "Stable."

I laugh, mostly from relief. "It doesn't feel like a lie on my end."

She looks relieved too, but then she frowns. "If we did that, then you'd be caught up in this. I don't want to do that to you."

"People know we were dating. I'm in it regardless."

"Yeah," she says. "But you shouldn't have to leverage your career to save mine. I can't ask that of you."

"You didn't ask. I'm offering."

Her eyes squeeze shut. "Yeah, well. Maybe you shouldn't."

I hold my breath for a moment. Her response bothers me, but it takes me a minute to figure out why. "Don't do that. Don't try to spare me."

She grimaces. "I love you. Of course I want to spare you."

I shake my head. "You're telling me I shouldn't want to be with you, shouldn't want to accept the consequences of whatever that means. And I get that you're scared, but really it's just an excuse to pull away, isn't it?"

She looks wounded, and I worry I'm being unfair. But then

she nods. "Yeah, okay. I can see that."

"And regardless," I say, "it's my career, and my call what I do with it."

Anna-Marie closes her eyes. "Or," she says, "we can get completely wasted and deal with what to do tomorrow."

The agent side of me wants to say that we need to get on top of the situation immediately, but the boyfriend side wins out. And honestly, getting wasted sounds pretty great right now. "I assume the store in town has beer?"

Anna-Marie rolls her eyes. "There are three things we will never be short on in Everett. Cows, guns, and beer."

TWENTY-TWO

Josh

By late afternoon, Anna-Marie and I are lying in the hammock beneath the trees on the far side of her father's backyard, her head at one end and mine at the other, both with the other's legs tucked up under one arm. We're each on our second bottle of a local Wyoming brand called Steer Beer. I'm trying to balance the half-full bottle on my forehead and Anna-Marie has installed Tinder on my phone and is giggling adorably while trying to set me up with random girls in Wyoming.

"Okay, here's one," she says, holding out a picture of a blond woman with a boa constrictor draped around her shoulders. "She's a herpetologist."

My beer bottle slips. "A *what*?"

Anna-Marie gives me a wicked look. "A person who studies reptiles. What did you think?"

"I think using the word herpetologist as a come-on has the opposite effect."

"Fine." Anna-Marie swipes left. "You're picky, Rios."

I get the bottle balanced for a second, and then have to grab it to keep it from falling in the dirt. "I used to be good at this in college."

Anna-Marie gives me a skeptical look, and twists a lock of

her long auburn hair around her finger. Neither of us is what I would call wasted, but her cheeks have turned slightly pink, and she seems much more relaxed than she was. "Were you? Did you ever do this when you *weren't* drunk?"

I laugh. "Maybe not." I down the rest of the beer, and then wave at my phone. "Give me that back. I'm taken."

"I don't know," Anna-Marie says, holding up the phone again. "Hannah makes a living selling cat sweaters on Etsy. That's never going to get old."

I don't even look at the picture. "Left."

Anna-Marie shrugs. "All right, Rios. Your loss." She finishes her beer and I open another one for each of us.

I'm starting to feel warm all over, and generally happy to be right where I am with no desire ever to move. Of course, much of this is probably just being with Anna-Marie while nothing and no one appears to be trying to kill us. And even though we said we were going to deal with the press issues tomorrow, I can't help but bring it up again. "You should let me tell the whole world we're together. Forget the PR stuff. I just want to show you off."

She smiles. "I don't hate that."

"See? I'm right. I'm always right." It's supposed to be a joke, but her face grows serious.

"What if we break up? What then?" She takes a long drink of her beer, as if she wants to forget she said that.

"You mean if you decide I'm not worth it?"

Anna-Marie looks startled, and it's my turn to swig my drink. Maybe I'm a little more buzzed than I thought I was. Though Anna-Marie influences me to say things I shouldn't more than alcohol ever has.

"If you break up with me," I say. "I'll still be your agent." I'm not sure if this is what she's asking, but it's true, and I probably should have been clear about it before.

Anna-Marie shakes her head. "You may not want to."

"At least I'd still get to see you. If you decide you can't make this work, it's not like I want you out of my life."

She rubs my shoulder with her bare foot. "*You* might end it, though. You might find someone else, or decide you're not in love with me, or—" She takes a shuddering breath, and I run my hand up and down her calf.

"You're worried I'm going to cheat on you, right? Because of your dad. But I'm not going to do that, so I don't know what would happen if I did."

Anna-Marie swirls her beer around and around. "No one goes into a relationship thinking they're going to do that," she says. Her voice is angry, but I don't think it's directed at me. "But what if you're unhappy, or you decide you've made a mistake? What are you going to do then?"

"I'm going to *talk* to you about it," I say. "We'll figure out why I'm not happy and work on it. And if that doesn't work then we'll get counseling, we'll take a trip, we'll talk it out until it does." I shrug. "My parents have been married for thirty-six years. And they don't always like each other, but they do always work it out."

Anna-Marie looks up at me, but I can tell she doesn't quite believe me. "But if you're not in love with me anymore, why would you *want* to do any of that?"

I smile. "Because I know if I loved you once, I can love you again. We'd just need to figure out what went wrong. And that might mean we have to make changes in our lives, but I'd want to do that." It's at that moment that I realize how much I mean this. I've never been with a girl I wanted to change my life for, but even before I left for Wyoming, I was starting to think of Anna-Marie as a person who might be worth giving up my basement evenings for, even the basement itself. The fact that I don't have to feels fantastic; I can't imagine not being willing to make other changes for her, if I need to.

"I'm still scared I'll mess it all up somehow," she says quietly.

I want to brush this aside, but she's said it before, and I know she means it. "I'm not so easy to scare off," I say. "If I'm still here after dealing with Patrice, and that moose, and Lily's sausage—which I'm kind of pleased made her sick, by the way, because maybe she'll never do that again—and not to mention that god-awful t-shirt they all had me wearing—"

"Oh, god." She covers her eyes. "Why aren't you gone already?"

I smile at her. "Because there's only one Anna-Marie Halsey. You can't be replaced."

She holds up my phone again. "Are you sure? Because Tracy enjoys sharing long bubble baths with her two standard poodles."

I snatch the phone and tuck it under my arm. "Do you know how long I spent looking for you? I almost went home early from that party where we met, you know. I was *this* close to not meeting the girl of my dreams, and instead going home to my basement and doing whatever it is I do down there—"

"Which you still haven't told me," Anna-Marie says, poking me with her toe.

"Yeah, well. I've already quoted you the entrance fee."

I'm worried this will scare her, but she just smiles and finishes her beer, and then tosses the bottle beneath the hammock and settles in.

"So why did you stay?" she asks.

"Because I figured I needed to at least make the rounds once, see if there was anyone I needed to talk to. I set my phone to vibrate after fifteen minutes, and told myself I'd give it that long, and then I could head out. I was crossing the room, and then I see this girl at the bar, and she's beautiful, and then she says something to the bartender and they both laugh, and I wished it was me making her smile like that." My own bottle clinks as it joins Anna-Marie's beneath the hammock. "And I've never wanted to stop."

Her blue eyes crinkle at the sides as she smiles. "I may have seen you noticing me and said something to the bartender just to get your attention."

I like this idea, that we both noticed each other before we

even spoke. "But you didn't know who I was, because I remember the shock on your face when I told you my name."

"And you said you recognized me from somewhere, but it was just a line. You had no idea who I was."

"I always use that line at parties," I say. "Because the worst thing you can do when you're hitting on an actress is to never have seen her before."

The buzz is settling in now, though I still think half of it comes from being with her. Or maybe it's that the alcohol gives me an excuse to say all the things I want to say but know I shouldn't.

"You should marry me," I say. "Then I can show you the basement."

Anna-Marie laughs. "I thought only a ring was required. We have to be married?"

"Fine, don't marry me. Move in with me and never move out. We can have kids and own a house together and everything but never be married."

She squints. "Wouldn't that make it a commonwealth marriage?"

I laugh. "Only if we do it in Canada."

Her face grows serious. "Is that what you meant when you said we could skip a step? Move in together?"

I pause. "I was thinking more along the lines of the ring."

I expect this to terrify her—this conversation has clearly gotten away from me, and I should put a stop to it before I say something that puts her off for good. But instead she sighs. "We can't get married. We'd be one of those horrible celebrity couples who names their kids after places they've had sex."

I laugh again. "We would! What brand is your dad's bathroom sink? Grohe? Moen?" I'm pretty sure I'm mispronouncing these words—the latter of which sounds like "moan."

Anna-Marie giggles. "It's not too late to add Shane's lawn to the list of possibilities."

"Ha!" I say. "Yes, please. Let's name a child after *him*."

"Not him," Anna-Marie says, jabbing a finger in the air. "His desecrated foliage."

I stare at her, awed that I'm dating a girl who downs three beers in minutes and then uses words like "desecrated" and "foliage."

"Moen Rios," she says. "Actually, I think my dad's sink is a Kohler."

"Huh. It might be the influence of the alcohol, but I actually like that one."

"Kohler Rios," she says. "See, I told you we were those kind of people."

I shrug. "I can live with that."

Anna-Marie looks down at her hands, which are resting just above my knees. "Anna-Marie Rios," she says, like she's trying it out, and my head spins in a way that has nothing to do with the beer.

Anna-Marie Rios. God, I love the sound of that.

Anna-Marie shakes her head, like she's suddenly self-conscious. "I probably shouldn't change my name, though, right? I mean, professionally."

I'm afraid to move or breathe or speak, like we've fallen under some kind of spell, and the slightest thing could break it. "You could. If you wanted to."

She's actually considering this, and my whole body feels like it's floating. "I think I'd want to. If that was okay with you."

It's all I can do not to get down on my knees and beg her right now. "Tell me you'll marry me," I say. "Even if it's just pretend. I just want to hear you say it."

She looks at me, and I swear on her face I see both longing and trepidation. "I can't do that. Can I?"

I'm surprised at how much I want it—the future, yes, but also to hear her say the words. To be able to imagine this possibility after a week full of stress and disaster. "No consequences," I say. "I swear. In the morning, nothing's changed. Just for today, let's talk like we're ready for this."

I'm afraid that this request—which, let's face it, is as crazy and desperate as I am—is going to be the thing that tips her over the edge into panic, but instead she smiles. "Okay," she says. "Let's get married, and have babies."

"Named Kohler. A girl?"

She nods. "A girl named Kohler. And a few more as well. None of them named Shane's Lawn."

"Definitely not. And we'll live in LA, and you'll be famous, and I'll work my ass off to keep the roles coming."

"And we'll be one of those adorable couples everyone is afraid will break up, but we won't."

"No," I say. "We won't."

We look at each other, and while hours ago Anna-Marie said we were in hell, this feels like exactly the opposite.

"And somehow," I say, "we'll find time from our busy lives being rich and famous to still drive our children to soccer practice."

Anna-Marie giggles. "That one's on you. I don't drive in LA."

I blink at her. "What?"

Her giggle grows louder. "I never told you, because I don't tell anyone. I'm terrified of driving in LA."

"You drove all the way out here—"

"No," she says, stabbing a finger in the air. "I took an Uber out of town, and *then* rented a car and drove to Wyoming."

"You don't have a car? I thought the driving you to work thing was because you wanted to stay over at my place."

"It is," Anna-Marie says. "But your car was a perk. And not because it's a nice one. Just because it runs."

I can't help but laugh. "All right. So we'll have a nanny who drives. I don't think I can handle all the carpooling alone."

She nods. "Exactly. Or I'll pay more for Uber. Either way."

"*Or*," I say, "as you get more visibility you can stop taking cars with random people who might stalk you, and instead learn to drive in LA."

Anna-Marie looks horrified. "Josh," she says, "don't you care for the safety of our *children*?"

We both laugh, and I wonder how many more things about Anna-Marie I'll be able to discover over the years.

Which reminds me. "I never told you what my main fandom is. It may have something to do with what's in the basement."

"*Game of Thrones*," Anna-Marie says. "*Lord of the Rings*. No, *Star Wars*."

I shake my head. "Actually, it's *Harry Potter*."

Anna-Marie looks surprised. "Really?"

"Yeah. But I'm not answering any more questions about the basement or else you'll get it out of me."

"Can I ask just one question?"

I narrow my eyes at her, but I already know she can ask as many questions as she wants. "One."

"Why do you keep it a secret?"

I arch an eyebrow at her. "I don't know. Why didn't you invite me to fight zombies with you?"

She tilts her head, her face growing serious. "Okay, but I didn't have any vows about a man having to put a ring on my finger before I showed him my Xbox. How many people have seen your basement?"

I'm quiet for a moment. "Just Ben and Wyatt."

"Exactly. I keep the two halves of my life separate, but I date an equal number of guys who I might bring home and play *Death Arsenal* with, if the mood strikes. But you, you keep everyone out of your geek life. Why?"

My heart squeezes at the idea that there have been men she's dated who got to come home to her apartment and relax and play video games with her. Not that I haven't loved our lifestyle together, but something about that feels so intimate.

"I don't know," I say. "I guess it just . . . feels so juvenile. Like I don't want to admit that I never grew up."

Anna-Marie looks confused. "But you're a successful business person. You have a good job and a nice place and a really nice car. Lots of adults like to read *Harry Potter*."

Lots of adults do not have scale models of the Harry Potter

universe with a working Hogwarts Express. "What's in my basement is *really* geeky."

"Okay," she says. "But that's not the only thing you hide, is it? All the books are in the basement too, right? And you're so concerned someone might find one that you sweep the house before you leave."

Honestly, I rarely bring the books upstairs at all. "That's true."

She's quiet, waiting for me to explain, but I guess it's hard for even me to understand. I make excuses about my job, and maybe that's a reason not to have a bookshelf in my living room where I entertain clients. But if someone happened to see a book lying around, it shouldn't be a big deal.

But it is.

"I think it's partly because of my family," I say. "I wasn't kidding when I said they call me the college dropout. I mean, *they're* kidding. Sort of. But my dad is a brain surgeon, and my older brother Ray, he followed right in his footsteps. What they do is serious. It saves people's lives. And my mom is a professor, and Adrian is in financial advising. Did you know I started out majoring pre-med? I really thought I'd be a doctor like my dad."

Anna-Marie's eyebrows go up. "*Really*. Was your dad disappointed when you didn't?"

I shake my head. "No, he knew I didn't have what it takes. He never said it outright, but whenever I'd come home, he'd ask me if I was still pre-med. I started to get a complex about it, like he didn't think I could do it."

Anna-Marie looks so sad, and I know I'm misrepresenting my dad. "Not that he meant it that way," I say. "I think he just honestly thought I'd be happier doing something else. And he was right. But it hurt at the time, especially because Ray was doing so well in his residency. He actually got to learn with my dad, which sounded awesome."

Her concern hasn't eased. She rubs the ball of her foot against my hip. "Are you and your dad close?"

"Yeah. I mean, we all get along, except Adrian, who doesn't

get along with anyone, and doesn't come around much because he knows none of us think it was a spectacular life decision for him to abandon his wife and daughter. Before Adrian, I was the one with the fast lifestyle. My parents were always worried about it."

Now she smiles. "Worried about your lifestyle. Really?"

"Yep. I think they thought I was into the drugs, at least a little, until the time I yelled at Adrian at a club for doing cocaine."

Anna-Marie chuckles, and I crack a smile. "I know, right? I mean, don't get me wrong. I drink too much. But I know I'm genetically lucky I'm not an alcoholic, and I don't want to get caught up in anything that might be more habit forming."

"Mmmm," Anna-Marie says. "Am I part of this lifestyle they hate? Dating actresses and snorting blow?"

I laugh. "I think they're mostly used to it, now. But it's all of it, you know? My job isn't serious the way theirs are. My parents read the classics and scholarly articles and I read about orcs and wizards and lightsaber battles. I started keeping it secret when I graduated college and officially became a productive member of society, and I guess no one in my family ever suggested that was a bad thing."

"What about Ben?"

I shrug. "Ben thinks it's dumb that I hide it, but as long as I still show up for video game night, he's good." I smile. "Except since I've been dating you, video game night has turned into the night Wyatt and I binge all five daily episodes of *Southern Heat* on the DVR."

Anna-Marie's eyes widen. "You do not."

I laugh, and it sounds a little maniacal, and Anna-Marie leans forward to punch me in the arm. The hammock tips precariously.

"You're making this up," she says.

I shake my head. "No, I swear. Since the first week we were dating, actually. I mentioned to Wyatt that I was seeing you, and he showed me that he had all the episodes recorded, and we started it up. Ben grouses that we're never going to finish playing *Digital Devil 2*, but he hasn't staged a walk-out, so we just keep doing it."

"I thought you didn't watch my show."

"I know. And I wasn't about to tell you I'm addicted to it and thus ruin my masculine mystique."

"That is not a thing," she says, though she looks happy that I've seen it, and not too terribly irked I kept it from her. "You should know that I haven't actually read the *Harry Potter* books. But I have seen the movies."

I nod. "I can work with that."

"So which house were you sorted into?"

I cringe. "I actually haven't taken the sorting test."

"*What*?" Anna-Marie puts her hand to her chest as if she's completely scandalized, and I think she's only half joking. "How can it be your number one fandom if you've never been sorted?"

"I'm afraid I'll be sorted into Hufflepuff."

"Ouch," Anna-Marie says. "I could see it."

I kick her gently in the ribs, and she lunges for my phone, fishing it out from beneath my arm. "That's it. We're settling this here and now. Which house would you *want* to be in?"

Now this conversation is getting personal. Ben would mock me mercilessly for admitting it—and with good reason—but discussing how much this stuff matters to me feels like poking around in the dark recesses of my soul.

"Gryffindor," I say. "But I can't look. Trust me, I have agonized over this many times. It's for the best that I just don't know."

This doesn't deter Anna-Marie from pulling up the website on my phone. "Oooh! They have a Patronus quiz as well. Do you know what your Patronus is?"

I laugh. "I don't. That one I can handle, but you go first."

I flip around on the hammock and we cuddle up and answer a vague series of questions and wait an artificial amount of time to get our results.

“Mine is a dolphin.” She wrinkles her nose.

I smile. “That sounds like it suits your inner fourteen-year-old.”

“It does. I accept it. Now it’s your turn.”

When my results appear on the screen, I groan. “No. No, why is this even an option?”

Anna-Marie leans toward me. “What?” she asks, and I turn the screen so she can see.

It’s a pheasant. “This is not possible,” I say. “There is no such thing as an attack pheasant.”

Anna-Marie laughs. “Suck it, Rios. The internet has spoken.”

I groan again. “A pheasant. What does that say about me? I’m supposed to be protected by a bird that is literally bred to be hunted and killed?” I shake my head at the phone. “Pottermore, you have betrayed me.”

“Oh!” Anna-Marie says. “We should name a child Harry!”

“Harry Rios. The kid would be destined for copious back hair.”

Anna-Marie dissolves into giggles again, and I stare at her in awe, this woman who I’m so deeply in love with. This woman who has become everything to me.

“God, marry me,” I say. “Please, please marry me. I want to do this for the rest of my life.”

A soft smile plays at her lips. “I already said yes. At least today, while there are no consequences.”

I nod. “Then I think time should just stop right here. We should just be here like this forever.”

Anna-Marie nods. “Agreed. We’ll never move, and morning will never come.”

But of course it does.

TWENTY-THREE

Anna-Marie

I wake up with the oddest sensation of being on a boat, and it takes my slow-churning brain a moment to remember I fell asleep on a hammock, which is now swaying as Josh shifts. I'm curled up under his arm, my face on his chest. My mouth is fuzzy and tastes like too much beer, and I'm pretty sure I've been drooling onto his shirt, which is something I thankfully only do when I fall asleep drunk.

As I definitely did last night, though not so drunk I can't remember a startling number of details about our conversation.

Marriage. Kids, even.

And the worst part, the part that is making my slight hangover headache start turning into a pulsing drum of panic, is how amazing it had all felt. How it sounded to say my name with his—Anna-Marie Rios—and the expression of bliss on his face when he heard it. How I could picture it, like one of those cheesy film montages set in warm, soft-edged filters: him standing on a beach in a tux, grinning at me as I walk toward him in a flowy white gown; us playing video games on a couch we bought together for our new house; me bringing him his morning cup of coffee to wake him up and a little dark-haired girl named Kohler jumping up on the bed to "help," giggling as her daddy groans and starts tickling her.

I couldn't just picture it; I wanted it. Desperately. More than I've ever wanted anything in my life.

No consequences, my ass.

I sit up—carefully, because I don't want to tip the hammock and dump both Josh and me on the beer bottle graveyard on the ground beneath us. I'm trying not to wake Josh as I do so—I wish I could say this was from purely unselfish motives, but honestly, the panic is making it difficult to breathe and I'm not sure I'm ready to talk to him again yet. Not sure I can handle the words "ring" or "marriage" or even "Harry Potter" right now.

Apparently it's impossible to get out of a hammock without waking the person you're sprawled across, even if that person is Josh Rios in the dawn hours.

"I reject the morning," Josh groans, running his hand along my back. "I thought it wasn't going to happen this time." His dark hair is mussed from the hammock and his many, many attempts to balance beer bottles on his forehead throughout the evening, and his eyes are barely slits against the sunlight.

The sight tugs at my heart. How many mornings have we woken entwined like this, him barely awake, me filled with a warmth I refused to examine too closely because I was afraid of what it might mean?

And that was even before I went and fell in love with him.

"Damn rotation of the planet," I say softly, watching how the light filtering between the leaves above us plays on his face.

"Mmmm," he agrees sleepily. "Where do you think you're going?"

Nowhere, I want to say. Nowhere without you, not ever again.

My pulse spikes, and I clear my throat, because it has suddenly gone so dry it might be a wildfire risk in there. "Coffee," I manage, this time having to force the smile. "I'll see if anyone's started coffee yet."

"I won't say no to that." He rubs his forehead, and before I can change my mind and curl up next to him again, I work my way out of the hammock.

I can hear voices from the house, so apparently at least someone's up this early, but I don't really care who. I just need to get away for a minute. To think. To breathe.

The screen door bangs shut behind me as I enter the kitchen, which is thankfully empty—the voices seem to be coming from upstairs. I open the can of off-brand coffee that is a far cry from the gourmet kind at Josh's place, but hasn't killed either of us so far. My hand trembles as I go through the motions of making the coffee.

I'm just scared, I tell myself, trying Josh's labeling thing. It's okay to be scared. I've gone through a lot this week, and the whole world has seen me naked and thinks I have a sex addiction and also that I cheated on Shane and damn, why did that song he wrote have to actually be *good*? But more importantly, I'm Josh's girlfriend, and I love him.

I love him, and he loves me, and it's going to be okay.

It's going to be okay.

By the time the coffee is brewing, I'm feeling more in control again. Calmer. I slowly breathe in the aroma, pretend I'm back at Josh's place. Pretend, maybe, that it's *our* place, and I'm about to crawl back into bed with him and—

"No! I don't want to go!" Ginnie shrieks from upstairs, sobbing, and I nearly spill the coffee I'm pouring as I jump. Her feet pound down the stairs.

"We are going now, whether you like it or—dammit!" This sounds like Tanya, and it sounds like she's in tears. I set down the coffee pot, just as Ginnie dashes by the kitchen and out the front door.

"Tanya," I hear my dad say, though it's far softer than the rest. "Don't go, just listen to—"

"*No,*" she says, and I can hear the fury in that one syllable. "I don't want your excuses, Bill. Save them for *her*. We're going."

I grip the edge of the counter, because I feel like I've been punched in the stomach. I'm dizzy from the déjà vu of hearing variations on this over the years.

Shit. Shit, Dad, *why*?

My dad doesn't beg or argue—I've never actually heard him do so when his wives or girlfriends leave him for his cheating. And so the only sound for a few moments is the thump of the suitcase Tanya is pulling down the stairs. She turns back only to say "Byron, get Ginnie's suitcase too, please."

"Mom, why can't we just—" Byron starts, his voice filtering down from the hallway upstairs, but Tanya cuts him off.

"We are leaving now, and we will talk about it on the road."

I can't see her face as she passes by the kitchen, her bobbed hair hanging over it, and she's rolling her suitcase, which isn't completely zipped up and has clothing sticking out from the sides where it was hastily crammed.

She yanks the suitcase hard when it catches on the weather-stripping at the front door, and a simple blue cotton bra and long feather earring that is hooked to it fall to the ground. She either doesn't notice or doesn't care, and the suitcase thumps down the wooden porch steps.

Numbly, I walk to the stairs and pick up the bra and the earring. I can barely bring myself to look upstairs, but when I do, my dad isn't even there anymore. He's gone back into his bedroom, and closed the door on this relationship like so many others. All I see is Byron bent over an open little-girl's suitcase decorated in bright butterflies, stuffing in clothes and sparkly shoes, looking like he wants to punch something.

I don't blame him.

From the door down to the basement, Cherstie is peering out, as is Aunt Patrice behind her, both woken up from the commotion. They meet eyes with me, clearly questioning, but it's like I can barely see them, let alone answer them.

I swallow, my throat so tight it feels all but closed up. My eyes are stinging, my fingers gripping the bra until my knuckles are white. I walk out onto the porch. Tanya has thrown her suitcase in the bed of one of the pickup trucks—I didn't realize one of those was hers, though it makes sense—and has wrangled Ginnie into the car, though my heart still cracks open from the girl's sobbing. Tanya slams the car door, and I flinch.

How many times have I heard car doors slam like that, cutting off the sound of crying or shouted expletives?

Tanya leans against the truck door, her head down and her eyes closed, arms folded across her chest, and it looks like the truck is the only thing keeping her from collapsing. I make my way down the steps toward her and she looks up at hearing the crunch of my sandals on the gravel.

Her face is blotchy, shiny from streaks of tears, her eyes puffy and red. She looks younger than ever. She swipes at the tears angrily as I approach.

"I—I . . ." I have no idea what to say, and I can't even form words. All I can do is hold out the bra and the earring, which she takes from me, her lips pressed tightly together.

She shakes her head. "You were right. God, I should have—I should have done lots of things. I should have not been an idiot who thought this would be *different*, and—" Her voice breaks, and she looks up at the sky, tears leaking from the corners of her eyes.

It's like I can still hear the echo of her voice from the other day: *He's a good man, and I love him. And I think that's worth the risk, don't you?*

"I'm sorry," I manage. "I'm so sorry." My voice sounds like a little girl's, just this squeak, and I feel my face burning from shame, though I'm not even sure why.

Because it was my dad that broke her heart?

Because I didn't somehow stop it?

Because I get to stay my dad's "favorite girl," even as he goes through woman after woman and leaves them all devastated in his wake?

The crunch of gravel sounds behind me, and it's Byron hoisting a faded backpack and Ginnie's suitcase. He glares at the ground, and climbs into the truck without saying anything or even looking at me. The door slams shut again.

Tanya's face crumples, as if she was only barely holding total grief at bay until both her kids were safely in the car. She takes a long shuddering breath, and I want to put my arms around her. But my arms feel like they're weighted with lead, and if I move they might shatter both of us.

"Me too," she says, with a nod. "I'm sorry, too. Take care, Anna-Marie. I wish . . ."

But she doesn't finish that, and she doesn't need to.

It doesn't matter what she wished, or what I wished, or what her kids wished. Because my dad did what he always does, and now she is joining the long list of women betrayed and gone.

Then she turns and walks to the driver side of the car, her spine unnaturally straight, her hands clenched into fists. She climbs up into the truck and it rumbles to life, and then they are gone, my almost stepmother and stepsiblings, and I hate myself that I didn't really say goodbye to any of them.

"Anna-Marie?" a worried voice calls, and it takes me a numb second to realize it's Josh.

I turn to see him standing on the driveway; he must have heard Ginnie's crying and the slammed doors and come around the side of the house. He walks toward me, his gaze never leaving my face. "Did Tanya leave?"

He must have seen Tanya leave, so it's clear what he's really asking.

"My dad cheated on her." I find myself hugging my arms to my chest, in the same position Tanya was, only without a massive truck to lean on. "She took the kids and left. He didn't even—he didn't even try. It's like he never cares." My own voice sounds distant, removed from me.

Josh's brows draw together. "God, Anna-Marie, I'm so sorry. I'm so—come here." He reaches for me, ready to bring me into his arms. Ready to hold me and comfort me and tell me he loves me.

But I take a step back.

Because my ears are still ringing from the slam of Tanya's truck doors as she left. I feel the pain on my scalp from when my mom would brush my hair as a child, after one of her fights with my dad, brushing too fast and too hard, tugging through the snarls like maybe this was one battle she could win. My eyes sting from the tears of every time I'd find Shane with whatever girl he broke up with me for, tears I'd never in a million years let him see. My face burns with the shame of opening Reid's wallet to slip a sexy note inside and seeing the picture of a pretty blond woman I would soon discover was his wife.

"I can't do this," I say, and the tears spill over onto my cheeks.

Josh freezes, his arm still reaching for me. "What?"

"This. Us. I can't—I can't do this." My voice is cold, a perfect match for the ice flooding my veins, pooling in my stomach.

And it's Josh there in front of me, Josh who swore he'd never cheat on me, that he'd never hurt me. Josh who I fell in love with, who I pictured a future with. He looks like he's going to be sick, and he's shaking his head and saying, "No, Anna-Marie, let's talk about this, okay? Let's—is this about last night? Because I know that wasn't real, okay? We never have to talk about it again."

But it doesn't matter if we don't talk about it, because now all I can see of that future is me yelling and crying and gathering up our dark-haired children into the car and trying with everything in me not to completely break apart where they can see.

"We knew perfectly well it would have consequences." I squeeze my eyes shut, to try to stop the tears and to keep from seeing his pain, because I can't handle that and protect myself the way I need to, the way I should have all along.

"Anna-Marie," he says again, and his fingers touch my elbow, just barely. "Please, let's just talk, let's just—"

"No!" I yell, jerking away from his touch. From him. Because I know what will happen if we talk. He'll make me believe again in things I never should have believed in the first place.

When I open my eyes, I see that his are red-rimmed, and my heart cracks.

"Why are you doing this?" he asks, his voice strained.

"Because I have to!" The words burst out of me, a tidal wave that won't stop until it's swept both of us under. "Because you're just like all the others! Because I'll trust you and love you and give you everything, and one day you'll find someone younger and prettier and you'll just toss me aside like I'm nothing. And I won't let that happen to me. I *won't*."

Josh's face pales, and then flushes. "How can you say that? After everything we've—how can you—?"

He stares at me, like he's waiting for me to tell him I don't mean it. But I don't—I *can't*.

His voice goes flat. "You really think that of me." When I don't deny it, he shakes his head and a dark look crosses his face. "Fine. *Fine*. If that's what you really think I am, then maybe you're right. Maybe *you're* just like all the others. Maybe you *are* replaceable."

Everything goes still. Even my heart, like the pain is so great it can't beat past it. "Leave. *Now*," I growl.

There's a beat where I think maybe he won't. Where I think maybe I'll beg him not to.

But I stay rooted where I am, silent, and he stalks off to his Porsche. Before I know it, he's gone too, his car disappearing down the street.

And I'm left standing alone in the yard, filled to bursting with so much pain and anger and regret, and yet somehow emptier than ever before.

TWENTY-FOUR

Josh

As I drive away from Anna-Marie's house, I know I should pull over and call Ben. I should do it now, and not drive first, because I'm not sure I can actually see straight, and I'll probably hit one of those damn antelope and end up marooned at Bleeker's Auto Shop while they order in parts for my Porsche.

I should not drive a couple blocks over and park in front of Shane's house. I should not slam the door of my Porsche and stalk down Shane's stairs, past the foliage that won't have my children named after it. I should not beat his damn balls against his door and wait, breathing heavy, fists clenched, for him to open the door.

But that is exactly what I do.

Shane opens the door and gives me one of his affable smiles. "Hey, man," he says. "Look—" But I don't give him another second to give me whatever excuse he's concocted for why he *had* to call TMZ and then *had* to write the damn song and put it up on YouTube. I shove him hard by the shoulders, and he goes flying back into his apartment, tripping over an amp and landing on his ass. He stares up at me wide-eyed as I plant a foot on his chest.

"You," I say, "are an asshole."

Shane holds up his hands. "Hey, man, I don't know what you've heard, but—"

"It's not about what I've heard. It's about what I saw you do to my girlfriend." Ex-girlfriend, technically, but I don't think that will have quite the same effect. "She *trusted* you and you *hurt* her. And for what? Just to get your stupid music a little boost. God, you've known her forever and you just threw her under the bus like she was *nothing*. She used to be in love with you, you know?"

Shane blinks at me. "Yeah, like five years ago."

I step harder on his chest, and he winces, but he's wisely not trying to get up. "Here's what's going to happen," I say. "I'm going back to LA, and I'm going to tell everyone I know what a worthless piece of shit you are. Forget about moving to LA. No one is going to let you play. I can't stop you from profiting for being a total asshole to a girl who did quite literally nothing to you, but not in my town. Not ever."

I shove him again with my foot, and then spin around and stalk out the door, slamming it behind me. I have no power to do anything I just said, and even though I've lived there my entire life, I have never before referred to LA as "my town."

Still, that felt good. So good that I get all the way down the block before the weight crushes down on me again.

You are replaceable. I would do anything to take those words back. To have the slightest hope that when we're both back in LA I might be able to call her, and we could figure this out. But no, for one horrible second I wanted to hurt her the way she hurt me, and I can't take it back.

I'm never going to forgive myself for this.

I manage to at least get out of the neighborhood—clutching the steering wheel all the way—before I pull over and call Ben.

"Hey, man," he says. "Nothing new, but the hits on the video just keep climbing, and a couple more outlets picked up the TMZ story. How are you guys holding up?"

"We broke up."

Ben is silent for a moment. "You what?"

"We broke up." My voice sounds strained, and I know I need to explain, but there's so much that goes into it I don't know that I can. "She's really afraid of commitment, right?"

"Yeah, Gabby told me the issues run deep. She says she's never even heard Anna-Marie consider commitment before you."

This should make me feel better, but it doesn't. "What, are you and Gabby like best friends now?"

"*No*. But she's cool. Wyatt and I hung out with her and her boyfriend last night. We talked about you. A lot."

I should probably be annoyed about this, but all I can think is how cool it would be to have Ben and Wyatt and Gabby and Will all be friends. It would be like taking two best-friendships and widening them into this whole community of awesome.

Except the link that would hold it all together is broken now. I'll be lucky if I can still be Anna-Marie's agent. There's no way we're going to be close. My chest aches and aches.

"Anna-Marie's issues," I say, "are because her dad cheated on all of his wives, and apparently his current girlfriend, who left today with her two kids."

"Classy guy."

I tighten my fists. Truth is, *he* was the one I wanted to shove onto his ass and then threaten. "Yeah. Things were going really well, and then Anna-Marie sees Tanya's leaving and she decides I'm going to do that to her and she kicked me out."

"Ouch," Ben says. "Jeez, are you okay?"

"No. I am not okay. We talked about what we would name our *children* last night. We were planning our whole lives. And now it's over."

"Damn," Ben says. And I know what he's thinking, so I say it for him.

"I'm an idiot."

"You're not an idiot. You're in love."

I shake my head. "Then love has made me into an idiot."

"Um, yeah. Remember that time I made you have lunch at the pool hall for four months straight so I could *not* talk to

Wyatt? Dude, he thought *you* were into him, because you kept calling him over and praying I would finally make a move."

"Yeah," I say. "It worked out significantly better for you."

Ben pauses, like he's trying to figure out what to say, and the hard truth is, there's nothing he *can* say that will help. "Maybe it's not over. Maybe she just needs time to think."

But I remember—will always remember—the look on her face when she told me to leave. "No," I say. "I messed up. She was yelling at me, telling me about all the shit I was going to do to her, and it hurt so bad that I yelled back at her."

"It's called a fight. Those happen."

I hold my breath. "I told her she was replaceable." I squeeze my eyes shut. "It's like—it's like her biggest fear, right? That I'll just go find someone else. That in Hollywood all actresses are replaceable, both personally and professionally. It was like the worst thing I possibly could have said."

"Why did you?"

My eyes are burning, and I'm pretty sure I'm going to cry, but I do still have to drive back to LA today. "Because I want it to be true. God, what am I supposed to do now? Go back to dating girls who don't get me? Keep looking like I'm *ever* going to find someone like her again?"

"You're going to get your ass back here, that's what you're going to do," Ben says. "Need me to meet you halfway?"

"Yes. And before we go back we're going to get completely plastered."

"*You'll* get plastered. And before you do, I'm taking your keys and your phone. No drunk dialing for you."

"I couldn't call Anna-Marie, anyway," I say. "A moose took her phone."

Ben pauses, and I realize I never told him about that. "Clearly you have more stories to tell me," he says. "I'm going to expect a full report."

"Don't worry. I don't think I'm going to talk about anything else for months."

Ben says he'll find out what town is halfway and text me a meeting place. With beer. I'm sure I'm going to want something stronger, but beer is a good place to start.

I drive down the road that leads out of town. I wonder what Anna-Marie is doing now—if she's going to stay there for the last couple days of her trip, or if she'll be doing what I'm doing and get the hell out of Wyoming.

I have my basement back in LA. I have Ben, and my family, and my job. But the idea of returning to the life I used to love fully aware of what I'm missing but with no hope of regaining it—

It's painful enough that by the time I reach the next town over, I'm crying.

I'm not sure I'm ever going to stop.

TWENTY-FIVE

Anna-Marie

For several moments I just stand there, staring after Josh, replaying those words in my head over and over and hoping eventually they'll lose all meaning: *You are replaceable.*

They don't. Each time is just as sharp, just as cutting as the first.

All the fury and pain I unleashed on Josh is still there, still waiting to be dished out to someone far more deserving of it. And I'm no goddamn martyr, able to just stand around suffering in silence. I stalk back inside the house, past Aunt Patrice who is standing on the porch wringing her hands. Past Lily, who, for once, doesn't seem to be exulting in my pain, but instead just stares down at her bare feet. Past Cherstie, who watches me with wide, sad eyes, and stutters out a "Oh, Anna-Marie, I'm so so sorry, I'm . . ." and trails off when I don't look ready to collapse into her arms for a hug.

It's not me she should feel sorry for. It's Tanya and Byron and Ginnie. It's stepmoms and stepsiblings of days past. It's my mom.

It's Josh, who I should never have let into the emotional minefield of all this in the first place, no matter how much he fought to be there. I knew better. We were only ever going to hurt each other.

And damn, does it hurt.

I walk into the house, catching sight of Uncle Joe in the kitchen, drinking the coffee I made out of the mug I had poured for Josh. But I storm right past and up the stairs, all my fury aimed for the closed bedroom door at the end of the hallway.

I don't bother knocking on my dad's door. I just fling it open and charge in.

"Dad, how could you—" My torrent of righteous anger is cut off with a strangled yelp as I trip over a big pile of fur positioned right inside the bedroom, landing in a less-than graceful heap beside said pile of fur. Who only stirs enough to lick my ankle. "Dammit, Buckley!"

Dad frowns from where he's sitting at the very edge of the bed. "Anna-Marie, pumpkin, are you—"

"No," I say, brushing off my dad's attempt to help me up. I push myself off the floor and stand up, and shit, one of the gold straps on my Ferragamo sandals has broken. And honestly, I barely even care, which is a real sign of how upset I am. "No, I'm not okay, Dad. I'm not. But you know who's really not okay? Tanya! Tanya is *not okay*!"

Maybe I should have planned this tirade out a little better. God, my parents got divorced when I was ten, so I've had like fourteen years to do so. But it's too late now.

"Pumpkin—"

"No! Don't use that 'calm down' voice with me! You cheated on her, didn't you? Of course you did, because you always do. Because no one is ever good enough for you, no one is enough—and why is that? Why the hell is that?"

My dad's expression, which was originally surprised and concerned, becomes hard. His blue eyes look gray in this light, like chips of granite. "It's complicated."

"It's complicated? Keeping your penis in check is *complicated*?"

"Don't you dare talk to me like that, Anna-Marie," he growls. "What happened between Tanya and me is none of your business."

I gape. "None of my business? She was going to be my

stepmom! I . . . I liked her! And you have to go and hurt her, and I can't—I can't have a normal relationship because all I know is what happens to women who date you!" My voice breaks, and I can still see Josh standing there, see the pain on his face, the hurt I gave him before he hurt me right back.

You are replaceable.

My dad's face is flushed, his hands balled into fists. Not that I think he would ever physically hurt me, but when he stands up, I take an instinctive step back. My dad doesn't get angry often, but when he does, it's like a force all its own.

And it has very rarely ever been directed at me.

"I am your *father*," he says. "You have no right to come in here and judge me. I have taken care of you your whole life.I made sure you had everything you ever wanted, even when I had to work extra hours to pay for it. You wanted horse-riding lessons? Vocal coaching? Done. Anything. You wanted to leave the *state* and go to Los Angeles and be an actress? Fine. I made sure you had the money to get an apartment, to afford headshots and clothes and new shoes and whatever the hell else you needed for auditions. I have loved you and supported you and cheered you on through everything. Because I am a good father. What else do you want from me, Anna-Marie?"

I blink, the fury settling into a fiery pit in my gut, simmering there. He's right. He has been a good father. But maybe that's not enough.

Maybe it never was.

"I want you to be a good *man*," I say. Then I turn and leave the room, limping slightly from the broken sandal. I make it to my room, and I shut the door.

And that's when I finally let myself break down and cry.

It's not the crying I do on *Southern Heat*—a few escaped tremulous tears, a faint shudder, a delicate sniffle, all designed for maximum on-camera sympathy and attractiveness.

No, this is real, honest-to-god ugly crying, full of wracking sobs and dripping snot and enough blotchy redness that my makeup artist would quit on the spot for easier work, like brain surgery. It's the kind of crying that physically hurts. And yet it's nothing compared to the pain I feel on the inside. How gutted I am, and how I know that nothing is ever going to be completely right again.

I lost Josh. No, I pushed him away with both hands. And maybe I'm sparing myself even greater pain later by doing so, but god, it hurts now. And I don't think it's going to stop hurting any time soon, not when I have to meet with him as my agent, and sure as hell not when I see him on the gossip sites with his arm around my replacement. Looking at her like he once looked at me.

Loving her like he once loved me.

I'm crying so hard I miss the first tentative knocks on my door. It's not until Patrice starts calling, "Anna-Marie, honey, you have a phone call. Anna-Marie, the phone," that I blink blearily and remember there's a world outside this miserable bedroom.

I fumble around for my phone before remembering that it's lying in pieces in a field, possibly under a sleeping moose's ass.

I manage to drag my achy body to the door and open it to see Patrice holding out the old cordless house phone, a big brick of plastic I'm surprised my dad still owns. Patrice's brow furrows when she sees me.

"Oh, honey, you look . . ." She trails off, the English language clearly failing her when it comes to a word that can adequately describe the awfulness of my appearance. She purses her lips. "Maybe Cherstie has some makeup that can help."

I yank the phone from her hand and close the door in her face.

"Hello," I mumble into the phone.

It's Gabby. I can tell before she even speaks, by the little heartbroken sound she makes. "I heard what happened, Anna," she says. "I'm so sorry. I'm so, so sorry."

"How do you—" A sudden spike of panic stops me. Was someone filming us? Is my awful breakup on the internet now too?

"Ben called," she says, and I let out a breath of relief.

Of course. Ben. Josh called Ben, probably to tell him how horrible I am and how he wishes he never met me.

But even in my grief, that doesn't feel totally right. Josh might wish that, but I can't picture him badmouthing me like that, even to Ben. He probably won't even badmouth me to his next girlfriend. Because I'm his client, and he's professional.

And more than that, he's just a deeply good person.

Something tickles my brain about that, but Gabby is talking again, and I force myself to pay attention. "—and I found your dad's number online, and oh my god, Anna, I'm so glad I got a hold of you."

"Me too," I say with a sniffle that is nowhere in the range of "delicate." It's not like Gabby can actually do anything about this mess—not like when I got fired on *Passion Medical*—but just talking to her, just knowing she's there . . . it helps. Not, like, a *ton*, but I'll take anything I can get. "I don't know how much I can even bring myself to talk about it right now, but I just . . . It's awful, Gabs. The things we said to each other . . ."

Another of those sad sympathy sounds. "Are you planning on coming back home soon?"

The pain hadn't allowed me much time to think about anything but surviving the next breath and then the one after that, let alone plan out my next moves, but now the answer is clear. "Yeah. I was only going to be here for another two days anyway, but—" I sigh. "My dad and I had this fight, and the whole family thinks I'm a sex addict, and now with Josh gone—I'm done. I'm coming home."

Home. Even with Gabby leaving the apartment, I can feel how true that is. LA is my home now, and it fits me way better than Everett ever did.

"Good." She sounds truly relieved. Which is when I notice the weird distant background noise that I first assumed was just this old crappy phone.

"Are you driving?"

"Um. Yes." She pauses, and then blurts out, "Don't hate me, but I'm actually with Ben now. On my way. Well, to Utah."

"You're driving with Ben. To Utah."

"Because that's where Ben is meeting Josh."

"Okay." I don't know how to respond to that, but even the mention of Josh sends a little stab in my heart.

"And you can meet us there and—"

"And what, Gabby?" Though I already know what she's going to say.

"And work things out with Josh, maybe." I can practically see her biting her lip nervously as she says this. "Because you love him."

"Yeah, I do." God, I'm only now getting a sense of how deeply true that is.

I love him. But Tanya loves my dad, as did my mom, once. Reid's wife loved him.

"I had reasons for what I did," I say. "And none of those were because I didn't love him."

Gabby sighs. "Okay, but just—think about it. Think about how happy you were with him, even when you were scared. And then, if you don't change your mind, well. I'll still be stuck in Beaver. So you need to come pick me up. And then we'll get through this."

"*Buffy* and wine and One Direction karaoke?"

"Of course." She gives me the name of some bar in Beaver they're headed to—I still have no idea why on earth this is their destination, but I'm too shell-shocked to care—and then she tells me she loves me. I say the same to her, and we hang up.

I slump down onto my bed and try to think about what she says, about how happy we were, but it feels so distant right now, even the parts that were just last night. All I can think of is Tanya hunched over, trying to keep herself from shattering, and Ginnie's sobs muffled by the car door. And Bryon's angry face, watching his mom hurt and unable to stop it.

And Josh, begging me not to end things, before his face grew hard and walled-off.

You are replaceable, he said, and then he left. Just like I told him to.

How can I even see him again after that?

He left so immediately that I realize there's probably a bunch of his clothes and stuff still in the storage room. So at least I can bring him that. And maybe apologize for hurting him. Maybe salvage our agent/client relationship, at the very least. I owe him that, no matter how much it hurts.

There's a knock at my door, and I groan. "Yes, Patrice, I'm off the phone. You can have it ba—"

The door opens and it's my dad there. He looks abashed, and what's more, his eyes look puffy and red, like he's been crying too.

I've never seen my dad cry. Ever.

"Can we talk, Pumpkin?" He shifts from one foot to another.

I don't trust myself to speak, so I nod. He walks in, Buckley trailing close behind him. Dad closes the door and paces the room a bit. He barely glances at the stacks of CDs and jars of makeup, but he takes in all the trophies on the shelf. Then the photos stuck in the edge of my mirror. One of them he pulls out and studies, and I find myself hoping it's not one of me and Shane.

I should seriously burn all those.

"I remember this day." He flips the picture around so I can see it. It's the only one of me and my mom and dad, all together, that I have. Mom notoriously hates having her picture taken, so she was always the photographer. It's not us doing anything special—no matching Mickey ears at Disney World or anything like that. Just us in the backyard, on that concrete patio. I'm about six and I'm putting on a show—of course—wearing a tutu and waving around a baton with glittery streamers. And Mom and Dad are sitting in those awful old foldable lawn chairs, laughing at my antics. I'm guessing Grandpa was the one taking the picture, since he lived with us back then, before Patrice and Joe moved and he went with them.

I shift uncomfortably on the bed. "Is this going to be one of those things where you tell me how you and Mom had some really great times, and how those were worth all the pain that came later?"

"God, no," he says, with a short laugh. "Your mom and I were miserable, pretty much from the beginning. The only great times we had involved you. We never really had anything in common besides how much we both loved the hell out of you."

That sounds about how I remember my childhood.

Dad sets the photo down on the vanity and stares at it some more. "It doesn't make it okay, what I did to her, though."

I look up, cautiously. My dad and I have never really talked about that, not directly. I think because I never wanted to know more. I wanted to think about it as little as possible, so that I could love my dad without being burdened by his bad choices.

Obviously that turned out to be a great plan.

"You were right, what you said before," he says. "I'm not a good man."

I cringe. "Daddy, I didn't mean that, like, you're not a good man at *all*, I meant—"

"I know what you meant. And you're right. I've hurt a lot of people. People I loved. I hurt *you*." He finally meets my eyes. "I think I always knew all this would affect you, but I convinced myself it wouldn't. That as long as I was a good enough dad, that if I provided for you and supported you and loved you enough, that'd outweigh all my mistakes. But it didn't."

I had all the things in the world to say to him before, it seemed—so many I was stumbling over them in my infuriated need to get them out. But now, I can't think of anything to say. So I just sit there, numbly, playing with the fraying edge of my jean shorts.

"I didn't want to hurt Tanya," he says, evidently seeing that if we're having a conversation now, he's going to be the one to lead it. "I didn't want to hurt any of them, not even your mom."

"Then why did you?"

My dad frowns and pulls out the chair at my vanity. It creaks when he sits down in it. "You know that intervention Patrice and the rest tried to have for you—"

I groan. "I'm not a sex addict, Dad, I promise."

"I know," he says. "But I am."

The shock is so great it jars me out of my grief-stupor. Though now it seems shocking that it wasn't something I ever considered before. "Oh my god. That's—are you serious?"

He nods glumly. "I figured it out after the divorce from Margaret"—his third wife, who had been the woman he'd cheated on his second wife with—"and I started going to a therapist. And from there to meetings. I've been in recovery now for two years. I know lots of people don't believe it's a real thing, and I also know it's not an excuse for the things I did. But I wanted to stop. I wanted to be a better man."

"Did Tanya know?"

"She did. I told her right from the beginning. God, I was scared to tell her. I'd never told anyone outside of my therapist and recovery group—still haven't, besides her, and now you. But she was—she was amazing. She came to a few meetings with me. She supported me through everything."

"And then you cheated on her, too." I wish I didn't sound so bitchy about it, now when my dad is confessing this deep, dark secret to me. But he's right—maybe I don't really get it and I sure as hell don't think it's an excuse.

He slumps forward, putting his head in his hands. "I didn't, actually. I mean, she found texts that were . . . yeah. Not great. I shouldn't have been texting that woman at all, let alone saying those things. I even drove to a bar last night, where I knew she would be. I sat there in the parking lot, and I hated myself for even being there. And then I turned around and drove home. I should have told Tanya about the texts, though. I messed up."

I pause. Maybe I shouldn't believe him, but I actually do. He sounds different, now. Honest, not defensive. Besides, I suppose at this point he has no reason to lie to me about it.

But I'm still finding it hard to forgive him—after all, not only did he keep this secret from me all these years, but he let them all have an intervention for me, and left me thinking he was ashamed of me.

Even though now I realize the shame was probably for himself.

"So is that it, then?" I ask, my tone still tinged with bitterness. "Tanya's gone, so on to the next one?"

He doesn't answer for a bit. Then, finally, "I don't know. I love Tanya. I'm going to do everything in my power to work things out."

"It didn't look that way. It looked like you just gave up."

"I know." He sighs. "I didn't know what I could do to convince her to forgive me. I still don't. But I'm done just giving up on people I love when really that's just an excuse to give up on myself."

I blink, tears burning again under my eyelids. God, how do I still have tears left? How am I not just some dry husk of bones and skin after all that bawling? I can't help but wonder how much of his self-loathing is the reason he's always wanted me to be perfect. Successful. Not like him.

"I heard you broke up with Josh," he says.

I nod. I had a feeling that's where this was going. I want to brush the topic away, because it hurts too much to think about, but I've never talked to my dad like this before—with him openly admitting he has problems. It's weird as hell, but also good. I might be happy about it, if I weren't also so miserable, and it feels wrong to shut him down when he's being so open with me.

"You know he's not me," Dad says slowly.

"God, I hope not." I swipe at my eyes. "I don't even want to consider the Freudian issues of *that* statement."

Dad chuckles. "You know what I mean."

"Yeah, I know." And it's true. Josh isn't a sex addict. His behavior isn't any more out of control or life-ruining than mine. And I believe him that he's never cheated on anyone. I believe him that he loves me, and that he would never want to hurt me.

But that doesn't mean he won't, and I already have proof that he *can*.

At least, I have proof he can after I hurt him first.

My gut squeezes tight, hating myself all over again for the pain I caused him. "I love him," I say, barely above a whisper. "But I'm so afraid."

The bed shifts as my dad sits down next to me. He puts his arm around me, and I settle in against him. And even though I'm still angry at him, he's my dad. It feels nice to curl up against him like I would as a child when we would watch TV together, or on summer nights when we'd sit outside and he'd tell me the names of the constellations—most of which, I'd later find out, he'd totally made up.

"I'm sorry I did that to you," Dad says. "Because I know now that I did. I made you afraid, and that kills me."

I let out a breath. "It wasn't just you. Relationships—they're always a risk, aren't they? And in Hollywood, it's like a million times worse."

"You're right. It's always a risk. And sometimes you get hurt. But it kind of seems like you're the one hurting yourself right now."

I want to argue with that. I want to tell him how I'm sparing myself all this future pain.

But god, can that really be any worse than how I feel right now? Can it really be worse than going the rest of my life wondering if maybe, just maybe, we would have made it?

"That boy loves you. That's clear to anyone who's seen you two together for five minutes," Dad says. "And I don't know him all that well, but I know you, Pumpkin. If you really love him the way I think you do, well. He's probably a pretty good man."

A thread of warmth makes its way through me. Josh *is* a good man. Not perfect; not some unattainable ideal. But good in the way I wish my father had been. Good in the way I wish Shane had been, or Reid.

Good in the way I wish I could be. The way I feel maybe I

can be when I'm with him.

"I don't know," I say, bumping my dad with my shoulder. "You weren't so sure I had good taste in high school."

Dad barks out a laugh. "I always knew Shane was a stage. It was just a stage that went on way too long."

I don't want to think about Shane, or the way he used me. It's far from the worst pain I'm feeling, but it still cuts deep.

"No kidding." I chew on my lip pensively. "Do you think Tanya will forgive you?"

"I don't know. At the very least, she'll talk to me, which will give me the chance to explain."

"How do you know?"

"Because she left her damn dog here," he says with a smile, looking over at Buckley, who has made himself into a trip hazard right in front of my door this time. The dog snores and rolls over. Dad looks back down at me. "So what are you going to do about Josh?"

It's the same thing Gabby wanted to know, that I couldn't answer then.

Think of how happy you were with him, she said. *Even when you were scared.*

It doesn't seem so distant anymore. Him and me, confessing all our geeky secrets on this very bed. Making love under the stars. Dancing close in a crowded club. Swinging in a hammock and talking about a future that felt so real I dreamed I was there.

I want to be there, in that future. I want to try to have it, even though I'm terrified I might lose it.

Even though I'm terrified I might have already lost it.

"Do you think it's possible?" I ask. "For two people to love each other enough that they can actually make it work?"

Dad lets out a breath. "I sure as hell hope so. And I'm finally willing to fight for it."

"Me too," I say, and it's amazing how sure I feel suddenly—not that it's all going to be all right, but that I need to try.

My dad smiles, and pulls me in for a hug. "I'm glad to hear

it," he says. "And maybe we can get you back here sometime before another four years pass."

"Okay. Just not for another Halsey reunion. I think I need at least a decade before I do this again."

He chuckles and stands up, then he leaves the room, Buckley trailing behind him like a huge furry shadow. Of a mop.

When my dad is gone, I become a frenzy of nervous action. I pack up my suitcase, not bothering to carefully organize my makeup or wrap my shoes in towels to protect them from luggage marks—except my fave Tory Burch wedges, of course, because I'm not a crazy person—and then I find Josh's stuff in the storage room and pack up his bag as well.

Then I drag my suitcases down the stairs, where I find, once again, my whole family waiting around the living room. There's no banner or cheese platter this time, though, thank god. Just a bunch of mugs of coffee and Grandpa with a plate of scrambled eggs on his lap.

I do see something important on one of the side tables, though—the Golden Weiner statue. I grab it, and Patrice jumps to her feet. "Anna-Marie, you're not leaving yet, are you? The reunion's still not over—"

"It is for me," I say. "I'm sorry. I love you guys, I really do, but I need to go. I need to find Josh and I need to get back home. To LA."

Patrice is back to wringing her hands again, looking to Joe for support. Joe just shrugs. "Safe travels, darling," is all he says. "Make sure the Weiner makes it back for next year."

And to my greatest shock, Lily looks at me and smiles in a way that seems neither gloating nor bitchy. I'm not sure it's an expression I've ever seen on her face before. "Good luck with Josh," she says. And by god, I think she actually means it.

"Bye, Anna-Marie," Cherstie says with a grin, and I grin back, mentally wishing *her* good luck with that girl in the picture.

Patrice gives them all an irritated huff. "But her *problem*, we haven't even really fixed—"

"If you need to have an intervention, have it for me," my dad says, coming in from the kitchen. "I'm the one with the addiction, not Anna-Marie."

Everyone looks surprised, but Patrice's eyes practically fall out of her head.

"Bill? But—"

"Well, that actually kind of makes sense," Joe says, nodding as if deep in thought. This is not an expression Joe has often.

My grandpa sits up straight, glowering at his plate. "Who salted these eggs, the Russians? It's like you're trying to give me hypertension."

Dad squeezes my arm. "Love you, Pumpkin," he says and smiles, then turns back to the family firing squad.

"Love you, too, Daddy," I say, and then I load up my rental Nissan and leave Everett behind.

TWENTY-SIX

Josh

I'm almost to Ben's appointed meeting spot in Beaver, Utah—apparently the exact halfway point between Everett and his apartment in LA—when he texts me. I pull over to check and find that he's left me yet another link.

Two things, the text says. *First, Gabby came with me. Second, Wyatt just sent me this article. Looks like you're part of the story now. See you soon.*

I swear. I'm not sure why Ben thinks it's a good idea to bring Anna-Marie's best friend with him when I'm planning to drink myself into oblivion, but what concerns me more is the damn article.

I click on the link, and the first thing I see is a picture of me, clearly snapped with a cell phone, back at a gas station in Rock Springs. I'm waiting at the pump with a hand on my forehead, and I'm clearly crying.

I should have thought I might be recognized. In that area, everyone probably knows who Anna-Marie is. She's a local celebrity, and half of Wyoming is probably glued to the story.

And now here I am, corroborating Shane's tale about what a heartbreaker she is. Anna-Marie was right not to want me caught up in this, because I'm making it worse.

Apparently the only place to get alcohol in Beaver, Utah is a bar called the Renegade Lounge. It's only after I park in front of it that I realize we are two freaking hours from Las Vegas, and yet I'm getting drunk in a dive in *Utah* of all places, where apparently even the restaurants in town don't have bars.

Clearly this is an oversight.

Still, when I walk into the bar, I'm greeted by a bartender with a purple pixie cut. She takes one look at my face, calls me "babe" and tells me the first one's on the house. Across the bar I spot Ben sitting at a table across from a girl with blond hair who is currently looking at me like I'm a beloved dog she has to have put down.

I drag myself over to their table and collapse into a chair. Ben slings an arm over my shoulders, and I wish he wouldn't, because I'm going to start crying again, something Gabby will almost certainly report to Anna-Marie.

"Hey, Gabby," I say.

Gabby makes a sad puppy noise and throws her arms around me as well. The bartender brings me my drink and clucks her tongue at me. "One look," she says, "and I knew he was the one you were waiting for."

She must have, because without even asking she's made me a poblano-infused tequila, which is my favorite. "Thanks," I say.

Gabby cringes. "I may have told her the whole story. And showed her pictures. Well, I showed her pictures of Anna-Marie, and Ben showed her pictures of you, and then we pulled up the articles and—"

"Yeah. I get the picture." I eye Gabby. "Not that I have any hard feelings toward you, but what are you doing here?"

Gabby squirms. She's a cute girl, but not movie-star gorgeous. I don't know why, but I guess I'd always expected Anna-Marie's best friend to be the same physical type that she is. "I'm meeting Anna-Marie."

I glare at Ben. "Tell me this isn't some obnoxious *Parent Trap* scenario. I'm not going to let you guys trick her into having to see me. This is hard enough as is."

"No," Gabby says. "I called her dad's house and talked to her. She knows you're going to be here."

I groan and throw back my drink. "And did she say she wants to see me?"

Gabby and Ben are both silent.

I shake my head. "No way. I've humiliated myself enough." I point at Ben. "You are going to drive me to Vegas and I'm going to get trashed, and next week when I'm sober and my thoughts are sorted and I can be reasonable again, Anna-Marie and I are going to work out our professional relationship like adults."

Ben glares at me, and he shakes his head. "Finish your drink. But you can't have another one until she gets here and we sure as hell aren't leaving until then."

I sit back in my chair. Ben hasn't told me what to do like this since college, and back then only when I was already drunk. "Whose side are you on, anyway?"

"Yours," Ben says. "Always yours. But if you don't work things out with this girl, you're always going to regret it."

I slump in my chair and finish my drink and recognize that I'm generally behaving like a child. Ben and Gabby both order beers they don't drink and waters they do. I should just get up and go, but I've already been drinking, and I'm not sure even sober I was really in a shape where I should have been driving. And the truth I don't want to admit is that I don't want to go.

I want to see Anna-Marie, stupid as that is. I don't like the way we left it, and even though there's no way I can get through a rehash of the end of this relationship without further humiliating myself, I do owe her an apology. I never should have said she's replaceable when nothing could be further from the truth.

And so the three of us eye each other nervously and wait for the arrival of the girl I'm not sure how I'm going to live without.

TWENTY-SEVEN

Anna-Marie

I drive all day, not stopping for anything other than gas station breaks just long enough to fill up my car and empty my bladder. I don't know how long Josh is planning on hanging out with Ben before getting back on the road, but considering they're meeting in Beaver, of all places, I doubt I have much time to catch him. And even though I could easily get a hold of him once we're both back in LA—and I've had time to take a shower, which I desperately need—I can't bear the thought of waiting that long. Of him going to sleep tonight without knowing that I still love him, that I want more than anything to have him back.

And I can't bear the thought of trying to go to sleep tonight without knowing if that's even a possibility.

I drum my fingers on the steering wheel nervously. I do a *lot* of nervous drumming on the steering wheel during this drive—I'm like Mikey that time he did some coke before one of Accidental Erotica's concerts and drummed so fast he reached the end of the song about ten seconds before the rest of the band. And then he punched his fist into one of his drums and collapsed.

Probably a good thing they got a new drummer.

I turn on the radio and eventually that Alec and Jenna song comes on, the one about forever love, and this time, now, I want to believe. Maybe they *will* make it. They sure sound like they're in love. Maybe Hollywood and fame and money isn't a relationship death sentence. Maybe the only real death sentence is giving up.

I force myself to slow down, to go over the speech I've prepared to convince Josh to give me another chance. My speech is not great—I'm an actress, not a writer—but I'm prepared to pepper it with any number of geek references, if necessary. I'm not above using *Harry Potter* quotes to my advantage, and I can even do a decent Hagrid impression if I get really desperate.

God, I'm thinking of using a *Hagrid* impression in my impassioned plea. Clearly, I'm about a hundred miles past desperate.

I just want him back, him and the possibility of that future together. I just want him to not replace me. And if I can't have those things, then I want him to at least know how sorry I am to have hurt him. How I wish, for his sake, that I had been an easier woman to love.

It's well past dark by the time I arrive in Beaver, and pull into the parking lot around back from the Renegade Lounge. Josh's Porsche is in the parking lot—two teenagers are eyeing it with awe—so I know he's still here. I should be breathing a sigh of relief, but instead I'm even more nervous. And doubting the wisdom of not taking some time in one of those gas station bathrooms to put on some makeup. At least before I left Everett I threw on a new shirt—not to mention non-broken shoes, a pair of cobalt blue Coach heels—and slapped on some deodorant. I'm not sure if that's enough to combat the funk of eight straight hours in a rental car, but I'm not backing down now.

I take a deep breath, grab the Golden Weiner, and head around to the front of the bar. Gabby is standing just outside the front door, pacing nervously.

"Anna-Marie!" she cries, throwing her arms around me. I

hug her back tight, because god, I need a best friend hug right now. "How are you?" she asks, pulling back and frowning at me.

"I don't know. I guess it depends on what Josh says. He's—he's still in there, right? I saw his car, but—"

"Yeah, he's in there with Ben." She eyes me hopefully. "So when you say it depends, you mean . . ."

"Yeah. I was an idiot, and I want to work things out."

Gabby looks surprised. "You're not too scared anymore?"

"I'm terrified. But Josh is worth the risk." It's true, I can feel it all the way down to my fashionable heels.

Gabby lets out a little squeal and hugs me again. "I'm glad to hear it. Ben and Wyatt and Will and I are Team Joshamarie all the way. At least, Will was until Wyatt pointed out that our couple name would be *Wabby*."

I snort-laugh into her shoulder, though it comes out half as a sob.

Joshamarie. God, what I wouldn't give to have that moniker top my Google hit results forever. "I don't know if he's going to be glad about it."

Gabby squeezes me. "I'm sure he will."

I wish this comforted me more, but the truth is, Gabby is not the best source on whether a guy would forgive me. She's blinded by best-friend loyalty and a pervasive (though untrue) belief that I could have any guy I wanted, at any time.

She lets me go, and I remember our last sane conversation, before everything went to hell. "God, Gabby," I say. "How's Felix? I didn't mean for you to come all the way out here if he needs you at—"

Gabby rolls her eyes. "He's dodging me. He's living in this dive out in Hyde Park and working at a convenience store—I'm guessing for drugs, because otherwise I don't know how he's affording them. Me being in LA wouldn't change anything." She looks down at the gaudy gold-painted foam hot dog statue in my hand. "What on earth is—no, never mind. Go get Josh. We can talk later."

"Trust me. We will. Probably for days." I smile, comforted a little by the fact that if things go terribly with Josh, at least Gabby's out here waiting to help pick up the pieces.

And I get it, in a way I didn't fully before. She always will be, no matter where she lives. Just like I'll always be there for her. She may not be my roommate for much longer, but she'll always be my Gabby.

The Renegade Lounge is a pretty typical small town bar, a lot like the one I used to work at before leaving for LA. Bright neon beer signs, carpet that looks like it's been salvaged from a seventies-era casino. The smell of smoke and alcohol, the clatter of pool balls and the clink of glass against the bar. It's fairly busy for a weeknight, which probably means it's the only bar in town.

I grip the Weiner tightly, looking around. A few guys sitting at the bar eye me openly, and one with the overly-confident bearing of an ex-high-school football star who now runs the local car wash stands up and starts heading my way. I glare at him to warn him off, but he's clearly a few drinks past good judgment.

"Hey gorgeous," he says, running a hand through his thinning hair. "I think the last time I saw legs that long, I was dreaming."

"If you think you have a chance here, you still are." I try to step around him, but he plants himself in front of me.

"Hey, no need to be like that. How about you give me a smile?" He grins, reaches for my arm, and is about to get a hot dog statue to the face and a knee somewhere lower when a sharp voice stops him.

"Kevin!" A woman behind the bar with a dyed pixie-cut and dark purple lipstick slams a mug down on the bar, loud enough the other guys behind him jump. "Back off of her. And you tell one more woman in my bar to smile and you'll be taking your Coronas intravenously, got it?"

Kevin narrows his eyes at her, and gives me one last ogling look as if in defiance, but retreats back to the bar.

I nod my thanks at the bartender, and she smiles at me. "He's in the back there," she says, jutting her chin towards the back of the bar, currently obscured by clumps of customers. It's clear she knows who I'm here for. I'm guessing they probably don't get a lot of out-of-towners here, not to mention ones as hot as Josh.

I make my way around tables and pool sticks, and then freeze when I see Josh. He's sitting at a table up against the wall, staring down at the empty glass in his hands. He looks miserable, his shoulders slumped and his dark hair falling over his eyes. My already broken heart manages to break further.

I did this to him.

I wonder if I should leave before he sees me. If I should just leave his life and stop hurting him.

But I can't. And more, I won't. Not until I've tried to fight for us. If he wants me to leave then, well . . .

I swallow past a throat that is painfully dry, and walk to the table.

There's a good-looking guy with light brown hair and a threadbare but still shockingly bright green shirt sitting next to him. Ben, obviously. I've never met him before, but even if Gabby hadn't told me Ben was here I would have known it was him; Josh and I laughed at length one night when he was telling me about how Ben acquired that hideous t-shirt on clearance at Goodwill and insisted on wearing it pretty much nonstop just because Josh hated it so much.

I'm glad Josh has someone like Ben in his life. Someone to pick up the pieces if I can't put them back together.

Ben sees me first, and sits up straighter. He nudges Josh, and says something to him. Josh looks up and we meet eyes and I feel tears well in mine.

Damn it, Anna-Marie, I tell myself. *Don't cry. You've done enough of that. Just make it right.*

"Hi," I say, when I get close to the table and find my voice. "Um. Hi, Ben."

"Hey," Ben says, but he doesn't look particularly thrilled to be meeting me, and I don't blame him after what I did to his best friend. This definitely isn't how I'd hoped to make a first impression on a guy Josh considers his brother. Ben clears his throat. "I'll—uh, I'll let you two . . . I'll go find Gabby."

Josh gives him a look that has the faintest trace of amusement, but when those dark eyes find me again, that trace vanishes. There's just that expression of sadness, of deep, deep loss.

I know that feeling.

I don't bother asking if I can sit; I just pull out a chair across from him and do. Ben claps Josh on the shoulder once and walks off without looking at me. If I do manage to fix things with Josh, I have a feeling I'm going to have to do some serious damage control with Ben.

I shift in my seat uncomfortably, and then set the statue on the table. "So I brought your Weiner."

And despite the misery etched into his expression, Josh actually laughs. God, it feels good to hear him laugh again. To be the one to make him laugh.

He picks up the statue and then sets it back down again. "I feel like there's a literal emasculation joke in that somewhere."

I smile. "In a giant foam hot dog? I think you're reaching, Rios."

"Yeah, well." His smile drops, and he looks back down at his glass. "I've always had a habit of that."

I draw in an unsteady breath. "Josh, I—" I start, just as he says, "I'm sorry about the picture—"

We both cut off, and there's a beat of this intense awkwardness that's downright painful. I just need to get this out, but I can't help but ask. "Picture?"

He sighs and pushes his phone at me across the table. "I figured you hadn't heard yet, what with the moose stealing your phone."

There on the screen is yet another internet gossip site. The page is scrolled down too far for me to see the headline, but there's Josh, leaning against his car, his hand holding the bridge of his nose. You can't see his face super clearly, but he's definitely recognizable and he's definitely crying.

"Josh," I say. "I'm so sorr—"

He shakes his head and takes his phone back. "You don't have to—"

"Let me go first, please. I just need to—I want to—" I can't seem to get the words out. My carefully prepared speech has vanished from my brain and I'm half tempted to blurt out "Yer a wizard, Harry," and run. But Josh just nods, looking increasingly broken with each fumbled syllable, and I force myself to continue. "I'm sorry," I say. "I'm sorry for what I said, for how I hurt you. I'm sorry I messed it all up like—"

"No, Anna-Marie," he says, shaking his head. "You didn't mess it up. Or at least, it wasn't just you. If I hadn't driven to Wyoming, if I hadn't intruded on your life like that . . ." He lets that hang there, and my lungs seem to clench. He regrets coming to Wyoming entirely. Of course he does.

Still, I need him to know. I need to try.

"I shouldn't have yelled those things at you," I say. "It wasn't fair, and—you never gave me any reason to doubt you. I was so scared, and mad at my dad, and the truth is, he's the one I should have been yelling at." I pause, running my fingernail along a crack in the table. "I mean, I did, after you left. Yell at him."

Josh's eyebrows raise. "Really?"

"Yeah. It didn't go well. At first, anyway. Then we talked, and . . ." I shake my head. I can tell him all the details—and will, if he wants me in his life enough to know them—but I don't want my issues with my dad to derail this. Those issues have derailed enough of my life. "Anyway, it was like I needed to finally say all the things to him that I've been keeping inside for years, you know? And he needed to hear them. And he did."

Josh's lips quirk up in a faint smile. "I'm glad. The only thing I did before leaving town was shove Shane."

My mouth drops open. "You *what*?"

He winces, and actually looks ashamed of this, though really I'm wishing I'd been there to see it, and possibly done some shoving of my own.

"Yeah, I may have barged into his house and shoved him onto the floor and stepped on him while telling him what an asshole he is and that he'll never work in *my town*." He rolls his eyes. "I didn't stick around to find out if he bought that." Josh looks down at the table, like he expects me to be angry about this. And maybe I should be, but I'm not.

"Thank you. For defending me. For always defending me, to everyone. I—I love that you care enough to do that."

He leans back in his chair and nods, but he won't meet my eyes.

"The other thing about talking to my dad," I say, "is that it made me realize how wrong I was to accuse you like that. You're not anything like him, and I know that. And I'm sorry I said you were."

He lets out a breath. "I'm sorry. I didn't mean what I said. When I said you're—" he stares up at the ceiling like he can't even look at me "—*replaceable*. It's not true. It will never be true."

The tears prick at my eyes again, even as my heart swells with the first gasping sense of hope. "Really?" I can't help but ask.

He looks back at me, his brown eyes soft. And reddened from crying tears of his own. "Yeah. Really. Losing you hurts like hell; that's the only reason I said that in the first place."

I nod, and brush away a tear that has leaked out. It does hurt like hell, but for the first time, I think maybe that's a good thing.

Maybe it's supposed to hurt when you lose someone you love. Maybe it means you're really in it.

"Okay," I say. "Okay. So I know I hurt you, and I'm a giant ass"—here he opens his mouth like he's going to contradict me, or possibly make some comment about the relative smallness of my ass, but I'm too afraid to let him speak before I've finished—"but if you were willing to give me another chance, I promise I'll do better."

His eyes widen, and his lips part again, but I keep going.

"I mean, I'm still messed up. And I'm still scared. But I love you, and I want to be with you, and I'll go to therapy or whatever to work on my issues, which, you know, I should probably have done years ago—"

"Okay," he blurts out.

But my mouth is running too fast for my mind to process his response. "—And I promise I'll actually talk to you about my fears instead of yelling them at you, and I know I'm not the greatest communicator and I have a tendency to throw shampoo bottles in people's food, and there's no way I'm going to be perfect at this, but I know now that I want to fight for us and—wait, what did you say?"

He blinks and swallows before answering. "Okay. Yes. Definitely yes."

My heart skips a beat. He looks so much like a stunned deer in headlights—or maybe a stunned naked actress in headlights—that I feel the need to clarify. "You . . . still want to be with me?"

With that, a slow grin spreads over his face and he gets up from the table just enough to take me in his arms and kiss me. And all that pain from our fight, all that anxiety I felt driving here, all of it drains away with his lips on mine, with our bodies pressed together. I am no longer fear and loss; I'm—*we're*—hope and love and everything that feels right in the world.

We make out long enough that people in the bar start whistling and cheering, and when we pull apart, I'm pretty sure I see a few people with their phones out.

But I don't care if *these* pictures end up on the internet. I don't care about anything right now, except Josh. Whose wide grin back at me—and yeah, maybe his hand at the small of my back—is making my knees weak.

"So you're my boyfriend again?"

"God, yes," he says, then chuckles. "Though we pretty much suck at the whole boyfriend/girlfriend thing, don't we?"

"It just—" I still don't fully know how to explain this, but I want to. "I guess being a girlfriend feels like constantly auditioning. Constantly wondering if I'll get the part."

Josh puts his hands on my waist, holding me close. "Halsey," he says. "You've got the part."

My heartbeat speeds up—a surprise, because it was already going faster than Mikey's coke-fueled drum solo. I bite the inside of my cheek. "Then maybe we could skip that step."

If I'd thought Josh's grin was wide before, it's nothing compared to now. His eyes gleam. "If you insist."

And then we kiss some more, despite the attention of the bar's patrons and the thumbs-up from the smiling bartender. We don't mind being the center of attention, Josh and I.

Especially if we're there together.

TWENTY-EIGHT

Anna-Marie

We arrive at Josh's place late in the evening the following day; neither of us were particularly interested in doing anything after leaving the bar other than finding a hotel and spending the rest of the night—and well into the morning—wrapped up in each other. Ben and Gabby didn't seem to mind, even though they had to get a room for themselves, and then Gabby had to drive my rental car back, which left Ben by himself in his car—all so that Josh and I could drive back together.

They really are incredible friends, and we owe them big time. For my part, I will definitely do better at overlooking Will's issues with personal hair care property. And be legitimately happy for Gabby for her new living situation—which will be easier now that I really know our friendship isn't limited to crappy apartments and even crappier coffeemakers.

We walk into Josh's living room, and he turns on the lights. He drops his duffel bag full of clothes near the door, and holds up the Golden Weiner. "I'll need to find a place of honor for this. Especially since as good as the carne asada was, I think your uncle Joe's hot dogs actually beat the ball park's."

I smile. "Worth the drive?"

He looks back at me, and his smile turns tender. "Definitely."

I laugh, looking around Josh's living room, thinking of the Weiner resting on the dark wood coffee table next to the designer glass and pewter chess set. Or poking up from behind those bespoke mason jars he paid way too much for.

And that's when it finally occurs to me what this place is missing—it's *him*. Not that he isn't the guy who fits with classy, expensive decor, or the guy who needs to have an upscale place he can entertain clients. That's definitely Josh Rios. But only part of him. And even before I knew that Josh has read every *Harry Potter* book at least a dozen times, I could tell his living space wasn't reflecting the whole of his personality. It's missing the Josh who tries to balance beer bottles on his head when he's drunk. The Josh who does goofy French lobster impressions. The Josh who loves my snort-laugh.

The Josh who is actually proud to have won a foam hot dog statue at my family reunion.

"I'm sure we'll find the perfect spot," I say, and catch him grinning at me. I realize I said 'we' like I'd be involved in his decorating decisions. I realize I want to be, and not because I actually care all that much about decorating.

He sets the statue down on the granite-countertop bar separating the kitchen from the living room. "Do you want a drink or anything?"

I raise my eyebrow. "I think you know what I want. And I think you're stalling."

"Maybe *I* need a drink." He runs a hand through his hair.

He's nervous. Like actually, seriously nervous about this. Which, you know, makes sense. A man's secret basement is a big deal. And if it was anyone but Josh who had a secret basement he was terrified to show me, I might actually be worried myself.

I give him a smile. "If you're not ready yet—"

"No, I want to show you. I've just—I am worried this may actually send you running. I really wasn't lying about being the *biggest geek in the world*."

I step forward and put my arms around him. "Just promise

me you didn't fake Alan Rickman's death, and really he's chained up down there, dressed up as Snape and brewing potions and sneering."

Josh smiles down at me. "Nothing illegal down there, I promise. Just criminally nerdy."

"Then I doubt we'll have a problem. I am, after all, the girl who wrote *Death Arsenal* fan fiction. And not just, like, years ago, either."

"Fan fiction I still need to read."

"Basement first, Rios. Though . . ." I pause, my heart beating faster.

He looks a little concerned, so I decide to plunge ahead.

"I don't have a ring yet," I say. "Isn't that breaking the rules?" We talked around this quite a bit on the long drive here—how we're in this for good, how maybe neither of us, but particularly me, do well with a lukewarm level of commitment. How we both want something way more long-term than 'girlfriend' implies—something more like forever.

We haven't, however, gotten into cut and carat-level specifics.

He lets out a small breath, and smiles. "I'm willing to bend the rules. Especially since it's probably a little late for Tiffany's to be open." Then he tucks a strand of hair behind my ear. "That being said—how soon do you think you might want a ring? Or, you know, a certain formal and life-changing question?"

My stomach feels fluttery, and though some of it is still residual fear, it's mostly just excitement. And a kind of pure, perfect happiness.

I look into his warm brown eyes. Eyes I want to still be looking into well past when we're old enough the rest of our bodies aren't worth studying all that closely. "As soon as you just can't take not proposing to me another second," I say, and he makes a little groan.

"Are we *sure* Tiffany's is closed?" he says, reaching for his phone.

I laugh. "No more stalling."

He presses me tightly against him and sighs into my hair. "Yeah, okay. Basement first."

And even though I'm dying to see the world's geekiest secret in this basement, I regret the moment he peels away from me, the moment I'm no longer in his arms. Luckily, I know it won't be long before I'm back there.

God, I've gotten clingy. Me. Clingy.

It's a good thing Josh doesn't seem to mind. Because with him, well—neither do I. Not anymore.

Josh strides over to this gorgeous mahogany screen behind his sofa, carved with intricate patterns. He reaches behind it and pulls a key from inside one of the carved whorls.

"Nice," I say, admiring the hiding spot. No one is ever going to explore every nook and cranny of that screen, and even an aggressive dusting by the cleaning service would probably miss it. I follow Josh to a door toward the end of his short hallway that I always assumed was some sort of utility closet.

He turns the key and opens the door, flipping on the light over a set of carpeted stairs. "After you," he says, and I head down, my excitement building with each step. As I reach the bottom step, I turn into the room, and—

And it's a big bookcase, crammed with books. And a ratty-looking La-Z-Boy that could have been lifted from my dad's basement.

Definitely not the geek mecca I was expecting.

"Um . . ." I start, not sure what to say. "That's a lot of books."

"You sound disappointed." There's a teasing note to his voice.

"Confused, mostly. I mean, you're clearly a big fan of the Star Wars expanded universe" —one whole shelf is packed with trade paperbacks from that line— "but I don't think this makes you the geekiest person alive."

"Well, I *was* thinking about getting a TV and Xbox down here, and maybe the entire collection of *Death Arsenal* games . . ."

My eyes widen. "Seriously? Because that would be—" I cut

off, noticing another door to the side of the bookshelf. "Wait, is there another room?"

"There may be, yeah. And another hidden key." He pulls out a hardcover copy of *Harry Potter and the Chamber of Secrets*, and removes a key paper-clipped to the cover flap.

"Wow. I'm surprised there's no retinal scan." I squint as I notice something on the armrest of the recliner. It has splotches of something translucent that glistens and makes the fabric crusty. I poke at it. "Is that . . . dried glue?"

"It is. I do most of my work out here, in the chair." He's back to looking nervous again, and swings the other door open. "For this."

I straighten and walk toward the door, and now I can barely speak at all.

Almost the whole second room is taken up with a table upon which rests the entire Harry Potter world in miniature. Incredibly detailed miniature, everything rendered in the most loving perfection, from the dusting of snow along the gabled roofs and cobblestones of that little town where Harry drinks butterbeer (I can't remember the name, sadly) to the goalposts of a Quidditch field to the tall spires of Hogwarts Castle itself.

And around it all chugs a small train that starts moving when he flips a switch under the table. It's the Hogwarts Express, and I can almost imagine the little kids inside, eating chocolate frogs and waiting to start school again for another year.

I'm barely breathing as I'm taking it all in, as if the faintest breath will knock over the tiny figures in their robes shopping for wands at Diagon Alley, or blow down the spiders dangling from the trees in the forest outside of Hogwarts. And maybe it will—I don't know how delicate all of this is.

But I do know one thing.

"This is *amazing*," I say, my voice a reverent whisper.

"Really? You really think so? Because you don't have to—"

He cuts off when I look up at him. "Did you really do all this? Yourself?"

A shy smile tugs at his lips. "Yeah. I mean, it's a lot of work, but it's not that difficult once you get the hang of the techniques."

"Could you teach me?"

He looks stunned, his mouth gaping open. "You'd—you'd want to do this with me?"

I worry I've crossed a line, assumed too much. This is his thing, and showing it to me is one thing, but letting me make my own tiny wizard figurines—something I never thought I'd have a desire to do, but well, here it is—might be more than he wants to share. I'm about to deflect.

But then I remember something we talked about in the car ride back—one thing among hours of talking about everything and nothing. Talking about my dad's revelation, and Shane's well-deserved shoving. About how we could have handled that fight better, and how we wanted to handle things like that better in the future. About the fact that we really could both use some therapy to figure out how to do this better. About how we're going to mess up, probably a lot. But we're going to work it out, and we're going to do so together.

And as part of that, we talked about how we need to be open with each other. We need to be willing to tell each other what we want. We need to be willing to admit to *ourselves* what we want (this one is, admittedly, more for me).

"Yeah," I say. "I would. If that's okay with you."

"Um, yeah," he says, with a surprised laugh. "Yes. That's more than okay. I'd love that. I just hoped you'd not hate it, but the thought that you'd actually want to be part of this with me—" he shakes his head.

"Well," I say with a smile. "I think we already established that I'm the perfect woman. At least, most of Wyoming heard you yell that."

"And all of LA will too, once we get on that talk show I booked," he says, stepping close to me and folding me back in his arms. "Though I will keep myself from actually yelling. Or jumping on couches. But I think we can get our story out there, told the way we want to tell it. And look damn good doing so."

"There are definite advantages to dating your agent. Especially if that agent is you."

"I tried to tell you that, Halsey." He presses his forehead to mine.

Honestly, I'm less worried about all of it now that Josh has worked out a plan and gotten us all sorts of PR opportunities to set things right. We'll tell the world our side of things, and I'm actually pretty confident we can work all this to our favor, professionally speaking.

And personally speaking, well, I feel like things are already in our favor.

"So, speaking of that Xbox and collection of *Death Arsenal* games . . ." I pull him back into the other room. "Maybe you don't need to buy all that stuff. Maybe I could just bring over mine."

Josh nods, as if thoughtfully, then sits in the recliner and pulls me down onto his lap. "You could. In fact, while you're at it, you could just bring over all your stuff. If you want."

There's that fluttery feeling again. I hope it never goes away.

"Says the guy who hasn't seen my massive shoe collection," I tease, leaning in so close I can feel his breath on my lips.

"Says the guy who will find room for it all," he murmurs, his hand stroking down along my thigh. "Because he is crazy in love with this amazing girl, and wants to share his whole life with her."

His whole life. *Our* whole life, the way we love it. Having a blast and looking glamorous at clubs and parties and premieres, then coming home—to *our home*—and unwinding down in this basement. Playing video games like I've imagined before, and now I can also see us painting miniatures and laughing at spilled glue splotches on the shaggy carpet. Going to work at jobs we love, and coming home to each other, who we love even more.

And that's just the beginning.

But before I can picture even more—like *damn* I'm going

to look good with a nice fat halo-set oval cut on my finger—our lips meet, and our hands are roaming each other's bodies with increasing urgency. I'm straddling him, my knees brushing against crusty glue patches and chip crumbs and I don't even care—even though I know very well there's a divine set of sheets on a very comfortable bed upstairs.

All I need, for now and for always, is Josh. And he's right here with me, and I believe him when he says he always will be.

And besides, this La-Z-Boy *does* recline.

ACKNOWLEDGMENTS

There are so many people we'd like to thank for helping make this book a reality. First, our families, especially our incredibly supportive husbands Glen and Drew, and our amazing kids. Thanks also to our writing group, Accidental Erotica, for all the feedback, and particularly to Heather, our first genuine superfan.

Thanks to Michelle of Melissa Williams Design for the fabulous cover, and to our agent extraordinaire, Hannah Ekren, for her love and enthusiasm for these books. Thanks to Dantzel Cherry and Amy Carlin for being proofreading goddesses, and thanks to everyone who read and gave us notes throughout the many drafts of this project—your feedback was invaluable and greatly appreciated.

And a special thanks to you, our readers. We hope you love these characters as much as we do.

Janci Patterson got her start writing contemporary and science fiction young adult novels, and couldn't be happier to now be writing adult romance. She has an MA in creative writing, and lives in Utah with her husband and two adorable kids. When she's not writing she can be found surrounded by dolls, games, and her border collie. She has written collaborative novels with several partners, and is honored to be working on this series with Megan.

Megan Walker lives in Utah with her husband, two kids, and two dogs–all of whom are incredibly supportive of the time she spends writing about romance and crazy Hollywood hijinks. She loves making Barbie dioramas and reading trashy gossip magazines (and, okay, lots of other books and magazines, as well.) She's so excited to be collaborating on this series with Janci. Megan has also written several published fantasy and science-fiction stories under the name Megan Grey.

Find Megan and Janci at www.extraseriesbooks.com

Other Books in the Extra Series

The Extra
The Girlfriend Stage
Everything We Are
The Jenna Rollins Real Love Tour
Starving with the Stars
My Faire Lady
You are the Story
How Not to Date a Rock Star
Beauty and the Bassist
Su-Lin's Super-Awesome Casual Dating Plan
Ex on the Beach
Chasing Prince Charming
After the Final Slipper
The Real Not-Wives of Red Rock Canyon
Su-Lin and Brendan Present: Your Wedding
All-Night Dungeon

Made in the USA
Coppell, TX
23 October 2020